The Length of Our Staircase

Betsy Naglich

ISBN 978-1-09807-823-2 (paperback)
ISBN 978-1-09807-824-9 (digital)

Christian Faith Publishing, Inc.
832 Park Avenue
Meadville, PA 16335
www.christianfaithpublishing.com

Printed in the United States of America

In memory of my mother, Dolly Naglich. Being a mom doesn't mean you had to give birth to the child. A mom is any person who mentors a child and worries each day about the outcome of that child's life. Thank God for moms!

Contents

Chapter 1

The Airport

Rose couldn't believe she might miss her flight. The one time she really needed to get home. Not only was the traffic bad, but the cabbie also fumbled with the credit card transaction, and then his trunk wouldn't open to unload her suitcase. To top it off, the flight was leaving from the farthest gate. She shouldn't have used the employee standby ticket for this trip. Standby is just not the way to fly when you definitely need to be home at a designated time. What if she doesn't make it to the gate prior to the ten-minute pre-flight deadline? She wondered why her mom thought this would be the perfect way to travel and the perfect job for Rose. Yes, back in the sixties, it was romantic and thrilling. Not too many people flew back then, everyone dressed up, and the food service on board was impressive. Today it is far less romantic. Almost everyone has been on a plane, and many people fly regularly. She had to admit that, most of the time, she enjoyed it. Her mom was right. It was just this one time that it was not working out to her expectations.

Running through the airline terminal, Rose spotted the monitor, which showed that her flight to Chicago was on time. She continued to walk fast and was determined to get to the gate before it closed. Rose was dressed in her business attire—as dictated by the airline company—so it was impossible for her to run, although as fit as she was, she knew she could have made it quicker!

Arriving at the gate, she saw that there was a line of customers waiting for service. The gate attendant seemed frustrated. The flight was going to take off in fifteen minutes, and there were still customers making changes. Finally, Rose was second in line. Behind her was a disgruntled customer swearing under his breath. "Come on, people, move it along. How long does it take to get a seat and print a ticket?"

She didn't want anyone else to get in front of her because her standby seat might be lost to a paying customer, but as a good employee she turned around. "Excuse me, sir, would you like to move ahead of me? It appears you are in a hurry." Rose strained to put on a smile.

The angry man moved ahead of Rose without thanking her. She continued to wait patiently, and it was finally her turn. With a smile, she handed her standby ticket to the gate attendant. "Hi, I'm flying standby. I should be on your list."

Relieved that she had a nice customer, the gate attendant smiled back at Rose. "Yes, I see your name. By the way, thank you for letting that irritating man go through before you. He was one of the worst customers today!"

"No problem, I wanted to help. I also wanted him to stop causing a commotion. I need you to get your work done, so that I could get on the plane too," Rose said in jest and smiled.

"Well, thanks! Look, your kindness paid off. You are in the first-class cabin for your trip home!" The gate attendant handed over the ticket to Rose.

"Wow, what a nice surprise! My mom would be happy. She told me to work for an airline, so that I could travel the world in style." Rose remembered how her mom was always pushing her to get a job with an airline.

"Tell her I said she was a very smart lady!" The gate attendant was happy to hear that there were still people who loved to fly!

"Oh, thank you. I wish I could, but she died seventeen years ago, back in 1981." Rose had a little sadness in her voice.

"I'm sorry to hear that. Was there any other good advice or requests that she made?" The gate attendant was packing up her desk, ready to move to the next flight going out.

Rose was the last in line, and she knew the gate attendant had time to listen. So she continued. "Only one last request, and it was a whopper! I compare it to that big piece of chocolate cake at the end of a meal. You want it, but you know you've already gone over your calories. You hate to think what the scale may say in the morning if you eat it, but it may be the best cake ever! So should I eat it or not? Would I be missing anything? It's a big decision!"

"The gate is closing, you better run!" The gate attendant didn't want her to lose her seat.

"Thanks again." Rose bent over to pick up her bags and scrambled to the gate. She grabbed her carry-on bag and purse but paused to hear the last thing the gate attendant wanted to say.

"Hey, about your decision. I think you should go for it, or you may always wonder, *what if.*" The gate attendant waved, shuffled her papers, and started off to her next gate.

Rose continued walking but looked back with a smile. The door closed as she rushed down the gangway to reach the plane.

Once aboard, she greeted the flight attendants. An older man in front of her was having a problem getting his bag up to the overhead compartment. Rose helped push the bag up and closed the compartment for the man. He thanked her and continued to his seat. She spotted her seat and moved toward it. Her carry-on was small, and she crammed it into a small space to try to leave the bigger spaces for the paying customers. Finally she sat, took a deep breath, and smiled. She got lucky and would make it home after all.

The flight attendants swiftly worked to make sure everyone was seated, bags were stored, and all doors and compartments were shut tight. The safety demonstration was given, and soon they were ready for departure.

After takeoff, one of the flight attendants appeared with a glass of wine for Rose. "I noticed you were helping the customers, and I wanted to thank you!"

Rose graciously reached for the glass of wine. "It wasn't a problem. I saw you were busy with others. I like to help out since I am a fellow employee."

The flight attendant moved to serve other customers. Rose adjusted her seat, grabbed a brochure out of her purse to read, and settled back for a long flight. She was in such a hurry that she had forgotten about the stressful day she had in store for her the next day. It felt good to finally relax.

"Good afternoon, everyone. This is Captain Smith, your pilot. Today's flight to Chicago will take three hours and thirty minutes. We will be flying at an altitude of thirty-nine thousand feet. We should touch down at O'Hare at 5:30 p.m. The weather looks good, and we should have a smooth flight."

The passenger to her right noticed Rose. He was happy that he was sitting next to a cute, professional woman who looked about his age, which was fortyish. He was hoping he would be sitting next to someone who wanted to talk. He glanced over at what she was reading and commented, "I couldn't help but notice the brochure. Can I ask why you are reading it?"

"Well, it's a long story. Would you like to hear it? It starts back around thirty-four years ago." Rose thought it might be good to get another opinion about the whole idea. Sometimes it was easier to talk to a stranger than someone close.

"I've got three and a half hours until we get off this airplane. Sure, I'm all ears!" He smiled and was ready to listen. He needed a new story and friendly travel companion. He traveled for business, and sometimes it was monotonous. They clinked their wineglasses in agreement!

Chapter 2

The Farm

Nick drove down a rural farm road in his new 1963 Cadillac with his beautiful wife, Dolly, and their two daughters. Diane, a studious eight-year-old, was reading in the back seat, oblivious to the road or conversation inside the car. Rose, six years old, was the opposite. She sat with her head stuck between the gap of the two front bucket seats, listening and watching her mom and dad with open ears and eyes.

Nick watched the farms pass by and pointed to the next row of trees on the left. "Look, there it is, the next farm on the left, after the row of trees."

Dolly watched as the land passed by and exclaimed, "Is this all ours? How big is it again?"

"Yep, all of the land up to the next gate is ours. In order to see the back border, we'll need to get out and walk. It's eighty acres."

"I never thought we'd own this much land! What will we do with it all?" Dolly was amazed.

"Hang on, let me pull the for-sale sign out of the ground and unlock the gate, then I'll tell you my plans for the place." Nick pulled over to the gate of the farm. Dolly watched as her strong husband easily pulled out the for-sale sign. He popped the trunk and threw it inside. Then he unlocked the fence and climbed back into the car.

Nick started to finish his thought. "As we drive down the driveway, imagine a row of apple trees on the right side. We'll have tons of apples to eat and give away to everyone. You'll see the house and the barn as we get to the end of the driveway. They're really in bad shape, and I need to completely rebuild them. Look over there, an outhouse. There isn't even any indoor plumbing in the house. Believe me, it really needs a rebuild bad."

Nick continued to drive past the house and barn and then stopped. "This is where I am going to put two ponds and piers for fishing."

"Maybe we can get some sand and add a little beach area for the girls?" Now Dolly was imagining all sorts of things to plan, build, and enjoy.

Rose was still listening, with her head sticking into the front seat. She listened closely to the plans her father had made for the farm. She looked back and forth at them as they talked.

"Nick, wouldn't it be great to have a son to help out and enjoy our new farm too?" Dolly looked away, not wanting to hear the answer she expected.

"Dolly, we talked about that. The girls are enough." Nick was stern.

Dolly was sad and kept staring out the window. Rose noticed that her mom was sad and wanted to help. She didn't like it when her mom was sad, and she didn't understand why her dad didn't want to make her mom happy either. She thought that maybe it might make her mom happier if she tried to fish with her dad and do some work with him.

"Dolly, get the girls ready, and we'll park the car and walk around. Take the camera, and get some pictures too. We should save the pictures of how the farm looked on our first visit." Nick pulled onto a gravel area and shut off the car.

"Okay, Nick, I want to get a picture of you and the girls too!" Dolly reached for the camera case and got the girls out of the car.

They walked around the farm, looking at the different fields, the creek that separated fields, the duck blind site for hunting, and the sites for the horse stable and barns. They took pictures and enjoyed their very first visit. After a few hours, they got back in the car and closed the gate behind them.

As the year went by, the family came to the farm week after week. The projects they planned became reality. Little by little, the farm became a beautiful place. The house was a huge project, and Nick had some friends helping with the construction. He had his own pet projects that he worked on himself. Even though Rose was young and small, she tried to help her father in any way she could. She followed him around and handed him tools or fetched things. Dolly noticed Rose helping her father work and always smiled.

The following year, Nick planted the row of apple trees along the driveway as promised. Again, Rose was right alongside her father digging with her little shovel, noticing how happy it made her mom as she watched.

Each year, Nick progressed and completed the barn, the stable, the ponds, and the piers. As the farm improved, friends and relatives started to visit and enjoy the place. The pond was stocked with fish, and the kids started fishing. The sand was poured for the beach, and the kids started swimming. The more work Nick put into the place, the more enjoyment came out of it.

Next, the plans came together to make the farm a hunting haven. He added a duck blind by the pond and planted the thorny bushes that the pheasants would hide under and then added more trees by the creek for the deer.

The friends and relatives started to depend on the annual celebration at the farm. Nick roasted pigs and lamb, along with the usual staples at a cookout, such as hamburgers, hotdogs, and Dolly's world-famous potato salad. The farm became the place to be in the summer.

As the kids got older, there were minibikes, dirt bikes, snowmobiles, and golf carts. Nick bought the fun vehicles mainly for Rose's enjoyment. He loved watching her learn to ride each one and conquer them. As she grew older, he started to challenge her and started buying the minibikes with manual gears. Rose learned to change the gears all by herself while her father watched. She struggled and the bike died out, but she just kept trying, and hours later she was buzzing around the farm on the new minibike like an expert. Nick loved watching his little tomboy. He loved her spunk and stubbornness.

Next, Rose learned how to shoot a gun and hunt for pheasant and rabbit. Nick showed her the safety lessons once and then just kept loading the clay pigeons over and over until Rose started to hit some. Finally, she got the hang of it. Pretty soon she turned into a decent shot. Another success for Nick and his daughter.

Rose started bringing her friends to the farm to enjoy all the fun. One of her best friends was Cindy. Cindy and Rose rode the minibikes to town and all around the farm roads. Memories of a lifetime were made together. They sang songs while riding down the farm roads. They hunted for butterflies, ducks, and boys! They played hard and constantly laughed!

The farm had kept their life busy and active, but as the years went by, the relatives visited less and less frequently. Their children had activities like baseball and ballet, and they found that they couldn't get to the farm on the weekends anymore. Slowly, the farm got lonelier and lonelier. Nick and Dolly spent more time at the farm by themselves.

As Rose turned into a teenager, she was less interested in the sports and activities that her dad enjoyed. She started to date and got interested in her education. She decided that she wanted to become an accountant and knew she'd need to go to college. Her schoolwork became a priority. She still wanted to make her parents happy but had less time to do it. Instead of working alongside her dad and fishing with her mom, Rose brought her boyfriend, Don, with her to the farm. He worked with Nick and loved to fish, so she could sit and study for school. Things worked out beautifully. Everyone seemed to be very happy, until one day when she was at the farm and her mom wanted to talk.

"Rose, sit down with me and talk." Dolly was a little melancholy.

"Okay, Mom, but just for a while. I want to get back to my studies. I have a test next week in chemistry and want to get an A. It's important that I do really well during my last year in high school, so that I can go to college." Rose was determined to get straight A's.

"I know that is important, but you can spare thirty minutes for your mom too. I've got something to show you. Look, I found this ad in the newspaper. United Airlines is looking for flight attendants.

It says that you need a high school education and you can apply." Dolly loved to travel and enjoyed trips with her two daughters when they were younger. She would've loved for Rose to become a flight attendant.

"Mom, you know that I want to be an accountant!" Rose loved bookkeeping class during her sophomore year and thought she'd like to pursue it as a career.

"Well, airlines need accountants too." Dolly was eager for Rose to give it a thought.

"Okay, Mom, I'll think about it. What are the plans for this weekend, Mom? Who is coming down to the farm? What are you cooking?" Rose tried to change the subject.

Dolly sighed. "Rose, the days of the big parties and all of the activities here are over. Everyone is running around with their growing kids, and they don't have time left to come to the farm."

"Oh, Mom, you are exaggerating. I am sure if you called people up, they would love to come to the farm and have fun!" Rose was sure that there were people who would still enjoy a weekend on the farm.

"Rose, you don't understand. It's not that easy anymore. People are staying in the city around their houses. The years of the family activities here are over." Dolly had tried to continue the cookouts each year, but as the years went by, the turnout was less and less.

Dolly got up and walked over to the sink to wash some dishes. Rose felt bad that her mom's life on the weekends at the farm had slowed down and become less enjoyable.

"Is there anything I can do? I bet some of my friends would love to come to the farm this weekend." Rose tried hard to make her mom's mood change and get her excited about having people out.

Dolly finished the dishes and walked back to the table. She hesitated, but she finally talked to her daughter about what she wanted.

"Rose, remember that orphanage down the street from your part-time job?" Dolly doodled pictures on her tablet while talking. She was always writing lists and doodling. She kept a list of the calories she ate, things needed from the store, and other chores that needed to get done.

"Yes, Mom, I know the place you are talking about. Why?" Rose had started working a year ago and would drive about fifteen minutes to her part-time job in the next city.

"Well, maybe you can stop there and ask if they will let you bring a little boy to the farm? Maybe there is a boy there who needs a home. You can pick him up and bring him to the farm. Maybe a boy who would love to spend some time fishing?" Dolly was hoping for a positive answer from Rose. She knew it was a stretch but wanted to suggest it anyway.

"Mom, I really don't think they would allow a teenager to take a boy out of the orphanage and bring him to the farm to fish." Rose felt like rolling her eyes but didn't want to upset her mom. How could a sixteen-year-old be trusted with a child from the orphanage?

Dolly was sad and walked away from the table. Rose knew that her mom always wanted a boy. She tried hard over the years to do the things that a boy would love to do to make her mom happier. She fished, hunted, and worked alongside her dad, just like a boy would have done. She thought that would be enough, but her mom was still yearning for that little boy she never had. Rose sat and was silent. Her mom continued to work around the kitchen.

Chapter 3

The Drive Home

The plane was just about ready to land in Chicago. Rose was finishing up the story to her new friend in the next airline seat.

"That was a great story. You must have had a nice childhood with the farm in your life!" The friendly passenger was truly interested in what Rose had to say.

"Yes, the farm was a great place, but as the story told, there was always something missing from my mom's life." Rose stopped and gazed straight ahead.

"Did telling me the story bring you closer to your final decision? Are you going to go through with adopting an older boy who needs a home?"

"Yes, I think our conversation helped me know that this is something I have to do for me and for my mom." Rose put a smile on her face. She had come to a decision that had taken a long time to make.

"Well, good luck to you. I hope everything works out as planned." The smile Rose had shown was catchy and appeared on his face too.

"There are a few more obstacles that I need to clear up before things can work out as planned," Rose pondered.

"You have a good head on your shoulders. I am sure you will get through anything you need to and make your dreams a reality." He touched Roses arm lightly to share his approval.

"Thank you for your kind words. You were a great companion on this flight. I will remember you." Rose started preparing to get off the plane.

The flight attendants prepared for landing. They came down the aisles and picked up the trash and glasses from the passengers. The seat belt sign illuminated. The pilot gave the final talk about the arrival in Chicago.

"Please put on your seat belts and prepare for landing. It is seventy degrees in Chicago. We should be at the gate in ten minutes. Thank you for flying with us today. We appreciate your business." The pilot ended the announcement and shut off the speaker.

The plane landed and taxied to the gate. The passengers were waiting impatiently to get off the plane and go forward with their lives, especially Rose.

The plane stopped at the gate, and everyone started to hustle, grabbing their suitcases and other possessions. She popped her seat belt and stood to run out of the door as soon as it opened. The flight attendants thanked everyone as the passengers moved toward the door and out of the plane. Rose also thanked her fellow employees for the nice treatment while she was on board. She walked quickly down the gangway and out into the airport.

It was a Sunday evening, and the airport had already started to clear out for the day. She moved past other people as she scurried to the exit. She was fit and walked fast. She learned to walk fast to keep up with her father at the farm. He was a tall man, and he didn't slow down for her. It was her job to learn to keep up with him, and she did. Just like everything else Rose tried, she usually got things accomplished!

She jumped on the shuttle to the parking lot where her car was waiting for her. It wouldn't be very long now. She just needed to get home and see how everything was going. She had only been gone for two days, but things might have gone downhill, even in that very short amount of time.

She found her car, threw the suitcase in the back, and got on her way. Luckily, the traffic home was light. She turned on the radio and listened to pop music. She wondered what she would find when she arrived home.

Driving up, she noticed that the outside of the house was just as it was when she left. The neighborhood was quiet. Everyone was winding down for the weekend, probably getting ready for the evening and the start of the new week. They were all inside their houses. Rose loved this neighborhood because each house was different. They were all four bedrooms and nice-sized lots, but the design of each was unique. She loved her house, not for the design, but for the placement on the eight-acre pond. She could look out the window while washing dishes and see the pond. The pond was stocked with fish, and all the kids in the neighborhood would either catch fish or watch others catch fish. Their deck faced the pond, and when she sat on the deck, she felt like she was back on the farm. She hoped that she could stay in this neighborhood and in this house forever. The house wasn't really her style when she first saw it, but it grew on her, especially the pond view.

As she approached her driveway, she saw the trees and bushes that she planted. Some of the plants and greenery she selected for the landscaping reflected her memories of the farm. She parked the car inside the garage. The floor in the garage was carpeted, which was unusual. Her house was a model home, and this was the office. She kept the garage carpet clean and looking like new. When they had parties, the garage was used as a party room for all the children that came over. They could play games and have fun! The carpet guarded against bumps and bruises if they fell. It turned out to be a cool addition to the home.

Rose grabbed her things out of the car and walked into the house. She heard the loud sports shows on the TV. It was always the same. Each day a different game on the TV. It was either basketball, football, or baseball. There was never a movie, except for the movies about sports, like the movie *Rudy*. The movie about the boy who dreamed of going to Notre Dame to play football. She wished her husband would pursue the dreams he watched on TV. She thought he would love to have a son like Rudy, but he didn't want children. It hadn't turned out like she thought it would. Yes, they traveled and had had many fun trips, but his idea of fun was the drinking, not the destination itself. Her idea of fun was the travel and excitement of the destination. Why did everything for him always result in partying? It was worse than ever now with his recent health issues. He shouldn't even be drinking any longer. The doctors had advised him to stop drinking because of the medications he was taking, but he didn't listen or hear them. He started having anxiety attacks two years ago, and instead of attempting to control his lifestyle, he just took more and more drugs.

She walked further into the house and noticed the empty bottle of rum on the table and the bottle of pills. She glanced over to see him passed out on the couch. As she got closer to the table, she saw a note. "Dear Hungywear, I promise I will be ready for the class tomorrow. I missed you." Rose was touched by the note. She wished he would come to his senses and stop taking the prescription drugs with alcohol. She climbed the stairs and got ready for bed.

Morning came quickly, and Rose prepared for a normal day of work. She got dressed, had a cup of coffee, and packed a lunch. Grabbing her gym bag and other items, she made her way into the garage. While driving, she thought of the wait for this day. This was the day of the first adoption class. Once she graduated from the adoption classes at Catholic Charities, she would be able to start looking for a child to adopt. She wished her mom hadn't died seventeen years earlier and could be here for this exciting day.

She pulls into the United Airlines parking lot. Her mom would be so happy that she followed through and got a job at an airline, but it was not such a shock; she always followed through and got the things she went after. Now she had the opportunities to travel like her mom wanted her to enjoy. Working for the airline was one of the best decisions Rose ever made. She made some great friends here and had been able to take advantage of the employee perks of travel.

She walked into the office and found Bettie already working.

"Hi, Bettie! You are here early." Rose smiled and waved at her good friend.

"I was so excited for you about the adoption class today! I couldn't wait to talk to you!" Bettie was a super happy person. She always wore a smile.

"I'm excited too!" Rose placed everything she carried into the office on her desk.

"How long are the classes? What time do they start tonight?" Bettie couldn't hold back her enthusiasm.

"The classes last for six weeks, just once a week for three hours a night. I also have to schedule a background check and fingerprints too." Rose sat down with a thump of exhaustion.

Bettie smiled. "You'll do fine. You are always so organized and prepared. They will see right away that you will make a great Mom." Bettie sat down.

"Thanks, Bettie, you are so sweet. I hope you are right." Rose showed her nervousness.

"How is Bob doing? Is he ready for the class tonight?" Bettie knew it was a tough subject but asked anyway.

"He promised me that he would go. Last night he left a note that he would be ready. He was passed out again last night. He had been drinking and taking prescription medicine again. I bet he doesn't go to work today either." Rose was fed up with her husband's behavior. Two years ago, the anxiety attacks began. She went with him for many doctor visits to find a prescription that would calm him, but not totally wipe him out each day.

"He will go tonight, Rose, he loves you. But he shouldn't be taking that medicine and drinking. That is just not good. He better get his act together and start going to work again. You deserve a good husband." Bettie also had a few problems with her husband, nothing as bad as Bob, but she could empathize with Rose about the problems she faced.

"Bettie, I have told him over and over again. He just doesn't listen to me. He doesn't listen to the doctors either. I tried to talk to the doctors, and they said that I cannot intervene. It's hopeless. I don't know what I think I am doing bringing a child into this mess." Rose sighed.

"Rose, you will be the best mom in the world, and if a child has you for a mom, he will be very lucky and nothing else will matter." Bettie reached and assured Rose with a touch on her arm.

"Thanks, Bettie, we better get back to work." Rose turned on her computer and smiled to say goodbye.

Rose worked all day while watching the clock. At four o'clock, she packed up and left work. She had received a call from Bob, saying that he would be ready. Driving home, she hoped he would be sober and prepared for the class. She hoped he would behave himself during the class too.

She pulled into the driveway, and all looked well. She parked and headed into the house. Dinner was waiting on the table, and Bob was clean and dressed nicely. He was sober.

"Hi, Rosie. Dinner is ready, so we can get to the class on time. I know it is important for you to be early. I made your favorite meal, and it's healthy and low calorie. I know how you like to watch your weight." Bob was trying really hard to please his wife.

"Thanks, Bob, I'm glad you are ready. You look great! Thank you for dinner too." Rose smiled and was relieved to see Bob was ready and active.

Rose sat down at the table and enjoyed the nice meal. She worked hard all day and was nervous about the class and nervous about Bob making it to the class. She could breathe a little easier, at least for tonight.

Chapter 4

The Hospital

In another city across the state, an ambulance was rushing down the street to a hospital. The sirens were blaring. Cars were pulling over. It arrived at the ER, and the medical crew rushed the patient into the hospital. It was early evening, and the emergency room was not crowded. Nurses and doctors were walking around, in and out of curtained areas. One of the curtained areas had a little nine-year-old boy. He had a bandage wrapped around his head. He was thin and dressed poorly. He appeared scared. His mother and grandmother were by his bed, also dressed poorly and unkempt. A doctor was holding the patient's board with his paperwork. He started asking some questions to get the story of how the boy's head was hurt.

"Are you the mother?" The doctor showed concern and was stern.

"Yes, I am, and this is my mother and Gabriel's grandmother," the Mom answered the question. She didn't like being questioned and was clearly annoyed.

"Can you tell me how this accident happened?" The doctor continued to add notes to the chart, pausing to ask questions.

"The kids were playing in the backyard, and one of them threw a screwdriver, and it hit Gabriel in the head." The mom gave only what was needed, nothing more. It seemed like she was used to being questioned.

The doctor scanned the papers. "Were you with the children when it happened? This is the fifth time this year that Gabriel has been in this emergency room because of an accident. I noticed that he also has lice in his hair." The doctor stared at the mother, looking for answers.

"Yes, we were both home, and we are home every day watching the children. We just turned our heads for a second and the accident occurred. We are trying to get rid of the lice too." The mother didn't care what the doctor thought, she thought she was right.

"I spoke to one of our social workers, and she is waiting for you in her office. I will finish with Gabriel while you go to see her. He'll be fine here with me." The doctor passed them a sheet of paper with the social worker's name and room number. He turned back to Gabriel while the mother and grandmother walked away.

"Gabriel, is there anything else you would like to tell me about the accident?" The doctor's face changed, and he presented a smile.

Gabriel pulled the covers way up to his chin and shook his head no. He was terrified.

"Have you been eating well? I noticed that you seem to be underweight. Do you get enough food?" The doctor never liked seeing children mistreated. It was one of the worst parts of his job.

Gabriel nodded, still with the covers up to his chin. He had been told by his mother how to answer the questions. He knew that if he answered incorrectly, he may be taken away from her. He didn't think he had a good home or nice stuff, but going somewhere else could be worse.

The doctor continued to write his notes and then told Gabriel to rest until his mom returned.

Meanwhile, in another area of the hospital, the social worker was speaking with Gabriel's mother and grandmother, going over paperwork, and asking questions. "Joyce, this is the fifth time Gabriel has come into the emergency room this year. It appears he is being neglected. We have told you what would happen if this neglect continues. He can be taken away from you and found a more suitable home. Do you have anything to add to the story about today?" The social worker was annoyed but had been in similar situations.

"No, we were watching the children. Gabriel was just in the wrong place at the wrong time. He shouldn't have been in between the other children."

The social worker continued her notes and looked up. "Since there is no other information that can clear this up, I have to explain that it is the duty of the parents to watch their children so that they do not end up in the hospital. I will have to update the file and start the proceedings to find Gabriel a better home."

Joyce and her mother looked at each other, not knowing what to say or do. They got up out of their chairs and walked back to get Gabriel out of the emergency room. All three of them walked out of the hospital and jumped into an old car.

They drove over to a used clothing store and parked. The three of them got out of the car. They walked into the store and started looking through the racks for clothes for the kids. Meanwhile, Gabriel went over to the used-toys' section to see if there was anything he could play with while they shopped. He spotted a book about Jesus. He didn't know much about Jesus because he was never taken to church or Bible classes. He had heard that Jesus was a good man and that he helped children. Gabriel thought that maybe Jesus could help him too. He took the book and lay on the floor underneath a clothing rack, so he wouldn't be disturbed. He started to read in a low voice.

"Jesus helps children. He brings them food if they are hungry. He clothes them if they are cold. He teaches them about God, his father. He tells children to pray each night before going to bed if they need his help, and he will hear them and help." Gabriel closed the book. He was going to pray each night for help. He had to do something. Things were not getting better.

Chapter 5

The Last Day of Classes

The last day of adoption class had arrived, and Rose was listening intently to the teacher as she went over the steps to find a child to adopt. There were basically two ways to go about adopting. She could wait until the local Catholic charity office had a child in need of a home, or she could look at the children who already needed homes located anywhere in the state of Illinois. Rose decided to take the bull by the horns and choose a child on her own. Catalogs were available filled with pictures and descriptions of the children that were waiting for homes. The teacher distributed the catalogs to the students who were interested. Rose started to page through the catalog, looking for possible matches, when she came across a cute boy named Gabriel. The description stated that he was in good physical health, up to date on his schoolwork, and was already a ward of the state. She marked the page and continued to look through the book for others. The teacher stated that more information about the children listed in the catalog was available by calling their individual social worker. She walked around the room to answer questions. At the end of the class, she handed out her card and wished everyone luck. The group mingled a little and ate the treats that were brought by each couple. They were all excited that it was the end of the class, but for Rose it was not the end. It was the beginning of a journey.

Bob and Rose drove home. Bob asked if she wanted to stop at a local bar to have a drink. Rose was not interested. She had never been interested in stopping at local bars to drink. She liked a challenge. She liked to accomplish things. She wanted to get home and start working on the chore at hand. She needed to start a spreadsheet listing the children she found in the catalog and start making phone calls. She wanted to start visiting the various available children right away. No time like the present to get things going.

The next day, Rose went into work and brought her catalog with her. She wanted to review more children during her free time during the day and also show Bettie. She got settled and started to work.

Bettie walked by her office and stopped. She was very excited for Rose, and she knew that the classes ended last night.

"Good morning, Rose! How are you?" Bettie was very excited to find out about the last class.

"I'm good, Bettie. What's going on?" Rose knew that Bettie was waiting for the news.

"Not much with me, but you have lots going on. Tell me about the class last night." Bettie sat down and waited to listen.

"Well, it's over and basically we don't have to go to that office anymore. It's in my hands now. I have this catalog, and I'm free and approved to inquire about any children in the state that need homes." Rose fanned the pages of the catalog to show Bettie the enormous task at hand.

"It looks like you have already started your homework. What are you doing there?" Bettie caught a glimpse of the spreadsheet.

"You know me. I'm an accountant through and through. I made a spreadsheet of the children I have found that seem to be a good fit for me. Here, take a look." Rose handed the paper and book over to Bettie.

"Awww, it's heartbreaking to see all of these children in this book. How often do they publish this book? Are they all still available? I wonder how fast they find homes for them. It just seems like ever-changing information." Bettie was finding it hard to believe they published this book many times a year.

"I think the catalog comes out quarterly. I'll have to call the social worker responsible for each child to see if they are still available and to find out more about them.

"Okay, so who have you picked so far?" Bettie wanted the rundown on the children Rose was interested in adopting.

Bettie looked through the book at the pages that were marked. She paged through one by one and studied the children that Rose had selected. She stopped when she got to the picture of Gabriel. "This one is cute. I see you have him marked. Are you going to call his social worker?"

"Yes, Bettie, you have a sharp eye. Gabriel is high on my list. I will call today and see if he is available. I've called on a few others already, and I have an appointment this coming weekend to visit a brother and sister who need a home." As usual, Rose was quick to get a task completed.

"I didn't think you wanted two children. Do you?" Bettie wasn't sure two children was a good idea.

"Well, Bettie, I don't. But when I called the social worker, she told me that the child I inquired about had a sibling, and they try to keep the children together as much as possible." Since I had already called, I felt it was my obligation to go and visit. It will be good experience too."

"Rose, I think that would be very hard for you, but I do see the value in it for the two siblings." Bettie wanted Rose to think twice before throwing herself into another difficult situation. It was hard enough for Rose to deal with the problems with her husband, Bob, and his drug problems.

"Well, this is a first visit, so it's just getting my feet wet and seeing how the whole system works." Rose just needed to get the ball rolling. She wasn't expecting to adopt these two children.

Bettie and Rose continued to look through the pictures until it was time to get back to work. Bettie went back to her office, and Rose picked up the phone to make another call.

Chapter 6

The Group Home

Saturday arrived, and Rose and Bob drove to the city to a group home where the first boy they inquired about lived. His sister lived in a foster home, not the group home, but she planned on meeting them at the group home. The boy was seven and the sister ten.

When they arrived, they were greeted by the group-home administrator, who explained about the life of the boy and girl. His parents were heavy alcoholics and drug users, and the two children developed fetal alcohol syndrome. The facial features were affected, and they had small eye openings and thin upper lips. They had behavioral problems because of permanent damage of the brain. The boy was much worse than the girl. He was far behind in school and could not read or write yet.

The administrator took them out to see the boy. He didn't have regular social skills and didn't even know how to greet new people he met. He was very slow and very small. His sister joined them, and she seemed normal except for her facial features. The couple who took these children would have their hands full, and with Rose working, she didn't want to get into a situation that was too complicated.

They spent about one hour talking and listening to the girl while she told them about their past life. She seemed pleasant. Rose and Bob listened closely, visited, and then left the group home to start to drive back home.

"Tell the lady we'll take the kids." As always, Bob made a snap judgement, not thinking about the problems it would cause.

"Bob, they are way too much for me or us to handle. I am looking for one child who can attend regular school and take part in normal activities. I could not give those two children all the love and attention they deserve. We'll keep looking." Rose was used to him always jumping into things too quickly without a thought.

"Okay, but I thought you wanted to adopt right away." Bob's intention was just to make Rose happy as fast as possible. He knew his behavior had not been the best lately.

"I do, but it has to be the right child." Rose wanted to take the time and make the right decision for them and for the child.

They drove on quietly and returned home.

At work on Monday morning, Rose got a visit from Bettie again. Bettie couldn't wait to see how the first visit with a child worked out.

"Well, how did it go, Rose?" Bettie had been thinking about the event all weekend. She could hardly contain herself.

"Not too good. Well, what I mean is that the boy we visited over the weekend did not fit in well with my situation. You know that I will keep working, and that boy needed loads of help. I wish I could help him, but that would not be the right move. He needs someone who has more time to devote to him." Rose was sad about the child's situation.

"That's okay. Don't worry, there is probably someone out there looking for that little boy. You can't do everything, Rose." Bettie knew her friend had good intentions yet couldn't help every child; she needed to find the right one.

"I know, but it was such a sad situation. I really wanted to help." Rose had a sad look on her face.

"How was Bob during the visit?" Bettie knew it was time to change the subject. She wanted to turn Rose's thoughts away from the sad situation.

"Surprisingly good, but at the end of the meeting I knew he wasn't enjoying the time spent visiting the child because he just wants me to adopt the first child I see, no matter if it is a good fit or not." Rose was a little frustrated with Bob's reactions.

"Did you get to speak with Gabriel's social worker yet? He seemed like he would be a good fit!" Bettie had thought Gabriel was a better fit and maybe even the right choice for her friend.

"Yes, I did, after you and I talked last week I was able to schedule a visit for next weekend with Gabriel." Rose's face changed to a smile.

"Where does he live?" Bettie was excited that there was another visit with a different child so soon.

"His hometown is a five-hour drive from here. He has been living with his foster mom for eighteen months. He has been with her for eighteen months." Rose rattled off the facts.

Bettie and Rose kept talking about the upcoming visit with Gabriel. She told Bettie more about Gabriel and then spoke about Bob. She confided in her friend about Bob's unstable condition, his constant drinking, gambling, and debt that was growing. Rose knew that her fun and wonderful life with Bob was over, at least for now, but that didn't mean that Rose couldn't do something fulfilling for herself. If she got Gabriel, he'd have a good mother and at least half of what he needed, even if Bob would never be a great father.

Chapter 7

The Visit to Rivertown

"This sure is a long drive. I hope it's worth it. I hope you like this kid better than the one we met last week." Bob was sitting in the passenger seat while Rose drove. It was plain to see that he did not want to be spending his time traveling this far to find a child, certainly not on a Saturday. It just wasn't his cup of tea. This was exactly the reason that Rose had a hard time making the decision to go through with this adoption. She knew he really did not want a child; he was just doing it to make her happy.

"Bob, I just want to do my homework and find the right fit for you and me. Taking the first kid we see isn't good for us or for the boy." She had to find a boy that Bob was enthused about and then maybe it would make a difference.

They drove five hours, stopping for a few breaks, and then arrived in Rivertown. Once upon a time, this town on the Mississippi was booming, but now much of the industry had closed. The main area in downtown was run down and looked like it needed a facelift. They pulled into a Holiday Inn with a swimming pool under a dome. Rose had picked this hotel, thinking that if the visit went well, maybe Gabriel could come to the hotel and swim with them.

They checked in and got their room key, then dropped off their suitcase and checked the time. There was just enough time for lunch, which was a good thing because Bob always loved to stop for a beer. The first meeting was going to be in the Children Services office with the social worker and foster mom. Then, if they both liked Rose and Bob, they would get to meet Gabriel. They headed out to the car to find a place for lunch and one beer and then to find the Children Services office.

When they arrived, they were escorted into the back-meeting room. There they were asked many questions to determine if they would be good parents. Rose answered most of the questions, but Bob did jump in occasionally to describe their house, yard, pool, and the lake behind their house. Things seemed to be progressing well, and Rose was keeping her fingers crossed. She found out that Gabriel's foster mom was trying to get him out of this old, run-down town. She wanted to make sure he was in a good home that would give him opportunities and liked the thought that he would be moving to a big city. She seemed like a fine lady who had been fostering children for several years. It gave her a good feeling to find homes for children and to be a part of their lives.

The social worker asked Rose and Bob to step out of the room for a minute while they discussed Gabriel. Rose and Bob went out to the front porch of the building to wait. After about ten minutes, they were interrupted by a rambunctious little boy who jumped over the railing and ran into the building. Another social worker appeared and brought them back inside the office. They were introduced to the cutest kid ever, who appeared to be full of life and happy! They were both surprised to meet this fun child.

Things went well with the short meeting, and they were told that they wanted Rose and Bob to go home and discuss whether they would want a second meeting. Rose was a little disappointed that she doesn't get to spend much time with Gabriel but understood that the social worker was trying to do her job correctly. They said their goodbyes and went on their way.

Chapter 8

The Book

Rose was excited about the second visit with Gabriel. He seemed like such a fun, special child. He seemed normal in his speech and actions too. She could imagine having Gabriel as her own son. This boy seemed athletic, jumping over the railing like he did. Bob would love to have a kid who excelled in sports. Finally, a link that might get Bob on board with this whole experience!

The next step included making a book that would tell a story about Rose and Bob's life to explain to Gabriel what a new life with them would be like. Rose was very creative, and she couldn't wait to start the book. She carefully imagined the pages in her mind and started compiling a list of everything she wanted to include in it. Next, she'd make a shopping trip to the craft store to buy everything she needed. Then, she'd find pictures showing many of the things they did, the house they lived in, and their dog Duke. Duke, their very special dog, a golden retriever who was trained well and loved everyone. He had been waiting for a boy to play with for a long time. Duke would be extra excited! A complete family picture: Mom and Dad with their son and dog. Just like a Norman Rockwell picture. Rose remembered her collection of the famous artist's work when she was a teenager. Before making the book for Gabriel, she'd have to go to work. The fun part of that would be telling Bettie the news.

She arrived on time on Monday and got right to her work. She had been extra busy since they started the cruise business. They've hired new staff and have written all new procedures, and she kept financials for two companies now, the cruise company and the meeting company for the airline. After an hour or so, Bettie stopped by for the news. She was very excited and plopped right down in Rose's chair in her office.

"Well, tell me everything! Did you meet him? Did he like you? What am I talking about, of course he liked you! Tell me, tell me!" Bettie was giddy with excitement.

Laughing, Rose said, "Slow down, Bettie! Yes, I met him. We had a meeting, and then afterward we were allowed to see him. We'll go back next week for another visit, but he seems perfect!" Rose was smiling and felt good about the situation so far.

"Oh my god! I am so excited! What is he like? Did he look like the picture? Does he want to move out of his town?" Bettie could not stop the questions. You would think that she was going through the experience herself.

Rose smiled. "Yes Bettie, he looked like his picture! I didn't really get to talk to him. Next week we'll meet again, and I have to bring a book with me with pictures showing our house, our life, our dog and everything!"

"I am thrilled! This is going to work out so well for you! You so deserve this Rose. I'll leave you to your work, so you can get out of here on time today and work on your photo album!" Bettie wanted this to work out for Rose so badly. She knew Rose wanted a child and she would make such a good mother. Bettie encouraged her as much as possible.

"Thanks, Bettie!" Rose quickly said her goodbye and went back to work. The day would be long because she wanted to stop for all the supplies and get that book started.

She worked hard all day long and got to leave on time. One stop on the way home to the craft store to buy an album and scrapbook paper with little pictures on each one. Every page would illustrate the different things she wanted to describe in her book. Some of the paper had little airplanes on it, signifying her job and their travels. Other paper had little dog bones on it for the places she would put pictures of Duke. She also bought some very special paper for the very last page. She had an idea that would be perfect!

Rose carried all her supplies into the house to find Bob asleep on the couch again. Another day of pills, alcohol, and sleeping. She just couldn't believe he was throwing away the great job he had and their great life. She didn't know why and what would happen to him, but she just couldn't stop living for him. She had to carry on and continue to accomplish and do the things she loved.

She shut off the loud sports program on TV and went into the dining room, away from Bob, to work on her project. Was this all a lie? Should she even be doing this? What would Gabriel think of all this? She had asked these questions a million times to herself but determined that Gabriel's life would be better than it is now, even if Bob slept all day.

The book was coming together just as she planned. It started with pictures of their house, the yard, the pool, and the pond. The next section showed Rose in her office and all her fellow employees who were also waiting to meet Gabriel. Another section showed their cabin in Wisconsin and various fishing pictures and their boat. The last section displayed places they have traveled to, including Disneyworld. Most importantly, the very last page of the album looked just the way she imagined it.

It was getting late, and she packed up everything and went to bed. It was another day closer to Saturday, and she could not wait to give Gabriel the book. She hoped it would make him say yes and pick her for his new mom.

Chapter 9

The Second Visit

Saturday arrived, and much to Rose's surprise, Bob was up and ready to get on the road. Even though he had a problem with drugs and alcohol these days, he did show that he loved her by going through the adoption process. She hoped things would get better.

The drive seemed shorter this time. They took the same route and got to Rivertown on time. This time they knew that the meeting would only be one hour, and they decided to make the five-hour drive back right afterward. They had a little time before the meeting, so they stopped at a different restaurant for lunch. Here they talked to the locals and learned more about the town and history. After lunch they drove around the historical section of the town and passed by some beautiful old houses. One of Rose's dreams was to someday own an old historical house and fix it up. She loved to watch those shows on TV about restoring old houses. Bob had no interest in any of this, but he did appreciate the old streets and the beautiful houses. Some of the houses had flowers out front. She thought about her mom's love of gardening and the bleeding hearts, peonies, poppies, roses, and lilies that filled the yard of her childhood home. Rose had a few flowers and planned to plant many more. She planted a row of rosebushes along the back of the deck, but it would be a long time before they grew to a size that would create a beautiful display.

They headed to the fast-food restaurant where they would meet Gabriel, his social worker, and his foster mom. It appeared that they were all there waiting as they pulled up. Rose picked up the album she made for Gabriel, and they walked in to meet them. They shook hands and sat down. Bob asked everyone if they would like anything to eat or drink and then went to order something for everyone. The social worker started to talk and explained that Gabriel has had a good week and was excited about the new things that were happening in his life. He had a choice of whether to look for a new family or to stay in foster care until he was eighteen. He chose to look for a new family. Rose was happy to hear this.

Bob came back to the table with the order and sat down. Rose presented the album to Gabriel, and he started turning the pages. He was especially excited about the pages with Duke and the pool. He had learned to swim while living with his foster mom, Sally. She took him to the YMCA each day while she went to work. He had made some new friends there. He also swam with Sally's nephews, who lived nearby and had their own pool. Leaving his foster mom would be a painful experience for Gabriel, but Rose didn't really understand this just yet. Children need stability in their lives. Gabriel had had several foster homes and had gone to several schools. He had not had any stability in his life up until now in Sally's house. This was the best it had been for him. He probably would not understand why things must change again. Life was pretty good with Sally.

Shyly, Gabriel asked, "Will the dog be mine?"

"Yes! Duke has been waiting for a boy just like you to be his friend. He likes going for walks, sitting outside, and just being a little lazy in front of the TV." Rose hoped this will be key in getting him to say yes to adoption.

Gabriel continued through the book until he got to the very last page. This page contained a large heart cut into puzzle pieces. The heart represented Rose and Bob's heart and all the people they love already. There was one piece outside of the heart with Gabriel's name on it. Gabriel was so smart. He took that piece of the puzzle and put it right inside the big heart where it belonged. Now the heart was complete, and Gabriel fit perfectly inside their heart. He closed the book, hugged it, and didn't let it go. Everyone was watching him and loved what they saw. It appeared to be a sign that the match would work, and that they would become a family. Rose was thrilled.

The social worker instructed Gabriel to take the book home and go through it carefully. She wanted Gabriel to ask questions and to be sure that he wanted to go to the new home. Rose and Bob were instructed to give it thought too. The next visit was set for the following weekend, and they were taking him to the state fair. They would be able to spend the entire day with Gabriel. They shook hands, giving Gabriel a hug, and left for their drive home. Everyone had smiles on their faces and Rose had a tear in her eye.

Chapter 10

The State Fair

Another weekend in Rivertown started. Rose and Bob drove down Friday night and checked into the Holiday Inn. Bob was better this past week. He made a few sales calls for work and was happier. He was a great cook and made one of his special meals, his famous Italian gravy. He put care into his spaghetti sauce as it cooked slowly all day long, and he used the best fresh ingredients and sausage. Not too long ago he started a cookbook with some of his favorite recipes and paired them with a drink and a rock and roll song. Bob loved his music. Before he started having anxiety attacks, Rose and Bob would go to lots of concerts. They were in the front row for Van Halen and many others. Those were some fun times!

The morning arrived, and they drove over to Sally's house to pick up Gabriel. As they drove up, they saw Sally and Gabriel outside waiting for them. Gabriel had on a windbreaker-type jacket zipped up to his chin. Rose thought that this was a little strange since it was going to be ninety degrees out today but thought maybe it was because of him being a little scared. Gabriel went through many episodes and types of abuse. It would be natural for him to try to protect himself, even if it was only with a jacket.

Bob stopped the car, and they got out. They greeted Gabriel and Sally excitedly. Sally explained that Gabriel was so excited he had to come outside and wait. Rose was very happy to hear that Gabriel was looking forward to their time together. They said their goodbyes to Sally and jumped in the car. Gabriel sat in the back seat.

"It's going to be a two-hour drive to the fair. Have you even gone to the Illinois State Fair before?" Rose was trying to make conversation and get Gabriel to talk more.

Gabriel answered quietly, "No."

Rose continued, "There are going to be lots of animals to see and carnival rides too."

Bob added, "They will have great hot dogs, snow cones, and cotton candy too!"

"I love hot dogs," Gabriel said with a big smile.

"Great, then we'll have to get you one." Bob enjoyed feeding people good food. He got back to driving and put a CD in the player. They all sat back and enjoyed the ride.

Driving into the state fair was crowded, and Gabriel sat up in the back seat and looked out the window. Rose asked, "Have you ever seen so many people before?"

Gabriel responded, "I was in a parade once, and there was a crowd watching me. It was the Dogwood Parade."

"That must have been fun!" Rose said as she smiled at Gabriel.

Bob paid for the parking and fit the car into a spot. They got out and started walking to the gate. Bob paid for the tickets, and they went through the entry line.

They spent several hours walking through the barns, past all the tents, rides, and food trucks. Gabriel got a hot dog and some cotton candy. He seemed to love his food. Rose stopped and bought him a souvenir. They passed a display of bicycles, and Gabriel stopped to stare.

"Do you like the bikes, Gabriel?" said Rose curiously.

"Yes, I like the stunt bike. It's cool!" Gabriel said excitedly.

"Maybe you can get one someday. Come on, it's almost time for the horse races." Bob had been waiting for the horse race since they arrived.

Rose made a mental note of the bike and grabbed Gabriel by the hand. They walked over to the arena. Bob asked Gabriel to pick a number from one to eight.

"Aaaaaaaaaaaaaaaah, six," said Gabriel hesitantly.

Bob walked over to the window to buy the ticket. He put five dollars on the number-six horse to win. They all climbed up to the grandstand and waited for the horse race to start. Bob read the racing form. Rose watched the horses walk around the racetrack until she spotted horse number six.

"Look, Gabriel, there is your horse!" Rose tried to add some excitement to the experience.

"He is beautiful! Is he going to run against the other horses?" Gabriel had never been to a horse race and asked some questions.

"Yes, there are eight horses in this race, and we are going to watch to see who comes in first," Rose explained.

The announcer started naming the horses as they walked by and got into the gate to wait for the start. Rose, Bob, and Gabriel waited patiently for the race to start.

The announcer started. "And they're off! Number one, Billy Boy is off to a quick lead, but number two, Hello Dolly is right behind Billy Boy giving him a run for the money. Number six, Cindy's Beau, is coming up and Lucky Lou, horse number 4, is giving them a challenge. They are coming up to the home stretch, and it's Hello Dolly followed by Cindy's Beau and look, it's horse six, Cindy's Beau has just gotten a burst of strength and is in it to win it. He takes the lead and wins it by a length with Hello Dolly coming in second."

Gabriel, Rose, and Bob all stood up to cheer and scream as their horse had won the race! Gabriel couldn't stop jumping up and down. "He won, he won, he won!" shouted Gabriel.

Bob said, "Yes, now we have to see how much he pays out! He was not supposed to win this race. The money should be pretty good."

"We are going to win some real money?" Gabriel was very excited and had a huge smile.

"Yes, watch the board over there, and soon it will tell us what we won." Bob pointed across the field to the large board that displayed the results. They watched closely, and the winning horses and the payouts were added to the board. Bob stood up. "Let's go get the winnings."

They approached the ticket window, and Bob stood in line while Rose and Gabriel waited for him. He returned with sixty-six dollars. Bob gave the money to Gabriel and said that since he picked the horse, it was his money to keep. Gabriel had never had that much money. He looked at it with surprise and asked if he could really keep it. Bob and Rose told him that it was his to spend it on anything he wanted. Gabriel was super happy and stuffed it into his pocket. Rose told him to be careful with it.

The hours went by, and it was time to leave the fair. They spent whole day there and they are tired and hot. Gabriel still has the jacket zipped up. Rose didn't believe how he could be comfortable, but it was not her place to judge. They piled into the car and started to drive. They were going to stop at a restaurant for dinner. Gabriel had told them that he loved ribs. They had done some research and decided on Damon's Ribs, a sports restaurant with big-screen TVs and great ribs. They also had trivia games on the TV. Gabriel was amazed at all the TVs that were on the walls. The waiter brought them menus, and they started to look to see what they would order. Rose asked Gabriel what he wanted, and he decided on the ribs. He also ordered mashed potatoes and corn on the cob. Rose stuck with a chicken breast and broccoli. Bob ordered a steak.

While they waited for their meal, they got a trivia-game control and started answering the trivia questions. Bob showed off his vast knowledge of sports trivia. Rose was pretty good at geography, and even Gabriel answered some questions correctly about TV shows. They ended up with the highest number of points in the restaurant. Gabriel thought they got a prize for trivia too. Rose told him that there were no prizes; it was just fun to play. Gabriel agreed.

The food arrived at the table, and Gabriel chowed down the ribs with gusto! Rose was surprised that for a small boy he ate so much. She just thought that he had a long life without food, and it would be easy to understand how he could love the tasty food he was eating now. It didn't worry her as she ate her healthy meal. She also knew they did a great deal of walking today, and it would make anyone hungry for a big meal.

When they drove back to Rivertown, they stopped to get gas. Bob got out of the car, and Rose talked to Gabriel. She asked him how he was doing in school. Gabriel said he got good grades and that he was the one who helped his brothers and sisters with their homework when they had lived together. Rose had no reason not to believe him. She told him that her only request if he came to live with them were good grades in school. Gabriel said that he would get good grades, and Rose was happy.

They dropped off Gabriel with Sally and told her all about the day. She was very happy to see Gabriel enjoying himself. He had had a hard life, and she loved him so much. She wished she could keep Gabriel, but she vowed to only foster children, not adopt. She wanted the children that she fostered to be placed in homes with both mothers and fathers. She was single, so she didn't believe that she should adopt a child. She was a good person.

Chapter 11

The Wait

Everything was back to normal on Monday. Rose was off to work, and Bob was still in bed. An hour's drive to work in the northern suburbs meant that her day started early. Rose didn't mind the long drive if she could start early to avoid some of the traffic. She arrived to work and found Bettie there, already waiting for the news.

"It had been a very long weekend for me waiting to hear how things went." Bettie waited impatiently with a smile.

Rose was always amused with Bettie's good-humored comments. She told Bettie all the details about the entire weekend. At the end of the detailed description, Bettie asked the big question, "What happens next?"

Rose explained to Bettie that everyone had to go home and think about what they want. Of course, for Rose the answer was easy. She wanted Gabriel. Bob wanted Rose to get what she wanted, if it didn't disrupt his life too much. The question was, what did Gabriel want? That was what they did not know yet. It was a big decision for a ten-year-old boy to make. He was going to have to move out of the town he had lived in all his life. Even though the family was dysfunctional, it was all he knew. Even though the town was not a booming, up-and-coming town, it was the only place he had lived and his hometown. Anyone would have difficulty with the change, but especially a child.

As they were talking, the phone rang in Rose's office, and Rose answered, "Hello, United Cruises, this is Rose. How can I help you?"

"Hi, Rose, this is Gabriel's social worker from Rivertown. I'm glad I caught you. I couldn't wait to give you the news!" The social worker had a happy voice.

Rose was pointing to the phone and shaking her head excitedly at Bettie. "Hello! I wasn't expected to hear from you so soon. I hope it's the news I've been waiting to hear!"

"Gabriel had a great time at the fair on Saturday. He feels comfortable with you, and he wants to come live with you and Bob." The social worker waited for an answer.

Rose was so excited; she could hardly speak but managed to say thank you and got more details. She understood that Gabriel had a small medical procedure to go through before he could move. They wanted to get that done and have Gabriel start school on time in his new neighborhood. It would be two weeks, and he would be moving in with them. After the six-month waiting period, the adoption could be finalized. She hung up the phone, and her head was spinning! Everything was working so fast and so easily. She never would have expected things to work out like this. She gave Bettie a big hug, and Bettie hugged her right back.

After the first few minutes of excitement, Bettie asked Rose if she was going to call Bob. Rose hesitated and then asked Bettie why she had to spoil such a great moment and remind her of Bob. She decided to wait to tell him until she got home. She hoped he had another good day and worked a little. She finished her day and headed home.

When she walked in the door, Bob was making dinner and singing. A welcome change! The table was set, and he offered her a drink. He told her that he received a few orders today and made a little commission money. He was proud of himself and happy for a change! They sat down to eat, and Rose told him the news. Bob was sure that Gabriel had fun and knew he would like them. He said he told Rose all along that Gabriel would want to come and live here. She agreed that he had said that and again felt a little relief. Everything did seem to be falling in place.

After dinner, Rose started a list of the things that needed to be done before Gabriel arrived. They had plenty of space upstairs, and one of the bedrooms would be his. They'd get a TV and some new clothes for him. Since he'd be starting school, he'd also need a backpack and school supplies. The list didn't seem too long, and they shouldn't have any trouble getting everything done in time.

Sally, the foster mom, agreed to drive half of the distance to meet Rose and Bob. They picked a truck stop off the interstate for a meeting place. Rose and Bob piled in the bicycle and their dog Duke into their pickup truck. They left with plenty of time to get there on time. As they drove up to the restaurant, they saw Sally and Gabriel waiting in the parking lot. Bob slowed down the truck and parked. As soon as he did, Gabriel was walking to the pickup truck, excited to finally meet Duke. Rose put the leash on Duke and brought him out of the truck. Duke liked Gabriel as soon as he saw him and vice versa. Gabriel wouldn't take his arms off of his new best friend, Duke. It was a heartwarming picture.

After letting Gabriel and Duke get to know each other, Bob brought out the brand-new stunt bicycle to show Gabriel. There was delight in Gabriel's eyes when he saw the exact same bicycle that he had his eye on when they were at the state fair. He couldn't believe it was his. Bob urged him to take it for a spin around the parking lot. Gabriel did a great job riding the bike. It was wonderful to see, since he never even had his own bike in the past. They said their goodbyes to Sally and packed everything back into the truck and started for home.

Although Gabriel had never been out of nearby communities surrounding his town, the scenery on the way to Rose and Bob's home was the same for him, cornfield after cornfield. There really wasn't anything to look at, and so Rose was able to talk to Gabriel about his school, YMCA, karate lessons, and life with his foster mom, Sally. They discovered that he had two half sisters and one half brother through his birth mother. He wasn't sure who his birth father was, but one of the possibilities included a man with six children, and they could also be Gabriel's half siblings. He had stayed with this man for a few months before he was placed with Sally, and that turned out to be the worst part of his life.

Gabriel told them that only one of those half siblings was in foster care. It was his older half sister, Melissa, who lived about two hours away, close enough for visits. Rose made a mental note to find out more about Melissa.

They pulled into the driveway and started to unload the truck. Rose took Gabriel into the house with Duke. They went straight to the sliding door at the back of the house to let Duke roam the backyard. Gabriel saw the pool and the pond. Another big smile appeared on his face.

Back inside, Rose showed Gabriel his room upstairs and helped him unload his duffel bag into the drawers and closet. He found new clothes and a new backpack for school. He saw the TV that was his alone and was very excited. Everything to him was picture-perfect. It was the best thing that had ever happened to him.

They went back outside and threw some balls into the basketball net in front of the house and then stopped and sat down for dinner. It was a great day! A day they would always remember: the first day with their new, perfectly normal, ninety-three-pound eleven-year-old son. One more day and a routine would begin. Gabriel was scheduled to start school at the junior high school right down the street on Monday.

Chapter 12

The First Day of School

It was Monday morning, and the first day of school came way too quickly for Rose. She had to go back to work, and Gabriel was going to be away at school all day. They all got up, had a nice breakfast, and drove to check Gabriel into the new school. It was only a two-mile drive to school but very unfamiliar territory for Gabriel. Rose wanted to stay home so badly, but Gabriel was eleven years old and capable of coming home from school himself. She did not want him to feel like she was treating him like a baby. She remembered how mean kids could be, and if she hung around the school the kids might call him names, and he would get off on the wrong foot. She would do anything to make life pleasant and normal for Gabriel.

The school administrator was in her office, and she checked Gabriel into the school. Bob signed the necessary papers, and then they headed off to show Gabriel where the bus was parked. He would take the bus home. Rose had asked Gabriel if he had ever ridden the bus, and he said that he had ridden it home from his old school. They stuffed Bob's business card into his backpack just in case there was a problem. Bob always had his cell phone with him for his sales calls, so he would be available. After they showed Gabriel the correct bus, a teacher escorted him to his classroom, and it was time for Rose to leave. They exited the building and went off to work.

It was a long, hard day for Rose. She was constantly thinking of Gabriel and how he might be doing at school. She called Bob, who was making some sales calls, but he had not heard a word. He would get home at 3:00 p.m. to be there when Gabriel got off the bus. She was relieved about that but still wanted to be home herself.

Gabriel got out of school and followed the kids to the buses. He remembered the bus that Rose and Bob pointed out in the parking lot and was sure he got onto the correct bus. Now it was just a matter of getting off at the right stop. The bus went through lots of subdivisions, and every one of them looked the same. Gabriel was confused and did not know where to get off. He just kept riding and riding around on the bus until he was the very last child on the bus. The bus driver noticed that he did not get off on the last stop, so she pulled the bus over and went back to talk to him. When she approached Gabriel, he handed her Bob's card and said that he just moved here and didn't know where he lived. The bus driver quickly gave Bob a call and explained the situation. Bob told the bus driver their address and subdivision and agreed to be waiting on the corner for the bus. A few minutes later, the bus arrived, and Bob waited for Gabriel to get off the bus. They walked back to the house, and Gabriel was embarrassed, so he did not say a word.

Back at the house, Bob made dinner and waited for Rose to get home while Gabriel lay on the couch and watched TV. Rose arrived at her usual time and ran into the house. She said hello very excitedly and went into the kitchen. Bob explained the whole story to Rose. She felt so bad for not being home and for making Gabriel ride the bus and getting lost on his very first day at school. She ran over to the couch and hugged Gabriel and told him she knew it must have been horrible. Gabriel smiled and felt a little better. Dinner was ready, and they sat down to eat. Hopefully, the rest of the first school week would be easier.

Chapter 13

The First Few Months

It was 10:00 a.m., and so far there was no call from the school nurse. It had become a habit for Gabriel to go to the school nurse whenever he was having a hard time with something at school. Each day Rose was receiving another call. She would talk to the nurse and then to Gabriel, and they both urged Gabriel back to class each day. When Gabriel came home from school, Rose would ask him how things went and if he was feeling better. Nothing else came out of the conversations. She figured that it wasn't that bad if Gabriel was missing thirty minutes of school each day. It could be much worse. She knew his homework was getting done because they would sit together to complete the assignments. He didn't seem to have any problems with the studies. What other problems could there be? It also didn't seem like he was behind in his learning at all either. Each night they sat at the dining room table and finished what she thought was needed for school the next day. He didn't struggle with anything. She had no other children, so when there wasn't any homework on any given day, she didn't give it a thought. She trusted Gabriel.

One night, Gabriel came home with a tough assignment. The homework consisted of creating a family tree. Gabriel hadn't even gotten a chance to meet his new family of aunts, uncles, and cousins. He had been taken out of his old family. He had to have felt like he had no family to put on the family tree. He was lost. Of course, Rose and Bob both helped and created a family tree with all kinds of branches. The thing was, Gabriel couldn't possibly explain the people on the tree, except for the two new parents he now had. The tree went to school, but they didn't really know what happened when it got there or if it got there.

Night after night, Rose and Gabriel sat at the dining room table and completed the homework, then Gabriel took a bath and went to bed. One night, Rose asked Gabriel if he ever had a horsey-back ride, and she found out he never had one. Beginning that night, Rose would carry Gabriel up the stairs to bed each night. When she started, he weighed 93 pounds and she weighed 135. When he reached 127 pounds, she confessed that she could no longer carry him, and he would have to climb the stairs himself. There was a little sadness, but she thought there were probably enough horsey-back rides those first few weeks to last a lifetime.

Gabriel liked taking baths when he first arrived. Rose bought him a few toys for the bathtub. Playing in the bathtub was a normal thing if you grew up in a middle-class family, but this was another thing that Gabriel never had the privilege to do. Most of the time, he didn't even get a bath. A bath was rare. During the time he lived with the man he thought was his birth father, there was no running water in the abandoned trailer. A bath was out of the question. After a few weeks Gabriel stopped taking baths and changed to showers. It was like all the pieces of Gabriel were at different ages, and they had to catch up to the age of eleven. One by one, each item was checked off the list, and his life was getting normal.

Bedtime started with reading each night. Rose read Harry Potter books to Gabriel. She would sit by his bedside on the floor and read out loud. They also read books about the presidents. Gabriel loved American history. One of their favorite books was *George Washington's Socks*, which was about a little boy who mistakenly went back into time and was with George Washington when he crossed the Delaware. George gave the little boy his socks to keep his feet warm.

This specific night, Rose was done reading a chapter and said good night to Gabriel. Gabriel responded with "I love you." Rose was shocked and returned the kind words right back. This was a moment worth all the work that she had gone through. This was the moment when she knew she had made the right decision adopting a boy like her mom had asked her to do so long ago.

The next day, Rose decided to bring Gabriel to her office to introduce him to all her coworkers, who were also people that encouraged her when she made her decision to adopt him. Gabriel had seen the group in the album that Rose had made for him when she had met him. Even though the faces were familiar, and he knew they were Rose's friends, he was afraid. Rose walked him around the office, and everyone thought he was adorable. She stopped to converse with Bettie, and when they were done talking, she turned around and Gabriel was gone. It had only been a few minutes, so he couldn't have gone far. They looked everywhere and finally found him underneath Rose's desk. Maybe meeting so many new people was too much for him. She felt she was making mistakes left and right. After acknowledging that he may need some space, Rose took Gabriel home.

Another day, Rose was cleaning out Gabriel's school backpack and found a letter for a conference with his teachers. It was in the evening during an open house at school. She wasn't sure whether all the parents received a letter for a private meeting, or if it was only some of the children. Either way, she was excited to meet some of Gabriel's teachers and hear how he was doing.

She drove over to the school, and Gabriel stayed home with Bob. Gabriel was nervous because he remembered that the only thing Rose had asked him was that he get good grades. Gabriel never had anyone who paid attention to his grades. No one even cared about his report card until he was living with Sally, his foster mom. There was so much going on at school, it was hard for him to concentrate on his studies.

Rose walked into the school and found her way to the classroom. She walked in and was shocked to find six teachers waiting to see her, all sitting in a row. She knew Gabriel had a different teacher for each class but didn't think that each one would be there to meet with her. It was like an interrogation. What was going on?

She sat down in the designated chair. The first teacher started. "Gabriel has many problems. We were trying to deal with them ourselves and not call, but it has gone too far."

The second teacher seemed frustrated and said, "He hides under his desk in my class most of the time. He never does his homework."

The third teacher was angry and said, "He threatened me with a pencil and threw down a podium."

The fourth teacher finally had her turn and said, "I found him at the end of the hallway in a fetal position."

The fifth teacher added, "He threw another child into a locker."

Rose was in shock! "Why haven't I heard any of this before?"

The first teacher answered for the others, "We knew you were a foster mom and didn't want to deal with any of these problems, but we have no choice but to ask for help."

Rose was angry. "Who do you think I am? I am Gabriel's mother, and I would have been here immediately at the sign of any trouble. This is not acceptable. Gabriel has been having trouble that could have been solved two months ago if you made me aware of the issues. Now it is two months later, and I am just hearing about this. He missed two months of studies because of you not giving me this information. What is wrong with you?"

The teachers were the ones who were shocked now. They all had their mouths open, not knowing how to answer. They usually found that foster parents at this school were just temporary parents and not the type who wanted to help.

The first teacher tried to dig herself out of the hole and started to apologize. "We didn't think you'd want to know, but now I realize we should not have assumed that you were uninterested. This was wrong of us. Sorry."

"Well, let's not worry about the past. What can be done to help Gabriel in the future? How are his grades? It can't be that bad. I had made sure his homework was done each night."

The teachers looked at each other, shocked again, and the second teacher added, "We haven't seen any homework being turned in to us."

Rose explained that she worked on the homework with Gabriel each night, but she wasn't sure if it was the right homework or all the assignments. She asked what could be done so that she knew the entire assignment each day. The teachers each offered to start e-mailing her the assignments, and they also agreed to personally ask Gabriel for his homework and look in his folder for the assignments now that they knew the work was being completed. They would each show Gabriel how to arrange his folder with the new assignments on the right and the finished assignments on the left. The meeting ended with everyone feeling better. Rose knew what had to be done, and she would make sure that she communicated with each teacher every day until things got better.

She walked into their home a few minutes later, and Gabriel and Bob were both watching TV in separate rooms. She walked right into the living room where Gabriel was lying with Duke, and she asked why Gabriel didn't tell her that he was having trouble in school. Gabriel just shook his head and didn't explain. Moving to a new home with new parents must have been more difficult that she ever thought. She gave him a hug and went into the kitchen to talk to Bob. Bob didn't understand why the teachers had not called either. He was not that enthused about homework, but he would have gone to talk to anyone of them if he was asked. Rose told him the plan for the rest of the school year. He felt bad for Gabriel too.

As the months went forward, Rose stuck with her plan and kept in constant contact with the teachers. The homework got done, and the assignments were turned in. After six months, Rose was in her office working on her computer, and she received an e-mail from Gabriel's homeroom teacher. She opened it up, expecting another assignment, but this letter was different. She kept reading and found out that Gabriel was to receive the Student of the Month Award for turning his grades completely around. She smiled and rushes to Bettie's office to tell her.

"Bettie, guess what? It's the best news ever!" Rose was slightly out of breath.

Bettie put down her work and listened.

"I just received an e-mail from Gabriel's homeroom teacher, and he is getting the Student of the Month Award." Rose was thrilled.

"Well, Rose, you two have sure worked hard for this. I expect great things out of Gabriel. He is one of a kind." Bettie nodded just to say she knew it would all come around.

"Thank you, Bettie, you are always upbeat and positive! You are a big part of this too. Every day when I come over and talk to you, you are supportive and give me the strength to keep going even when things look bleak." Rose wanted her friend to know how important she was to her each and every day.

"I just love both you and Gabriel and want good things for you both." Bettie was beaming with joy!

"As soon as Gabriel brought home the certificate, I'll bring it to show you! Now I have to get back to work so I can finish my day and get home!" Rose was really looking forward to getting home and giving Gabriel a big hug!

Rose worked until four o'clock and then shut down her computer for the day. The drive home seemed awfully long today. She anticipated the joy she'd see in Gabriel's face when he showed her the certificate. Pulling into the driveway, she expected him to be waiting anxiously with the award in hand. She shut off the car and didn't hear a thing. Grabbing her purse, she went into the house, and still there were no cries of joy. Gabriel was lying on the couch with a very sad face. Bob approached her and told her that the kids on the bus tore up his certificate. He had gone over to the house of one of the parents, and they accused Gabriel of shouting off his mouth and said he deserved what they did. Rose could not believe a parent of any child would approve of bad behavior and not try to help in any way. She walked over to Gabriel to hear his side of the story. As usual, he didn't have much to say. She comforted him and told him she would call the school and get another certificate tomorrow. Why couldn't this one day be free of problems?

After a sometime, Rose and Bob congratulated Gabriel on the Student of the Month Award, and Gabriel started to smile and clutched his hands together and acted like he was stirring a pot. This was a dance he did when he was happy! He called it the cabbage-patch dance. They smiled with him and hoped there would be plenty of these happy times in the future! Rose started to do the dance with him. Round and round they stirred their hands while laughing!

Chapter 14

The Certificate

Rose was working on the month-end financial numbers in the office when the phone rang. It was the school counselor informing her about the new Student of the Month certificate that was given to Gabriel today. There was more news. The counselor strongly suggested that Rose take Gabriel out of the public school and put him in a private school. Even though Gabriel improved enormously, he still would need special care, and the public schools were just not equipped to give him the care he needed. Rose had already thought of that solution herself before the call. A private or religious school might help Gabriel. He believed in God and wore a cross around his neck to give him comfort. Going to a religious school would most likely help Gabriel. When the counselor made the suggestion, it was the final push that she needed to make the change. She would start the application process right away. There were two schools that were close to their house. One of them was very popular and would be tough to get into, and usually there was a waiting list. The second school was farther away, and there may be a problem dropping Gabriel off there each day, but she would apply there too and get some of the questions answered.

Rose made another big push to get Gabriel involved in sports and other activities. She enrolled him in baseball and art classes. Nights were busy: dinner then Little League and one day a week the art class. After the episode on the bus when the kids tore up his certificate, she knew he needed more help socializing.

It was Wednesday, and they headed to art class in their Chevy Silverado pickup truck. Gabriel took his usual spot in the middle of the front seat, right next to Rose. They rode a few miles, and then he started to talk.

"Mom, when we get up to heaven, I am going to be a baby up there so that you can hold me in your arms." Gabriel stared straight ahead.

Shocked with this comment, Rose hesitated but then said, "Wow, what a wonderful thought. That would be a dream come true." They rode on quietly; some of the best conversations happened in the car.

The next day was batting lessons. Gabriel was built like a young Sammy Sosa and hit the ball really well! Lessons would improve his skills and give him a little self-esteem boost when the crowd cheered for hitting a home run! Rose found a batting coach about ten miles away. The coach was on a minor baseball league, and Gabriel was proud that he was learning from him. On the way home he was talking more than usual. It must have meant that he was happy.

"Mom, did you know that the guy I lived with for eighteen months who is supposed to be my birth father is a bad man?" Gabriel stared straight ahead when he said this.

"What do you mean a bad man? Did he do something wrong?" Rose had no idea what Gabriel was telling her, but she wanted him to feel comfortable saying anything, so she tried to stay calm and listen.

"He used to do bad things to the kids when Becky, his wife, went to work." Gabriel was opening up to her and trying to get something out.

Concerned, Rose asked more questions. "Can you tell me what happened?"

Gabriel told the story of the abusive behavior of Gabriel's possible birth father. He was abusive to all of the children in the abandoned trailer where they lived. The abuse was unbelievable and shocking. Not only did these children have to put up with poor conditions, no running water, little food, but also an abusive environment.

Stunned, Rose hesitated and said, "Would you be willing to tell someone about this?"

"Will they put him in jail?" It was obvious that Gabriel was angry with this man for what he did and wanted him to go to jail for it.

"I'm not really sure what will happen, but if you don't tell someone, he definitely won't go to jail, and that is not fair." Rose tried to encourage Gabriel to speak up.

"Okay, I'll do it. I'll tell whoever you want me to tell." Gabriel was finished talking. They drove on, and Rose made the appropriate calls when she got home. They were told to come right over to the DCFS office. Once they got there, Gabriel had to go into a separate room to tell the authorities what had happened at his previous home. Rose was also interviewed and was only able to tell what Gabriel had just shared. She had not known anything about this. None of the social workers had known either.

A counseling appointment was made for Gabriel because of the new information about his past. Meanwhile, Rose kept in touch with the DCFS office to track what was happening in the investigation. She wanted this man to be put in jail too.

From then on, Rose had flashbacks about the things that went on in that abandoned trailer even though she had never seen the horrors. It was so sad that Gabriel went through this and worse that he had kept it bottled up inside until now. For weeks she called the DCFS office to get updates. Finally, she was told that the man had skipped out of the state, and they can no longer do anything about what happened.

Rose did not accept that answer. She found the city that she assumed the stepfather ran to. He had taken his children with him. She knew the names of the children and called the police department in his new city. The police found him and the children. The children were questioned at school but would not commit the father for fear that they would be beaten or thrown out on the streets. It was a shame. There was nothing more that Rose could do. At least Gabriel was safe and would never live another day with this man.

Since his confession, he was ordered by DCFS to attend counseling. The first day of the counseling arrived, and Gabriel and Rose headed over. Fortunately, the counseling was offered as a free service since he was a ward of the state. He was apprehensive about going into the office with the psychologist, but Rose was not allowed to go in with him. She read some magazines while she waited. When it was over, Gabriel walked out alone. They made another appointment and then went to the car.

On the way home, Rose asked Gabriel some questions about his time with the counselor. He said the counselor asked many questions. One of which was whether he had any thoughts of suicide. Gabriel never had any thoughts of suicide, but he said, now that it was in his head, he was thinking about it. Rose thought, *Just what we needed. This is going from bad to worse.*

Gabriel also told Rose that the counselor thought that he was still living with the abuser and the abuser was Rose. Rose was furious. What in the world? Was there no communication between the DCFS office and the counselor's office? This counseling was worthless if they didn't even start off with the correct information. She made a mental note to call them to take care of the miscommunication.

The next day, she received a letter from the nearest Catholic school, which informed her that Gabriel was on a waiting list. It didn't look like he would get into St. Mary's. She thought about the counselor's mistake and wondered if they might be able to help his chances of enrollment into St. Mary's. She gave them a call.

"Hi, this is Rose, and I am calling about a visit my son had at your office yesterday." Rose gave the receptionist the information he needed to look up the visit.

"Yes, I see that we saw Gabriel yesterday afternoon. How can we help you?" The receptionist paused and gave Rose time to answer.

"Can I speak with the counselor that had the session with my son?" Rose didn't really want to explain about the mix-up to the receptionist because she knew she would just have to repeat the same story again.

"Sure, let me put you on hold and see if I can get him on the phone." Background music came on while the call was being transferred.

"Hi, this is Steve. I was your son's counselor yesterday. Do you have a question for me?" The counselor seemed hurried, like he was between appointments.

"Yes, after leaving, my son told me that you were under the impression that I was the abuser. The abuse took place two years ago when he was living with the man who was thought to be his birth father. Gabriel also said that you asked him about suicide, which he had never thought about, but he said that after the thought was put into his mind, he couldn't help but think about it." Rose was upset that these mistakes were made. She wanted an explanation.

"I am sorry that the information I was given was incorrect. I will call the DCFS office and clear things up before his next visit." He was ready to hang up but noticed that Rose wasn't ready to finish the call. There must be more.

Rose thought this would be a perfect opportunity to get some help to get Gabriel into the private school. "Can you do us another favor too? Since things did not work out during his first visit with you, and he may have even taken a step backward because of it, can you help us get him into a private school?" Rose was nervous about asking for help. She usually didn't ask anyone for help. She was always taking all the burdens herself.

The counselor paused. "What can I do to help?"

"Maybe a letter from you saying that he needed the smaller classrooms and more attention because of his past. Maybe a letter like that would help his chances of enrollment in St. Mary's?"

"I understand the situation, and I would be happy to help. Let me get that letter out this week. I will send you a copy of it." After explaining the whole situation, the counselor seemed more relaxed and happy to help.

Rose was a little relieved. "Thank you. I really appreciate it." She hung up the phone and was grateful that the counselor listened to her. Next, she'd call the other school—which was farther away, but smaller—and see what were his chances there just in case the letter didn't help at St. Mary's. Maybe that would be a better place for Gabriel anyway? Maybe this was all meant to be.

The smaller school, Holy Family, had just relocated and was soliciting for more students. They welcomed the opportunity to enroll Gabriel into seventh grade. Rose went ahead and bought the uniforms and made the doctor appointment to get all the necessary steps out of the way for him to start in late August.

She never heard back from St. Mary's until a few weeks later, the day school started. The phone rang in her office, and it was their administrator saying there was one seat left in the seventh grade for Gabriel. Since Gabriel was already set to go to Holy Family and even had a nice mom willing to drive him to and from school, Rose said no thank you to St. Mary's. She felt good about her selection of the smaller school and thought that it was a good thing he didn't get into St. Mary's right away, or she would never have found this smaller school where the administrator was so grateful for the extra student.

Chapter 15

The Adoption

The day finally came for Gabriel to be adopted by Rose and Bob. They sat in the lawyer's office, and he asked Gabriel if he was happy with his new home. Gabriel said, "Yes, I am." The lawyer told Gabriel that most likely he was being spoiled since he was new to the house and that the spoiling would lessen as time went by. This bit of information did not affect Gabriel's decision to be adopted. The papers were signed, and we celebrated the occasion with a fancy restaurant and a gift. The gift was a box with a small teddy bear inside and the date on the box. There was a card inside too. Gabriel hugged the teddy bear and cherished the box with the adoption date.

Things went smoothly for a while, and even Bob was going to AA meetings. Maybe things would work out after all. Rose had regular meetings with the school, and there were problems with kids bullying Gabriel, but most of the problems were minor and lessening.

It was getting close to Thanksgiving and time for Rose to meet with Gabriel's teacher. She said that she caught him looking at the cross in the classroom quite often. Rose had bought Gabriel a cross for around his neck too, so that he would always feel safe. It seemed to have a good effect on Gabriel.

Mrs. B, a nickname the kids gave her, said that she was concerned about something. They were putting on a Christmas play, and all the kids were asked to take part in the play. When it came for Gabriel's turn to select a part that he would like in the play, he said that he wouldn't be able to attend the practices after school and would not be in the play. Mrs. B thought that was odd, since she knew Rose was always open to everything. Rose was surprised about his answer too. She thought she had always given the impression that she would help in any way she could. Mrs. B thought that maybe Gabriel never had anyone bring him to practices in the past, and he was just programmed to say no. That made sense to Rose. Mrs. B. and Rose agreed to do what they could to get Gabriel into his very first school play.

Rose went home and talked to Gabriel about the practices and told him that he should be in the play, and she would gladly take him and pick him up, just like she did for the basketball practices and games. Gabriel was apprehensive but agreed to be in the play.

A few weeks went by, and Gabriel went to the practices. He had a small part in the play with very few words. Rose was looking forward to the event, which was held in the school gym. The bleachers were full of parents and grandparents. Rose found a seat close to the stage and sat down. This was a big night, Gabriel's first-ever play!

The lights were turned down, and the play started. Mrs. B. saw Rose in the audience and walked over to sit next to her when it was Gabriel's turn to be on the stage. He was beaming. There was a huge smile as he presented his part in the play. Both Mrs. B. and Rose had a tear in their eyes because they felt like they had a victory! They saw Gabriel happy and taking part in something with his schoolmates. It was awesome!

The night ended, and Mrs. B. pulled Rose aside once more. She said that they learned about angels in religion class that week. She asked Gabriel if he believed in angels. He did not have an answer. Mrs. B. told him that he should believe, because he had one in his life. It was Rose, his new mom. She said Gabriel smiled.

The night went south when they arrived at home. Bob was supposed to be at an AA meeting, but instead he had gone to a bar and drank. He was taking prescription medicine and was never supposed to drink. He was driving home, was in the wrong lane, and ended up with the company car in a ditch, smashed. The police gave him a ticket for drunk driving. This was not good. Bob couldn't tell his company about the accident; they would have to fix the truck themselves. Also, there would be lawyer costs to deal with the DUI ticket. These were problems that Rose just didn't want to deal with right now. It was a very happy day, and now Bob turned it upside down. She should have made him come to the play, but she thought the AA meeting was more important. Why didn't he go to the meeting like he should have? She was getting very tired of this whole mess.

Christmas brought mixed feelings. It was wonderful playing Santa for Gabriel even though he did not believe in Santa. She had a coworker write a letter from Santa in gold writing, saying that he had noticed all the achievements Gabriel was making and therefore left some great presents for him. Even though Gabriel came to their house with only one memento of previous happiness, a stuffed clown from his grandmother, Gabriel's closets and room were now filled with trophies from sports and all kinds of happy mementos.

Rose knew that one of Gabriel's favorite Christmas movies was *Miracle on 34th Street*. She brought the movie to life. In the movie, Kris Kringle left his cane in the living room. The little girl saw it and knew that it was really Kris Kringle who left the presents for her. Rose mimicked this action and found an old cane that she left beside her fireplace on Christmas morning. Even though Gabriel had been told that there wasn't a Santa Claus, seeing the cane made him think that just maybe there really was.

Chapter 16

The Boat

The summer was filled with happy memories. Bob was behaving after his DUI. The case was closed, and he got off easy. He was still able to drive and started making sales calls again. As a reward for good behavior, Rose and Bob purchased a fishing boat mainly for their cabin. The first time they used it was on a visit to see one of Rose's friends, who had moved to Wisconsin. Gabriel, Rose, Cathy, and her two girls went to a festival where Gabriel and Cathy's kids made some crafts and went on rides. Meanwhile, Cathy's husband, Dave, and Bob took the new boat to a lake. All went well, until Rose came back to pick up the boat. Bob and Dave had drunk during the day, and Rose had to use the truck to pull up the boat because they were unable to handle it. This was new for Rose, but she was a good driver and could do it. She backed up the boat and got near to it. Bob and Dave were unable to steer it into the trailer. She got upset that it was taking so long and hopped out of the truck to help. Meanwhile, she forgot to put the emergency brake on, and the truck was slipping into the water with Gabriel inside! She panicked, hopped back into the truck, and fortunately was able to pull forward with the trailer and boat on board. Phew, that was a scare! A day she would remember for a long time. Again, she was tired of Bob's tricks and irresponsibility. What was the future going to hold if this continued?

Because of the perks of the airline that employed Rose, they were able to take a Caribbean cruise. The cruise was wonderful and mostly uneventful except for the time Bob would spend in the casino. Since their savings were down because of the earlier accident and DUI, Rose was not happy with the wasteful spending in the casino. Maybe Bob thought he could win back the losses of the past year, but Rose would have been happier with mindful spending habits instead of hazardous gambling. A happy event on the cruise was Gabriel's second experience with fame. The cruise director called him onstage! They put Kermit the Frog on his shoulder, and Kermit asked him some questions. It was a cute skit, and Gabriel was smiling from ear to ear.

Shortly after the cruise was over, Gabriel started eighth grade. Mrs. B. still took a great part in his day to day life at school. She was an angel, and Rose was very happy to have her there with Gabriel.

On her way to work in September, there was a special announcement made on the radio station. A plane had crashed into the twin towers in New York. She wasn't far from work and proceeded into the office where people were just getting in and watching the catastrophe on the TV. A second plane hit the other tower! One of the planes belonged to her employer. It was a great tragedy. Many lives were taken. It was no longer considered an accident.

The phone rang in Rose's office, and it was Mrs. B. Gabriel was extremely worried that Rose was in the plane and was killed. Mrs. B. tried to reason with Gabriel that his mom worked in the office and was never on the planes, but he didn't get it. Rose was asked to come down to the school. Since no work was being accomplished in the office, her boss let her go home.

Rose arrived at the school, and Gabriel was waiting in the lobby for her. Mrs. B. came out shortly and was happy that Rose was able to come back to the school to get him. There were hugs, and then Rose took Gabriel home for the day.

The rest of the eighth-grade year went smoother. Mrs. B. encouraged Gabriel to go on the eighth-grade class trip. One of the chaperones was his basketball coach who he'd grown to know and like. Because of Coach Jim being on the trip, Gabriel agreed to leave home and take the class trip to Springfield with his classmates. Again, Mrs. B. thought this was a victory getting Gabriel to share some good times with his peers. Rose and Mrs. B. waved as Gabriel took off from the school parking lot on the three-day trip.

Rose went home and continued her normal routine while he was gone. She went to work and was completing the month-end financial numbers when Bob called her on the phone.

Bob was agitated. "Rose, I just called the police. There was a girl with green hair on a bicycle, trying to break into the house."

"That sounds weird. Are you sure she was trying to get into the house?"

"The neighbors also called the police. They are sending out an officer. Can you come home?"

Rose thought the whole thing was odd. "Sure, I'll be right there."

She told her boss about the circumstances, and luckily he allowed her to go home and check it out. She hurried home and found Bob in the driveway. He had his finger to his mouth like he was telling her to be quiet. He motioned with his other hand for her to come over. Rose got out of the car and hurried over apprehensively.

Bob said, "Shhhhh, look over there. There are snipers in that bush. They are waiting for the girl to come back."

Rose saw nothing. She just listened.

"Okay, now let's go inside and look in the back. The snipers also have a dog back there waiting for her to come back," Bob kept whispering.

They went through the house and looked out the back window. There was nothing there. The situation was worse than she suspected. Now Bob was hallucinating! She never ever imagined it could be so bad. The mix of drugs and alcohol was getting worse and worse.

In the morning, Rose told Bob the whole story, and he said that he often hallucinated, but not as bad. She told him to get help. He agreed that he needed help. It was time to pick up Gabriel, so she left Bob to think and drove to the school.

The kids got off the bus. Gabriel was happy to see her. He told her about all the things they saw. He said that he spent time with his basketball coach during the trip, and Rose was happy that he had an adult that he knew who would make him feel safe. They got in the car and drove back home. When they arrived, Bob had been drinking again. Rose was beside herself and dropped off Gabriel's bag and left for a movie with her son, not knowing what to do about Bob.

The next morning, she went to work as usual. On her way, she wanted to listen to some self-help tapes about living with an alcoholic. She grabbed a tape and tried to pop it into the slot, but it fell to the floor. Quickly, she bent over, and just as she reached the tape, she heard a bang. She had hit the car in front of her. The car was only going about five miles an hour because of the morning rush hour traffic, but she was still alarmed and ran out of the car to see the damage.

The car she hit was driven by a lady about the same age as Rose. She also climbed out of her car. They met at the bumper and examined the damage. There didn't seem to be any damage at all, but Rose burst into tears.

"Don't worry, I don't think there is any damage at all! We don't even have to call the police or the insurance companies."

Rose could not stop the tears from flowing. All her emotions came out at once. "I'm not worried about the car. I am having a difficult time with my husband. He is drinking and doing drugs, and it is getting worse and worse. I was trying to listen to some self-help tapes and accidentally hit your car."

"Don't worry, you need to help yourself. The best thing to do is sometimes the hardest thing. Have you thought about leaving him? Sometimes that is what is needed for him to understand the severity of the entire thing."

"Thank you for understanding. Yes, I have given it some thought, but we just adopted a son, and he is also having some difficulties. It would be horrible to leave Bob and throw another bad situation into Gabriel's life." Rose was getting herself together and able to stop the tears.

"Well, I was in a similar situation and found out that leaving the situation is sometimes best. Give it a thought. You have to do what is best for yourself and your son." The nice woman tried to comfort Rose.

They needed to get back into their cars and stop holding up traffic. They said their goodbyes and hugged. Rose did not expect to get support from a stranger in traffic. Sometimes people come to you just when you need them.

The next day, Rose accompanied Bob to his doctor's appointment. She had been told before that she didn't get to have any control of the situation since there had been laws passed that protect the patients' rights. She decided to go anyway with hopes that a doctor would allow her to give her side of the story. While Bob was in visiting his doctor, she asked to see the other doctor in the office. She knew the partner and had seen him in the past. He was aware of Bob's situation.

"Hi, Doc, thank you for seeing me. I know you are busy with your patients."

"No problem, Rose, what can I do for you?" The doctor motioned for her to sit down.

Rose was silent for a minute, but then decided to talk. "Bob is not doing well. He takes too much of this medicine and then drinks with it, which causes problems. He has smashed his truck, gotten a DUI, and is now hallucinating. He went to a few AA meetings, but doesn't go any longer. I am at the end of my rope. Can you advise him to take less of the drugs?"

The doctor looked at Rose with concern. "Well, it is not our choice. Bob has the right to say how he is feeling and how much medicine he needs to take. I can't decrease the medicine because you have told me it is too much. I need to hear that from Bob."

Rose was disappointed. She was anticipating this answer but prayed that maybe she could get the doctor to help.

"Rose, you need to take care of yourself and your son. This situation is very depressing for you. Do you want me to give you some medicine to help you through this difficult time?"

Rose did not want to make the matters worse and start taking medicine to control her moods. "No, thank you. I will deal with this problem. I know what I have to do."

Chapter 17

The Move

Rose watched one more time as Gabriel played with his dog, Duke, in the yard. She didn't think the last time watching her son play in the yard with his dog would come so soon. She also looked around at the pond she loved so much. She remembered the days fishing and cruising around on the paddleboat. The days when the pond was stocked with fish. Gabriel's first catch, a bass of about ten inches. There were so many happy days here. She loved the neighbors, loved the house, and loved watching Gabriel play with his dog. She was so disappointed that they had to leave.

The last eight months were spent painting, stripping down wallpaper, and getting the house ready for sale. It was hard. There were many new houses in the town, and people bought new first, before looking at the previously owned homes. After a few months of trying, she realized she had to make the house look new to compete with the other homes. She quickly started to paint all the rooms white and made her house look like a new model home. It worked. The house finally had a contract, and the only thing left was moving the buying family quickly to make it possible for Rose and Gabriel to move too.

The agent had told her that the family wanted to wait since Christmas was near, and they didn't think that Rose would want to move out just before the holiday. They were wrong; she wanted to move and start a new life as quickly as possible. Bob had taken the only job he could get in California and had been gone six months already. All the other employers in his industry had already heard about his poor work record. It was a small industry, and everyone knew each other. The only chance he had for a new job was in another state.

Bob did not fight the divorce, but Rose had a tough time getting the lawyers to agree with her. They all wanted her to fight for child support. She knew that Bob would most likely lose another job and didn't think it was worth the fight. It would be like getting blood out of a turnip. On the third attempt at finding a lawyer, she decided not to tell him about Gabriel and was able to get a thirty-day divorce. She agreed with Bob to split all the assets. His credit card bill with all his gambling losses was his to deal with, but other than that she split things fifty-fifty. He would not have to pay child support and was happy that was taken off the table.

Her old friend Don, from childhood, came to help Rose and Gabriel clear out the house. Don had been a good friend and spent some time with Gabriel building a chair in the garage too. It was nice to see Gabriel with some good male guidance.

Rose grabbed another of the last boxes and carried it out to the truck where Don was loading. The worst part was taking apart the pool table that was in the basement and carrying it up the stairs. It was a good thing the slate was in two pieces; otherwise, there was no way they would be able to take it. She had sold the pool table to her cousin Mary's family. She was happy that something would get good use, and she knew it would bring back some good memories when she saw it in the future at their house.

Time was going by, and she had to get to the property closing. Don climbed into the truck, and Gabriel, Rose, and Duke hopped into the pickup truck.

With a tear in her eye, Rose looked at Duke. "I am so sorry, Duke. I know you loved your yard. There isn't a yard where we are going, but I promise to walk you every day. I promise we will have a yard again someday."

Gabriel hugged Duke to console him. He was happy that Duke didn't have to be given away. The new town house had plenty of room for him and a walking path too. It wouldn't be so bad. The fights with Bob would be over, and they could all live happily from now on. It wasn't such a bad trade-off. Sure, he was disappointed that Bob had not come through for him. When Gabriel first met Bob, he was his hero. He didn't have to do much, just work and be there. Too bad Bob couldn't even do that.

A few days later, they were settled in the new town house, and Gabriel was watching TV. Rose was decorating, hanging pictures, and emptying the last of the boxes. She opened one of Gabriel's boxes and found a school paper titled "My Hero."

My hero is my Mom, she works every day, gets me to school, cleans and cooks too. My Dad used to be my hero, but he let me down. He drinks too much and does drugs. He left us. My Mom saves money, fixes the cars and cooks our meals…

Rose put the paper down and was sad. She didn't want Gabriel to end up without a father. She did, however, know it could happen. At least he was in a better place than he was back in his old hometown.

She got busy trying to vacuum the carpet when the vacuum stopped working. She is fed up with things breaking and being low on money. They used to have it all, but now she lived on a lot less money and scraped by without the comforts she had all her life.

She tried to take apart the vacuum cleaner to determine what the problem was, but the parts were stuck, and she couldn't get them apart. Suddenly, all her emotions came out, and she started to cry. Gabriel came over and told her he could help fix the vacuum. He had never fixed anything when she was around but sat and took it apart and put it back together. He got it running again. She was surprised and thankful and started to feel like things could get better. Maybe they would be okay after all.

The next weekend, they climbed into the car with Duke. They had one more thing to take care of, closing down the cabin. It had sold fast. She was lucky. The cabin was a great investment. They bought it for a low price, and the lake they were on was a great fishing place. During the years they owned it, they had rented it out. There was a journal in the cabin, and many people wrote how much they loved staying there. When the property was listed for sale, it sold fast and for the full price. The money would be split, and half sent to Bob. The rest was put in the bank, hoping to be saved to buy back a house for her, Gabriel, and Duke. She didn't like the fact that the town house had no yard and no garden.

The cabin was eight hours away, and they had a fun time in the car. They sang songs and danced. They did the cabbage-patch dance too. She loved the birch trees up north and all the lakes they passed on the way. She knew she would miss going up north in the future. The cabin would be gone and their house on the pond back home too. All the views of water were being taken out of her life. All the things that reminded her of the ponds on the old farm were going to be gone.

They arrived at the cabin and opened the door for the last time. The cabin smelled a little musty since they were not there to enjoy it this past summer. She walked in while Gabriel walked Duke outside. She looked at the little things hanging on the wall and the journal that held the memories of the cabin. The cabin was sold with all the furnishings, so all they had to get were the knickknacks and pictures on the wall, one stereo, and their fishing equipment. It didn't take long to pack everything in the car. They looked at the cabin, lake, and lodge one more time and said goodbye. It had been filled with happy times, and Rose would never forget the fun-filled summers there.

Chapter 18

The High School Years

Gabriel's first year of high school included friends, football, and girls! Rose was proud of his place on the football team, especially since it was Joliet Catholic, which had a strong history of championships. He was on the sideline much of the time, but he was learning. His body was growing into a football-type physique, and soon she thought he may be an important part of the team. He was also on the shot put team. He had a strong arm and broad shoulders. He did well, even without practice. His grades were average, but at least he was turning in his homework and not failing.

Since Gabriel was having a pretty good year at school, Rose thought it was time to get her life back on track. She heard others talk about online dating and thought she'd give it a try. She never had problems getting along with people, so she figured it would be easy to succeed.

Her first try failed. She met a man online that wanted a pen pal. She found out he was still married and was trying to leave the marriage but wasn't quite ready. Maybe Rose wasn't ready either, because having a pen pal filled her needs for a few months. She grew tired of having a friend online without having anyone to pal around with in person, so finally she gave him up.

The second try was better. She met a local man who loved to go fishing. She started going off on day trips, fishing with him, while Gabriel was out with his friends. It seemed to be okay, but soon

Gabriel rebelled and told Rose he was running away. Maybe he felt left out and wanted some attention. Maybe he was jealous of her new friend. It could have been influences of Gabriel's new friends too. He spent one night away from the house and came back the next morning. He never did that again.

His second year of high school included some good things and some bad. He decided to take up French. Rose responded by taking him to France for his Christmas present. It was a budget trip made possible by her airline employer, but fun too! On the plane, Gabriel put on all the things they gave him for the long flight: booties, eye mask, and the blanket. He was loving the first-class treatment. Rose took a picture of him with that big smile on his face. It was great to see that smile back. They struggled with the language while there but were able to see quite a few of the historical things and museums, as well as going on a river cruise. It was just the break they needed.

Football wasn't as successful. Although Gabriel filled out like a football player, he didn't like to run. Rose started to run herself in an attempt to get Gabriel into running. She got involved in a few 5K and 10K races and brought Gabriel along. He took part in the races but was fine walking. He did not feel the need to run. When football tryouts took place, Gabriel was not selected because of his lack of running ability. It was a sad day for both. Fortunately, his coach found a place for him running the camera and filming the team. These were important films that were reviewed at practices and sent out to colleges for recruiting purposes. Gabriel felt like he was still part of the team. The football practices ended, but he was still involved in the park-district baseball. He had less exercise each week and started to gain weight. He was still quite handsome and had no problem getting girlfriends.

One day, Rose's friend came over to help her repair a patio door in the town house. Gabriel was up on a ladder changing some light bulbs in the dining room. He walked by the ladder and looked at Gabriel's stomach that was sticking outside his shirt. He pulled Rose over in the kitchen and said, "You better watch it, Gabriel is putting on too much weight."

Rose was shocked and mad. She had kept him in sports, tried to get him running, and fed him food that was healthy. She didn't think she overindulged him in candy and ice cream. The problem was that Gabriel was now working part-time and had his own money. He chose to spend it at fast-food restaurants with his friends. She thought most of the other kids did the same and hadn't been worried, but now she was starting to be concerned.

She tried every way she could to get him interested in good health. Since his goal was to become a policeman someday, she decided to take him to visit a college that was known to be a good school for criminal-justice studies. Being a police officer also meant being fit. To apply, you needed to pass a power test and be within a certain weight range. Maybe if Gabriel focused more on the future, he would start getting in shape for becoming a policeman.

The open house at the college consisted of walking around to the different buildings and listening to talks about the various programs. They also visited the cafeteria, student rooms, and walked around outside on the campus. Gabriel didn't seem too enthusiastic. Maybe he didn't want to leave home. Maybe since he disliked school, he wasn't looking forward to another four years of school. She wasn't sure but marched through the drill. They visited the financial office, and she took home the information about the costs. She'd need to get a higher-paying job to be able to send him there.

During the walk around the campus, she noticed that he was dragging his feet and couldn't walk as fast as she did. She missed his youthful energy of the past.

In the next few weeks, Rose sent out résumés to get a higher-paying job to pay for college. She didn't want to leave the airline, but sometimes you must do things you didn't want to do. She was successful and secured a higher-paying job at a manufacturing company. The work was different from the airline. The days were longer, and she had to work Saturdays too. She saved the extra money she earned and wanted to buy a real house and save for college. Meanwhile, she had her old friend Don come over and help build a room in the basement for Gabriel to hang out with his friends.

Don was having some problems of his own, so he was grateful for the opportunity to get out of the house one day a week. He was going through a divorce, and they were sharing the house until the divorce was final. He had to remove himself out of his own house two nights a week, and his soon-to-be ex-wife had to do the same. On one of the days each week, he came over to Rose's and worked on the basement.

Gabriel learned while he worked with Don. Don was a jack-of-all-trades and taught Gabriel things that he would never forget. He learned a little carpentry, a little electricity, and how to use power tools. The whole adventure worked to everyone's advantage. Not only was Gabriel learning, but Rose was also adding value to her home for low cost. This would help her sell it when the time came.

Duke was walked at least once a day and had a small yard where he could lay in the grass while on a chain. Rose still wanted to make sure he had a yard again. Duke was getting older, and he was a good dog. Soon she wanted to give him that yard he deserved and possibly missed. Until then, Gabriel and Rose taught Duke some tricks. He would sit and lie down on command. They were teaching him to roll over and the hardest trick of balancing a milk bone on his nose and then trying to throw it up to catch it. After a couple weeks of training, Duke was getting the hang of the milk-bone trick. Gabriel put the bone on his nose, and finally he caught it! It was another small victory. Rose and Gabriel stood up and did the cabbage-patch dance to celebrate. They put their hands in a fist and drew them together and then pretended to stir a pot. It was a fun dance, and they enjoyed their victory.

Sadly, later that night, Duke started to shake out of control. "Mom, what is Duke doing? What is happening to him?"

Shocked, Rose said, "I think he is having a seizure."

"Will he be okay? What is going to happen to him?"

Duke stopped shaking and got up. He seemed to be lost and bumped into the wall. Rose let him walk outside to see how he would do. He seemed to be coming around. They watched him closely for the next hour. Things calmed down until later that night when the whole episode started again; only this time, it was much worse. He shook for a longer period. When it was over, he didn't get up.

"Let's get him to the vet." Rose grabbed her purse, and they both picked up Duke and got him into the car. He was still breathing.

Gabriel sat in the back seat with Duke. They drove to the neighborhood veterinarian. Both carried Duke inside, and they were given an examining room right away. They waited and anticipated the bad news.

A few minutes later the doctor came into the room to look at Duke. There was little response from him. He lay on the table very still and lifeless. It did not look good. The doctor said that Duke would not come out of this and would have to be put to sleep. Rose was almost ready to buy the house with the yard. Why did he have to get sick? Rose and Gabriel said their last goodbyes to Duke and left the veterinarian's office.

The ride home was silent. They would miss their good buddy so much. There would never be a better friend to Gabriel or a more loyal friend to Rose. They would remember him for the rest of their lives.

Chapter 19

The New House

It was moving day! The day that Rose had been yearning for the past three years. She would be back in a house with a yard and real neighbors! The house was in the same town, only three miles away from the town house. Gabriel would be close enough to his high school and friends. Nothing would need to change, except for having more room and a yard to enjoy the outdoors!

Gabriel and Rose did most of the work themselves to save money. They rented a storage unit and had been moving smaller items over for the last two weeks. All they had to move on the day of closing was the furniture that they could handle. Professional moved the three largest items: the piano, TV, and couch. Everything else was moved by Rose and Gabriel. They stuffed the truck to the maximum and then drove it over to the title company to sign the papers for the new house.

The paperwork went smoothly, and soon it was over. They jumped into the truck and drove over to the new house where the movers were waiting. The two men carried the piano, TV, and couch inside and then left. Gabriel and Rose worked the rest of the day, moving in the rest of the furniture and boxes. By the end of the day, they were exhausted. The beds had not been put together, so they both ended up sleeping on the floor. The next day they finished the work that needed to be done. They were off to a good start. The rest was just prettying up the home and making it a place they would enjoy.

Gabriel had friends over, and they enjoyed the pool in the back-yard and the finished basement. Things were going well, and then the phone rang. It was the school. The teachers wanted to meet with Rose. Graduation was only a few months away, and they needed to review his grades with Rose. One stair up and then another down. She was getting accustomed to how things worked. A major accom-plishment would then be accompanied by a small disappointment, but overall things were getting better.

The next day, Rose drove over to the school where Gabriel's name was on the large sign outside the school. He had won the Silver Presidential Award for volunteering at the day-care center for the underprivileged. He spent every day there after school until Rose picked him up, and he spent enough hours there to earn a very pres-tigious award. The school was so proud of his achievement, they put his name on their billboard outside of the school.

Inside the school the news was not as happy. Rose learned that Gabriel was failing science. He needed a passing grade on the final to graduate. The only way to do that was to get him a tutor. Gabriel understood and agreed to go to a tutor. He would go three days a week and plan to pass the final exam.

It was an intense last few weeks of high school. Rose did not want Gabriel to fail. She wanted him to get the diploma on time with the other students.

The weeks passed, and she was getting nervous. The day of the final exams came, and they waited on pins and needles to see if Gabriel would pass and get to graduate. The next day he came home from school with good news. He passed the science final and would graduate. When times got tough, he always came through. They did their cabbage-patch celebration dance in the kitchen. Things worked out again!

Rose's friend Joel came to the graduation with her. She told him that she was proud of Gabriel because when push came to shove, Gabriel always came through. She wished that someday he would give it solid effort at the start instead of only at the end. She knew things would improve.

They watched the ceremony, and Gabriel came to see them in the audience after it was over. Rose hugged him, and Joel shook his hand. Rose and Gabriel briefly did the cabbage-patch dance of happiness! They stopped quickly so his friends wouldn't catch them!

Joel wanted to know if Gabriel was prepared for the real world and brought the conversation back to reality. "Gabriel, what do plan to do now that high school is over?"

Rose answered, "We started to visit colleges for criminal-justice studies so that Gabriel could fulfill his dream of becoming a police officer.

"Gabriel, do you understand that policeman have to pass a physical test and maintain a good weight?"

Gabriel responded to Joel unenthusiastically, "Yes, I know. I'm going to work on both of those."

Joel was trying to get Gabriel to realize that he needed to take a good, hard look at what was needed to become a police officer.

Gabriel also added that he might join the Army and follow a few of his friends. Rose wasn't worried about that comment because he would fail the weight requirement.

Shortly after graduation, Gabriel turned eighteen, and Rose knew it was time for him to go back to his hometown. He often mentioned his background, and maybe getting in touch with some of his old friends would help him with some of the issues he was having. Maybe he could figure things out about his own future? It couldn't hurt, and it never hurts to have more people in your life.

She prepared for the trip by looking for his family online, gathering all the addresses she could find and compiling a list. She even paid $19.95 for a list of addresses connected to the name of his birth mother. They had been visiting with Melissa, Gabriel's half sister, through the years, but she did not have any relations with the old family either since she was in a foster home. Hopefully, if they found Gabriel's other siblings, they would unite Melissa with them too.

The day came for their trip back to Rivertown. They reserved a room at the hotel that they had stayed at when Rose first met Gabriel.

The hotel had changed names since then but was still standing. It was a five-hour ride, and they spent the time as usual, singing and playing trivia. They always had a good time on road trips.

On the way there, they stopped at an old Route 66 restaurant. Gabriel loved history and wanted to travel the old Route 66 someday with friends or girlfriend. Every opportunity they had the stopped at places that were on the old highway. They had fun looking at the old memorabilia. In the past, they had enjoyed going to the restaurants from the TV show *Diners, Drive-Ins and Dives*. Whenever they were on a road trip, they looked to see if any of the three Ds restaurants were in the town.

After their lunch they got back on the expressway to finish their drive. They checked into the hotel and started their journey to find Gabriel's old homes. The first-stop address turned out to be invalid. There wasn't even a building on the spot where the address should have been. They were slightly disappointed but drove to the next place on the list.

More luck arrived with the next address. "I remember this house!" shouted Gabriel.

"Let's get out and take a picture."

They jumped out of the car and snapped a picture of the house, then they were on to the next place on the list.

Gabriel didn't recognize the next address. This one had a recent-occupancy date on the list, so he never would have lived here with his birth mother. They walked up to the front door and rang the bell. While they waited, they looked around and found initials of his two half siblings carved into a pole on the porch. It was like in a movie. They were so excited, they forgot to get a picture of the initials. The front door opened, and an older lady came out. It wasn't his birth mother.

"Hi, do you know the last people who lived here and where they went?" asked Rose.

"Well, I remember the lady, but I have no idea where they went after they moved out of here. That was over a year ago."

"Okay, thank you for your help. We're looking for my son's birth mother, and this is one of the addresses where she lived," explained Rose.

They left the house and went back to their car. This was a wild-goose chase. They didn't have enough information to get them what they wanted. Next, Rose thought maybe a trip to the local library might help.

Finding the library was easy. Hopefully, they could find some-one inside who could help. Rose walked up to the desk and told the clerk the situation. She asked if there was any documentation in the library that could help them find the right address or current address. The clerk pointed them in the direction of the phone books, another dead end. She also gave them the address of the DCFS office. If any-one could help, they could. Rose took the number, and they headed out the door.

Never give up was always her motto. They needed to cover as much ground as possible while they were here in Rivertown. She knew it was important for Gabriel to connect with his birth family to feel whole. Also, he needed to think through the reasoning that he had been taken out of the family and placed in her home. He needed to know that it was the best thing that could have happened. When a child is taken from their home, they usually assume they were not wanted, or did something to upset someone. In reality, he was the luckiest one of the children. He was put into a loving home. His sib-lings stayed in their home with little food and poor living conditions. Most were also abused. She hoped that he would learn this from some of the people they visited.

The DCFS office was not busy, but they were very professional, and even though they seemed to have time to discuss Gabriel's his-tory at length, they didn't. They followed the rules, took his phone number and address, and said they would give it to any relative they had on their books. It would be up to the relative to call or not call Gabriel. On to the next stop.

Finally, they connected with a person from Gabriel's past. A woman who was working at family services, when Gabriel was there six to seven years ago, worked at a group home now. They visited for a bit, and she remembered Gabriel. She also took his phone number and address and said that she would see what she could do to find his birth relatives. This felt like a win. They may have found someone who would help. The group home also gave them another glimpse into a life that could have been Gabriel's, if he had not been adopted. It was time to go home.

Chapter 20

The Call with Joan

It was Thursday night, and Rose was spending an evening home when the phone rang.

"Hello?"

"Hi, Rose, it's Joan! How are you? How's the love life?"

Laughing, Rose replied, "Hi, Joan, same as usual, nothing happening at all. Same old, same old."

"What is wrong with these men? Can't they see? Are they all stupid? You are a great catch!"

"Oh, Joan, you are my biggest cheerleader!" Rose laughed. "Well, the guys are not beating down the door, I can tell you that!"

"Just wait, they will. They just have to realize how dumb they are being!"

"I'll let you know. What's going on with you?" Rose loved her Aunt Joan, who was her mother's sister. Joan had promised her mom that she would always watch and take care of Rose, and she had done a fantastic job. She was always happy and positive and accepted everyone for who they were, no strings attached!

"I'm making my weekly round of calls. I just got done talking to June, and you were next on my list. How is Gabriel doing?"

"He is doing well. We just got home from Rivertown where he was born. We were looking up his relatives but weren't so lucky. We left our names with a few people, so we'll see what happens."

"Have you gotten anywhere on that cruise we are supposed to be going on together? I've got my bags packed. I can leave tomorrow!"

"It's next on my list. I'm not so sure I can afford the Mississippi cruise. How about a Caribbean cruise?"

"Sure, Rose, whatever you find that is a good deal! Give me a call when you have the details."

"Okay, Joan, I love you! I'll call you soon!"

Rose had promised to take Joan on a cruise ever since she was getting the deals when she worked for the airline. Now, the deals were no longer available since she left for her new job. She has to find something. Joan was getting older, and she wants to make sure they'd go soon. It would be a good time since Gabriel was not in college yet.

Gabriel came up the stairs and asked who was on the phone. Rose recapped the call with Joan.

Gabriel was excited. "When are we going on the cruise with Aunt Joan?"

"Maybe right after you sign up for college classes." Rose was bringing up a subject that he didn't like very much.

"I have time, registration just started."

"Time is ticking away. You can't make pizza all your life. If you don't go to college, you will be stuck in dead-end jobs." Rose reminded him.

"I really wanted to go in the Army, not to college."

"Yes, I know, but your weight is too high, and you don't meet the requirements."

"I'll start a diet tomorrow. If we still had Duke, I could walk him every day for exercise."

Gabriel wanted another dog, but Rose knew that Gabriel didn't walk Duke when they had him. She didn't think he would walk him now. She sat down and stopped the conversation and let him go back to his video games. She didn't know how to get past this point. It was a constant argument between them. She knew the types of jobs he wanted and steered him to those classes. She had taken him to different colleges to entice him too. Nothing seemed to work. He didn't like school. He just wanted to try something different like the Army, thinking that would be better. She sat and gave the problem some deep thought, and then it came to her. Maybe they could both win? Maybe there was something that was in between what they both wanted.

"Gabriel? Since you are sitting at the computer, can you look something up?"

"Sure, what do you want me to look up?" questioned Gabriel without much enthusiasm.

"Look for military colleges. See if there is one that you would want to go see."

"Okay, I'll look."

Gabriel started to visit websites for military colleges. He always liked the South and steered toward colleges in the Southern states. He came across one that was in Georgia, Georgia Military College.

"Mom, I found one in Georgia that I wouldn't mind going to visit." Gabriel seemed a little interested.

"Okay, think about it a little more, and we'll see if we can set up an appointment to go down there." Rose was excited. She saw this as a breakthrough. Finally, she saw a little interest in Gabriel. It wasn't the Army, but it was as close as you could get to the Army. He could wear a uniform, live the same type of life, and go to college classes at the same time. This could be a win for both of them.

Just as they were finishing the discussion about the new school and new idea, Gabriel's phone rang. It was a number he didn't recognize and looked at his cell phone with question but answered it.

"Hello?" he questioned, not knowing who could be calling him. He listened, and in a few seconds a smile appeared on his face. He started to talk and then disappeared down the stairs into the basement room. A sometime went by, and then Rose heard him climbing up the stairs. He appeared in the living room with a broad smile on his face.

"Guess who that was on the phone?" he asked Rose excitedly.

"I don't think I could even guess. Why don't you tell me?"

"It was my brother Gary from Rivertown. One of the people we left my number with contacted him. He wants to see me. He wants me to come to Rivertown and visit. He gave my phone number to my sister too."

"Wow, Gabriel! That is good news. I'm so happy they found you! You should go back there and see them!"

"I will, Mom. I'll go right away."

"Okay then, you have a lot of work in front of you. You need to visit and reconnect with your brother and sister and then visit that military college and start planning your life. After that, I'll make some plans to go on the cruise with Aunt Joan. One day sure makes a big difference, doesn't it?" Rose thought they might finally be on the road to some good things. She paused and started to do their happy dance, the cabbage-patch dance, and Gabriel joined his mom.

Chapter 21

The Return to Rivertown

Gabriel loaded up his car and set out for Rivertown. This was the first time he was driving to his hometown alone. This was his time to connect with his birth family and find out why he was given away. He planned to stay in a hotel and visit with his half brother, Gary, and half sister, Hope. They were two and three years younger than Gabriel. They had lived with the birth mother and birth father. The birth mother would have lost them too, but their birth father stepped up and took care of them alongside the mother. Melissa, another half sister, had grown up in a foster home. She had been taken away from the home about the same time as Gabriel but did not fare as well. At the age they were taken away from their mother, which was nine or ten years old, they were able to make the decision whether to be fostered or adopted. Melissa chose fostering; Gabriel chose adoption. The biggest difference was what would happen when they reach the age of eighteen. In a foster home, the state stops the financing for your care. Many foster parents took on the fostering of the next younger child who needed a home, and the older foster child moved out at eighteen years old. Many young adults are not capable of supporting themselves at that age. There are no adults watching or helping them. Melissa wound up in shelters and in other bad situations. She was a mother of a few children herself at the age of twenty-one, without a father to help take care of the kids.

Gabriel arrived in his old birth town, hoping all would be good. He would gain the friendship of his siblings and maybe get a better understanding of the entire situation. He did not want to see his birth mother; she had let him down, and he was not yet able to forgive. His birth mother wanted to see Gabriel, but he avoided the situation.

He learned that Gary had type 1 diabetes and was not in very good health. Hope had a baby already. The child's birth father was in prison. The visit opened his eyes to new views. He started to share his opinions of the lifestyle he was living. Since his siblings knew nothing about a middle-class society, his ideas were not accepted. They only knew life one way. They lived on the welfare system. They lived in projects. They didn't have any dreams of going to college or getting a good job. Their diets were bad, and in general their life choices were terrible. This was the first glimpse Gabriel had into the way things could have been for him. It was the first time he may have had a thought that he was the lucky one. Sure, he was taken away from everything he knew, but he didn't have things so bad. He never had to worry about food or shelter. He always had someone there to help him. Even his new extended family cared about him and would help if needed.

Gabriel was curious about his heritage, and he tried to find out what his sibling knew. This was another part of finding out who he was. He wanted to find more relatives, hopefully some who were a part of a middle-class society, like all his new friends and family. He wanted to fit in. He wanted to know who his ancestors were and the country where they originated. None of the siblings knew anything. He couldn't gather much information on names either. All they knew were the grandparents, nothing more. It was up to him to research the background himself.

He came home with more ambition to educate himself and find a better life. Rose and Gabriel made the reservation to visit Georgia Military College with the intention of enrollment.

They flew into Atlanta and rented a car for the two-hour drive to Milledgeville. This town became famous when it was mentioned in *Pretty Woman* as Vivian Ward's hometown. It was also the home of Georgia Military College.

The college was established in 1879, and the campus contained old buildings showing its history. As they walked from one building to another, Rose and Gabriel felt the honor and achievement in the grounds and walls of the school. The greeters were dressed in full uniform and described their life at the school with pride. Gabriel was impressed. He always wanted to wear a uniform and carry that pride with him. This was a great compromise since he was not able to enlist in the Army, because of his higher weight. After the tour and stop at the admissions office, their day was over, and they drove back to the airport. The decision was made. Gabriel would attend GMC.

When they returned home, Rose finalized the details for Gabriel's start at the college and started making plans for the cruise with Aunt Joan. Gabriel would have a long winter break, and during that time, they would take Aunt Joan on the long-ago promised cruise. She put down the payment for both the college and the cruise. Things were more settled, and she felt more at ease. Maybe this was the start of a more stable life for them. Gabriel had found his birth family again and was enrolled in a new school.

Another blessing was Duke being gone. Rose didn't know what she would have done with a dog, with Gabriel being away at college. She was away from home at least ten hours a day with her commute and work hours. It was now better that there was no dog waiting home for her and Gabriel each day. Maybe someday Gabriel could get another dog, but now wasn't the time.

Life returned to normal for a little while. They prepared for the drive to school and bought the things that were on the list for preparation at Georgia Military College. Gabriel was glad to be leaving. He hadn't done well in high school and didn't make any lasting friendships there either. A few friends came over to play video games and watch movies, but it wasn't much of a life for him.

One night before leaving for college, Rose received a panicked phone call from Gabriel. He had been in a car crash on the expressway. He had a passenger, one of his friends. This was all Rose needed. Another unfortunate incident before school started.

She picked up a few things off the countertop and ran to the car. Gabriel had said the accident did not involve another car. He had been driving next to a car, and the driver of the other car kept pushing him over. He kept reacting by moving over to the right, and finally there was no more room to move except into the wall of the viaduct. The car was smashed and needed to be towed. Gabriel and his friends didn't even have a scratch: the airbag had inflated upon impact, and it worked, providing a safe and soft surface to shield them from damage.

As she approached the scene of the accident, there were flashing lights and a large gapers' block of cars gawking at the car in the ditch. She pulled on to the shoulder of the expressway and got out of the car to investigate. The policeman had already gone over the accident with Gabriel, and since there were no other cars involved, there were no tickets issued. It was just a matter of moving the car out of the way so that the traffic could start moving again.

Rose called a tow truck to come and move the car to her driveway. She would put it on Craigslist and sell it as is. She was sure someone would buy it for the parts. The bad part about it was that Gabriel would no longer have a car when he was home from college. The good part was that there would be one less bill to insure the second car.

The tow truck driver dropped off the car and came to the door for payment. He had his ten-year-old daughter with him. It reminded her of the times when she would drive with her father in his tow truck when she was little. She felt special when he would let her accompany him. She was sure that his little girl also felt special to be with her dad watching him work.

The car sat in the driveway for two days. She listed it right away and had several calls. It would sell on Saturday when she was home from work to see the buyers. In the meantime, she received a letter in the mailbox from the homeowner's association. The letter stated that she would have to pay a fine for having the car in the driveway. She would go see the president of the association on Saturday. The car had a license plate, was going to be sold, and wasn't causing anyone any harm. There were others with boats and things in their driveway for months. Why were they picking on her?

Saturday came, and the president of the association was very understanding and removed the fine. There were a few buyers for the car, and it was sold early that day.

In one week, Rose would be dropping off Gabriel at college and then driving back alone. A car wasn't really needed there. All the classes were on campus. Maybe what had happened wasn't so tragic, but Rose still felt a loss since that car had been good to her and Gabriel for ten years. Also, she didn't understand why Gabriel wouldn't have just pulled over to the side of the road or just slowed down the car. Why did he have to stay alongside a crazy driver? Lastly, why did the driver get away with doing this to two teenagers? Well, this would be a lesson to Gabriel, because money doesn't grow on trees, and she didn't have the money right now for another second car. She thought maybe both her and Gabriel needed space from each other, and him attending college in Georgia would be good for both.

The next week went by quickly. The car was packed to the gills. She took an extra day off work, so they could treat this as a mini vacation. There were a few touristy sites along the way. It would be an adventure, and some needed smiles!

They set off for the twelve-hour drive to Georgia. They sang and played games in the car to pass the time. They were on another adventure. Rose loved it. Seeing new things, meeting new people, and being free for a few days to experience something different.

There first stop was Nashville, Tennessee, and the home of President Andrew Jackson. When Gabriel had first arrived at Rose's house, she found out that he loved learning about the presidents of the United States. One of their favorite bedtime books was on this very subject. Through the years, whenever they were in a town near one of the presidents' homes, she took Gabriel to visit. This was another opportunity to see one of the stately houses.

At the Hermitage, Gabriel learned that he had a few things in common with the seventh president of the United States. Andrew Jackson fought in the American Revolutionary War. During that war, his mother nursed the soldiers, caught cholera, and died. She left her son an orphan at fourteen. Andrew Jackson was an orphan just like Gabriel.

Andrew Jackson also had the same piercing blue eyes as Gabriel's, but he had a fiery spirit and was known to be fearless. Gabriel was cautious and calm on the outside. Using his fiery spirit, Jackson became general of the Tennessee Militia in 1802. In the War of 1812, he led his troops to defend New Orleans against a large attack by the British, forcing them to withdraw from Louisiana. America soon realized the potential of Jackson. Learning about the president's and their part in the wars in the early life of the United States gave Gabriel the desire to enlist in the military and become a hero too.

President Jackson was known for laying the framework for democracy, paying off the national debt and acquiring new land for America. He was an inspiration and instilled the hope in Americans that anyone can succeed through hard work and natural ability. This is the part of the seventh president's legacy that Rose wanted to instill in Gabriel. No matter what your background was, you had the power through hard work and determination to become a success. Rose believed this with her entire soul.

The fun fact learned while visiting the Hermitage was about Andrew's beloved pet parrot, Polly. Polly attended the funeral for Jackson but had to be removed because he was cursing. This fact brought a smile to Gabriel's face, and again he realized that this president had a pet that he loved, just like Duke, Gabriel's dog.

They returned to the car, both having learned some important lessons. They were silent for a while and then recapped the stories learned at the historic home. Their next stop was Ruby Falls in Chattanooga, Tennessee, a limestone cave. This was a cave that was formed 200 million years ago. The stream that makes up the falls entered the cave sometime after its formation. The stream is 1,120 feet underground and joins the Tennessee River at the base of Lookout Mountain.

There was a long line waiting to get into the cave. Gabriel and Rose waited for their turn to go inside. It was rather scary being far down inside a cave with only one way out and many people who would be scrambling to move if there was a cave-in. They moved slowly and eventually saw the famous Ruby Falls. It was impressive.

Back inside the car, they did their cabbage-patch dance to music because they both felt happy. Another song came on the radio that had some meaning for both of them. It was a Kelly Clarkson singing. Gabriel mimicked the song and beat his hands on the dashboard while he belted the lyrics out loud. "Because of you, I am afraid." They both knew in their hearts that they were a bit more cautious because of the things that happened to them in recent years.

They drove on and knew, for just a few days, they had no cares and they wanted to enjoy every minute of it. The next stop was Georgia Military College.

Milledgeville's location on the Oconee River made it the perfect site for Georgia Military College. The river drew people to the town in the early 1800s. It was so popular; it became the capital of Georgia from 1804 to 1868. It now had a population of about eighteen thousand people. The Old State Capitol is on the National Register of Historic Places, along with as many buildings of the original city.

When the capital city moved to its new home in Atlanta, Milledgeville struggled because it lost its main purpose. In 1879, the leaders created a new purpose of a place of education. They established the Middle Georgia Military and Agricultural College, now Georgia Military College.

When Rose and Gabriel arrived, they took a tour on the Milledgeville guided trolley. Their tour included the Old State Capitol, St. Stephens Episcopal Church, and Lockerly Arboretum, all from the early 1800s. The tour was a great beginning to Gabriel's time at Georgia Military College.

After the tour, they ate lunch at the Huddle House, which would become a comfort stop for Gabriel on weekends when the college emptied of many of the students who would go home to visit with family.

Finally, they arrived at the college, and they were admitted to the room where Gabriel was assigned. It was on the second floor of a dormitory building called Jackson Hall. He would live in a building named after the famous president they just became familiar with on their journey.

It took them a few trips from the car, up the stairs, and down the hall before everything was out of the car and in his new home. After that, there was nothing more for Rose to do. She hugged Gabriel and said goodbye. She would miss him, and tears were just about ready to come out of her eyes when she turned and walked quickly out of the building. Gabriel had everything he needed there. He had a cell phone to call. She would add a little money each week to his checking account, but generally, he would be fed and educated while he was at the college. Hopefully, they would include exercise into his daily program, and he might lose some weight. She could only hope. The next time she would see him would be on the cruise with Aunt Joan.

Chapter 22

The Parade

Once home, Rose settled into her normal routine without Gabriel. She worked long hours at the manufacturing company as the controller and often worked weekends too. This didn't leave much time for fun, but she tried to take long bike rides and explore new trails when time was available. Another thing that Rose did was run in more races. She loved the 10K races because, although she was not a fast runner, she had stamina. She always finished in the top three in her age category, and it made her feel like a star! She hung her ribbons and medals in the dining room and was proud when she sat back and admired the number of races she conquered. Every day she ran around the neighborhood for exercise. It made Rose more confident each day.

Another pursuit was her dream of having a man in her life who understood Gabriel and her need to be involved in his journey. She wanted someone who wanted to share her dream, not watch from afar. That was the hard part. Many men who were divorced had children of their own, and they couldn't spend enough time with them. They were not really interested in spending time with Rose and Gabriel together. They wanted a woman who kept them company on the weekends in between visits with their own children. Much as Rose understood this dilemma, she wasn't satisfied having a part-time boyfriend, so she kept searching for her soul mate.

Financially, Rose was making it. Her salary from the manufacturing company and yearly bonuses were enough to send Gabriel to college and never take any loans. She lived meagerly. She restored old furniture, painted the house herself, and fixed anything she could around the house rather than hiring a professional.

Soon, another problem crept up. Gabriel was overspending at school. His account was overdrawn a few times, causing large fees in his account. She learned that on the weekends, he was lonely and would walk to the Huddle House to eat there when he could have eaten at the school for free. This caused two problems: overdrawn accounts and weight gain. The school recognized the weight gain and sent him to the school nurse to gain knowledge about diet and nutrition. It might have helped if Gabriel had the motivation to exercise, but he only completed the exercises and drills that were necessary, never going above what he was instructed to do. The school also tried to help him by giving him a part-time job on the weekends. He managed the equipment in the gym, and this gave him a little extra money, which ultimately helped Rose.

His grades at the school were the best ever. He won a scholarship for academics. For the first time in a long while, he was doing well in school. This was one of Rose's greatest wishes for him. She was proud.

She received a surprise from Gabriel. He was going to be in a celebration at the school. There would be a parade and other events, and he wanted her to come to see him. Of course, she accepted the invitation. When she arrived, she found Gabriel bigger than when she had left him. She was a little shocked because she thought he would be marching and doing drills like in the military. She wondered how in the world he could be gaining weight.

Gabriel told her all the food at the college was fatty Southern cooking. She was sure he piled food high on his plate and sought food for comfort. She didn't realize he was lonely and had trouble making friends. Because of his good grades and the participation in various clubs and activities, she had wanted to believe that things were improving. She also kept in contact with his sergeant via e-mail, and he had not given her any indication that there were major problems.

The parade was wonderful, and she was proud that he was staying at the college and would earn a degree. He would be the only one in his family with an education. This would earn him a better life. Her mother had always told her, people can take away everything, but not your education.

She returned home with some questions in her mind, but at least he was in school, gaining knowledge and moving forward with his life.

Chapter 23

The Cruise

Gabriel's semester was over, and he came home at Thanksgiving a little larger than when he left. It seemed the weight gain was still moving upward. This worried Rose a great deal. She imagined how well he would be doing if it were not for this inherited trait from his birth mother. Gabriel never discussed his weight that he had inherited from his birth mother. She had stolen a normal childhood from him, and now she was stealing his young adult happiness because she gave him the obesity gene. Rose always tried to encourage him to eat right, but she really didn't get much cooperation. Even if Rose purchased healthy food at home, Gabriel would go out and buy fast food when he was not with her. Suggesting groups like Weight Watchers or Jenny Craig did not accomplish anything either. He needed to want to get down to a healthy weight. Unless he wanted it, it wasn't going to happen.

The extra weight also clouded his mind preventing good decision-making too. Often, he was embarrassed or self-conscious about his size and therefore was concentrating on his feelings, instead of the task at hand. His weight caused havoc in many areas of his life.

Soon, they would be on the ten-day vacation with their dear Aunt Joan. They had not spent long periods of time with Joan, with exception of a weekend in Hilton Head a few years ago. Joan was very accepting, always smiling and easygoing, so Rose was not expecting any problems at all.

The day arrived, and they met Aunt Joan at the airport. Her daughter Karen dropped her off and arranged for the airport to give her a ride to her gate. Rose didn't realize that Joan had a hard time walking distances, and this would change the plans a bit.

When Joan arrived at the gate, she was her old, joyful self, making everyone smile and laugh. Rose knew right away that they would have a great time.

The flight to Florida boarded, and they set off on their journey. The first stop would be Orlando where Rose rented a town house for three days. Gabriel wanted to go to Universal Studios and Medieval Times. The town house turned out to be a fantastic first stop. They all had their own bedrooms. There was the perfect amount of space to stretch out and all be comfortable, which was just what they needed. Soon, they would be squished into a small cabin on a ship.

The first full day at Universal was excellent because they rented a wheelchair, and Joan got to ride around like a queen all day! They had a great deal of fun that included a make-believe Lucille Ball posing with Joan and Gabriel for a picture. They went on rides, ate some enjoyable meals, and saw quite a bit of the park.

The second day included an afternoon at Medieval Times. Joan was photographed on a throne, and their knight won the tournament. What could be for more fun!

They packed up the car and drove down to Fort Lauderdale to board their ship that would take them to Cozumel, Belize, and Key West. Joan was a riot. She had the best comments for everyone and was very proud to introduce her niece and grandnephew to all. This embarrassed Rose a little because Joan gushed over them, and Rose didn't feel like she was all that special. You couldn't stop Joan, though. She had a story for everyone and wasn't satisfied until she met everyone on the ship.

Each morning she would coffee klatch with new passengers. She wasn't picky. She chose anyone and everyone to sit with and made sure she brightened their day. Gabriel and Rose took this time to walk around and exercise their legs because Joan was seventy-five and not as mobile as they were. Rose liked to climb the stairs, but Joan needed to ride in the elevator. She didn't want to seem rude to Joan, but if she ran up the stairs, she would make it in the same amount of time as the elevator and meet up with Joan again.

Their first port was Belize, and they booked a river tour. This would give Joan an easy day. The bus picked them up at the dock, they boarded a boat for the ride and then were escorted back to the ship. Joan didn't need to walk at all. The second port was Cozumel, and Rose hired a horse and carriage to take them to the main part of town. There they had a quaint Mexican lunch and walked around the main square where they saw different artists selling their work. Gabriel bought a cross, one of his favorite types of souvenirs. They made their way back to the ship and stopped at a lively restaurant on the dock where they listened to fun music, took pictures, and had a drink.

That night on board, Gabriel went and played video games while Joan and Rose sat with a few glasses of wine and talked about men. Rose wanted a respectable life with a man who would be good to her. It was hard to find. Joan did not understand why good men weren't flocking to marry Rose. She had a good career, was smart with her money, a wonderful Mom, and looked fifteen years younger than her true age. Rose took care of herself, that was certain. She exercised every day and made sure she stayed at her ultimate weight. Her hair sported a great style, and she wore clothes that were up to date with the times. What wasn't there to love about Rose? Their conversation was memorable. Joan always made Rose feel like a princess. She was happy that they took the time to go on this adventure.

Their last stop was Key West. This would be the hardest stop for Joan because it was a smaller town, and many passengers just walked out to browse shops and visit the bars. Rose and Gabriel went ahead and picked up a golf cart. They came back to the ship and gathered Joan and then ride around the town.

As they approached the ship, Rose saw that Joan had made yet another friend. This time it was a young woman who Joan thought was exactly like Rose. I guess Joan didn't notice that this young woman with the same name and occupation as Rose was black, but that was just so typically fun of Joan! She was a wonderful woman. Rose got a kick out of the situation. They then climbed into the golf cart and left Joan's new friend on her own journey.

The golf cart was not ideal for them because the back seats were a little higher, and with the cloth roof, it was a little hard for Joan to see everything. She wished it would have turned out better, but Joan never complained about anything. It was much better to be on hot and sunny Key West than to be back in the cold Midwest, so who would complain?

That night, back on the ship, they relaxed and spent the last night of the vacation seeing a show. They all would probably admit that the small cabin caused them to learn a little too much about each other, but it was a trip that would never be forgotten.

Karen met them at the airport, and Joan reported a fun trip to her. They waited for their luggage, hugged, and said their farewells.

Chapter 24

The Funeral

A few months later, after Gabriel was back in school, the phone rang. It was her cousin Jack who very rarely called. Jack had some bad news. Joan had been taken to the hospital and had a heart attack. They were able to revive her, but then she gave orders to Karen that if it happened again, let her go. The next day it happened again, and Karen followed her mother's orders. Joan was gone.

Rose felt blessed that she had been able to share so much time with her mother's sister, Joan, during the last few years of her life. She also will always feel grateful to have had that cruise vacation to remember for the rest of her life. They had also shared Easter alone together at one of their favorite restaurants. That day, Joan had said goodbye like she never had said it before. Rose thought that she knew her time was short. She felt like she was the luckiest girl in the world for having Joan in her life. Not only her, but also for Gabriel. He found out what a wonderful person she was, and she had made a great impact on his life. She never judged, never spoke ill of anyone, was always happy, and wanted the best for all.

The funeral took place in the church where Rose when to grammar school and Joan was married. They drove past various important buildings on their way to the cemetery. Joan would be buried near her granddaughter who was taken before her time. Every Fourth of July, her birthday, she would be honored by her children and never forgotten.

Gabriel had come back from school for the funeral. There had been time enough for Rose to drive down and pick him up. When she had arrived, Gabriel was waiting outside the dorm with tons of luggage. She thought it was very strange, but because of the circumstances had not pressed the issue. They just piled in the luggage and drove back home. Now it was time for Gabriel to return to school, but he did not want to go back.

Because of this new problem, Rose thought it was time for her and Gabriel to visit a counselor. She knew he had gained more weight but didn't know any other reason for his resistance to go back to the military college. As far as she knew, he loved the school, loved the Southern town, and was doing well in his classes. What could have been the problem? She had paid a good deal of money to send him out of state, and this was the first time he was making good grades. She did not want to see it end.

The counselor asked them to describe the problem at hand and what they were wishing to gain from their visit. Rose told the doctor how proud she had been of Gabriel during his time at Georgia Military College. She knew he had always wanted a military life and the school fit that description. He had only two more semesters to finish to get a two-year degree in criminal justice, a career path he had chosen. She was clueless.

Gabriel did not shed much light on the whole problem. He just kept saying that he would not go back. If he was made to go back, he would just sit in his room and not attend any of the classes. Rose saw absolutely no point in pushing back only to waste good money because Gabriel did not go along with the program. They were at a standstill.

Finally, the counselor asked what Rose wanted from Gabriel if he were to stay home instead of going back to Georgia.

"I'd need him to go back to work in a job in his career path and go to school at night. I will even get Gabriel another car, but he cannot drop out of college."

Gabriel agreed. "I'll go to Triton College to finish up my degree. I just do not want to go back to Georgia."

That was it. The counselor brought them to an agreement. Gabriel wasn't going back to college. All the good grades, marching parades, and scholarships would be history. He wasn't going to finish. Rose was devastated. This was probably the biggest setback of all.

The car ride was silent. She couldn't believe that this good period ended, and for what? What could it be? Were their bullies at school making fun of Gabriel for his size? Why wouldn't Gabriel tell her everything that was going on with him? She really thought she deserved some answers, but that was not going to happen, at least not now, especially since Gabriel did not want to attend counseling sessions.

Gabriel applied and was hired at an armored-truck company as a driver and guard. The pay wasn't very good, but he was getting the type of experience he needed in the industry. He also signed up for classes at Triton College. He was being true to his word so far.

Chapter 25

The Visit with Cindy

Rose needed a break from the real world. It was time to go on a weekend trip with her dear friend Cindy. Cindy had been her friend since kindergarten. They had gotten in trouble together, cried and laughed together, all at different times throughout their forty-five years of friendship.

The plan was to drive out to Cindy's home in Indiana and then hit some wineries in Michigan. They loved seeking out new places and trying new things.

Cindy lived in a beautiful subdivision that was set on a ten-acre lake. Surrounding the lake were big, beautiful homes with decks jutting down to the water's edge. Rose loved driving through this neighborhood and seeing the houses being built. Each house was different than the next one. Cindy's was a ranch, off the water, but still lovely as can be. She had spent a great deal of energy planning the right details to make it an upscale house that was also not too much to maintain. It was brick and included beautiful beveled glass windows. The pantry door was a screen door that looked like it belonged on a farmhouse. White furniture in several of the rooms gave the house the perfect touch of feminism. The yard looked out at a small pond. It was the perfect setting. She wished she was back at her old house that included the pond in her backyard. Unfortunately, Bob had ruined that part of her life, or maybe it was because she allowed him to ruin it?

As Rose approached the house, she saw that the garage door was open as always. Cindy's house was always welcoming. She parked and went through the garage and called out for her friend. Cindy came to the door with a cup of coffee in her hand and her friendly dog, Chance, right next to her. Of course, she offered Rose a cup of coffee and some breakfast before they got on the road, but she declined, wanting to leave at the time they planned. They had a jam-packed schedule to conquer that day, and Rose didn't want to miss a thing.

Cindy called Chance to get into his cage on the back porch. She had him trained so well; he went in willingly, knowing that his master would be home in plenty of time to take him out. She was really a great dog owner, and Rose could not imagine her friend without a dog.

They climbed into the car and were on their way, Cindy still holding her cup of coffee with the napkin underneath. She sighed and started to relax. She worried too much and was always a little apprehensive before leaving her house to go anywhere, even this short day trip. Soon she calmed down and started to chatter. This was the Cindy that Rose always had fun around, the relaxed, fun girl.

"Well, what do you have on the itinerary today? Any place new?"

"Cindy, you know I always have something new, but we'll also stop at our favorite, the Round Barn Winery!"

"Oh good, I could use a glass of wine. I've had quite a busy week! This job is killing me. I've been there thirty-seven years, and I have never worked this hard. They just laid off another twenty-five people in my area and spread their work to the remaining employees. I can't believe how much I have to do each day. They also started to time people on their computers, so even though I work from home, they know exactly what I am doing each minute of the day. Gone are the days when I use to be able to do my yard work in the middle of the afternoon. They have me chained to my computer!"

Rose still thought that Cindy was a lucky girl. Just think of the ease and benefits of working from home. She didn't have to buy work clothes, didn't have to worry if her car was going to start or how many miles were on it and if she would need another new car soon. Working at home would decrease the amount she spent on gas, clothes, and car repair. All in all, it would make life so much easier. She wondered how her friend could complain so much. She wished her life could be a bit easier. The only thing that Rose didn't like about the thought of working from home was the lack of socializing with her work friends. She actually liked arriving each day to her office and kibitzing with her workmates! She thought the long drive and additional costs of going into the office were worth it. It also got her out so that she would exercise at lunch time and sometimes even after work on the way home. Rose loved being busy. She guessed they both had the life that was truly best for them.

"Cindy, everything will work out. I am sure you will organize your work to make it doable each day. How is the boyfriend?"

"Oh my god, everything is so wonderful! He is the man of my dreams. He is always bringing me presents and fixing things around my house. Did you notice how great the garage is looking? He just put up a new light fixture, and then he plans to paint the floor with that epoxy paint. It is going to look so awesome. After that, I am going to set up my old yard furniture in the area over to the left. That old dresser will be painted blue with chalk paint, and I'm going to paint the entire work bench too. It's going to look feminine, like a girl works in the garage, and I will love it!"

"What is he up to today? How come you have the day off to take our little day trip?"

Cindy frowned a little. "He is out with that old bunch of friends from high school. Really, can't he leave those people? It was thirty-five years ago when he was the football star of the school, yet he is still reliving those glory days of his. I am glad I don't have to be there today. I mean, it's time he moved on with his life."

"Well, this gives you time to spend with me. I am sure he is probably saying the same thing, why is she spending time with Rose!" They both laughed.

"How is Gabriel? How does he like the military school? Are his grades still good? Did he win anymore scholarships?"

"This is exactly why I needed a day with you. He quit school. I don't really know why. I am thinking because he has gained weight, and it is getting harder to do the exercises, clean his room, and maybe even sit in the classroom seats? I have no idea what is going on there, but he will not go back."

"I'm so sorry to hear that. I know you were so happy that he was doing well."

"He has gotten so big. Yesterday we were sitting over by the neighbor's house, and he sat on a chair and broke it. I was so embarrassed for him. He has to feel awful. I have tried talking to him about diets and exercise and sent him to Weight Watchers, Jenny Craig, and others. Nothing helps."

"Rose, Gabriel is such a good boy, sweet and kind. You two will figure this all out. I have faith in you!"

"That is why I love you so much, Cindy. You are just as nice and accepting of Gabriel as dear Aunt Joan. It is so sad that she is gone, but I am sure she is happy to see my mom up in heaven and tell her all about Gabriel. She loved him so!"

Rose was silent for a while.

"Speaking of Joan and my mom, remember all of those parties at the farm, the minibikes, and the boys we would chase!"

Cindy laughed. "We were such nerds! Remember some of the houses those guys lived in and the car they used to drive around? You had those bangs, and I had the weird glasses? We were quite a pair too!"

"We had such fun there. I can't believe I have known you so long and that we are still good friends."

"Come on, let's be happy. Let's just have a good time today and forget all of our troubles! Let's be Joan today!"

Cindy smiled and agreed.

Chapter 26

The New Car

"Mom, as Lisa was driving me home from school today, we saw a car for sale on the side of the road. It's an Acura, just like the car we had that was in the crash. Well, not exactly like it, but it is an Acura. It's only fifteen hundred dollars, and I can get a loan for it from the credit union. What do you think? That way I could get to all of my classes and get a job again."

"Well, Gabriel, we'll stop and take a look at it. If it runs and seems like it will last a while, maybe it's a good idea."

Rose knew they needed another car, and she didn't have much in her budget for it. If Gabriel was excited about this car and was willing to get the loan and work for it, it was probably the best option they had right now.

"Get your shoes on, and let's go out and see it." Rose grabbed her purse and got ready to take the ride to see the car. It would only take about fifteen minutes to go over and see it. Maybe they could buy it fast before another party got it.

As they approached the car, Rose thought it looked really nice. She was surprised at the condition of the car for the price. They pulled alongside of the car and stepped out.

It was a white Acura, small and kind of sporty, which is why Gabriel was probably excited about buying it. They walked up to the auto shop that was selling it and asked about the car. The man inside said the he fixed up cars that were in accidents that insurance companies totaled. He was able to buy them for next to nothing and then sell them to make a profit. They took a test drive in the car, and it seemed to run really well. She was happily surprised. They made the offer, and Rose gave the man a deposit and said they would be there the next day to pick it up. They left with a smile, and Rose thought this might be the start of something good. The next day she would call her good friend who she knew would help her. He could go over the car to ensure it was in good shape.

*****

"Pull her in slowly. I've got everything set up, so we can take a good look at this beast." Joel waved Gabriel into the garage and signaled when he wanted him to stop.

Joel was extremely thorough in everything he did. He was also very well organized. He probably had a list of everything they would check in the car and most likely spent the entire night reading up on the engine and specs of this Acura. He was incredible.

"It doesn't sound half bad. We'll go over it and make sure it is safe for you to drive."

Joel grabbed a book and a flashlight off his workbench and handed them to Gabriel. "I'll need you to read to me when I tell you. Each section we will review is marked with a Post-it Note. I also want you to shine the light for me when I need it. My eyes aren't what they used to be, and I need all the light I can get. Can you handle it?"

"Yup," Gabriel said quietly. He was always a little nervous around Joel. Joel expected a great deal from people, only the best. He wanted everyone to be responsible and pull their own weight. Help was something you needed only after you gave it a 200 percent try yourself. He was a tough guy.

They worked for a few hours. Gabriel was reading the car manual to Joel when he needed information and was shining the light on the various parts of the car, as they progressed. Occasionally, Joel would ask Gabriel a question.

"How much did you pay for this car?" Joel never made eye contact with Gabriel, just kept on working.

"I paid fifteen hundred dollars. I got a loan from the credit union for it, and I'm working as a security guard to pay the loan. I took a class to get my PERC card, and I'm taking more classes to get further into security jobs."

"Does the job give you benefits? You'll need health insurance."

"This job doesn't, but I'm going to apply for more jobs that pay for health insurance. After that I want to become a police officer."

"How much does a job like that pay, to drive the armored car?"

"It's enough to pay for the car and give me some spending money."

Joel thought for a minute. "You'll need more money if you want to move out of your mom's house someday. Also, what happens if something goes wrong with this car? You'll need money for brakes and other things too."

Gabriel was silent. He didn't like all the questions. It was hard enough just going to school and working without having to worry about the future and more things breaking on the car.

Joel closed the hood of the car. "It's time to take the car for a spin and see if we have it running better than it was. Let's go get a beef sandwich!"

"Good, 'cause I'm a carnivore and I devour meat!" Gabriel smiled at the decision. It was the most fun of the day so far.

The car ran like a top. They stopped for a beef sandwich and then made their way back to Joel's garage. They continued working for the rest of the afternoon and finished up. Gabriel backed out of Joel's garage with a heavy heart. He learned a great deal listening to Joel today. He needed to make more money, get a job with benefits, and to have a goal to move out of his mom's house. That was a lot of things to do. Too much for him to think about. He pulled into a fast-food restaurant for some comfort. Tomorrow was another day. He could think about making some changes then. In the meantime, he needed something to eat.

Chapter 27

The Trip to Missouri

Thanksgiving weekend snuck up on them quickly this year. There would be no event with their Aunt Joan now that she was gone. They would be on their own. In order to make things fun, Rose came up with the idea of going on a road trip on each future Thanksgiving weekend. One of the things she decided to start was having Thanksgiving dinner at a lodge that was built by the Works Progress Administration during the Great Depression. She was impressed with President Franklin D. Roosevelt and his ideas of how to get US citizens back to work. Gabriel had a love for history, so this would work for both.

The goal of the WPA during the Great Depression was to employ most of the unemployed people on relief or government aid until the economy recovered. To be eligible for WPA employment, an individual had to be an American citizen, eighteen or older, able-bodied, unemployed, and certified as in need by a local public-relief agency approved by the WPA. The WPA Division of Employment selected the worker's placement to WPA projects based on previous experience or training.

The Works Progress Administration built magnificent, uniquely American campgrounds, lodges, and cabins in state parks across the country. Some of the notables include Timberline Lodge, which was used in the movie *The Shining*, Monument Lake Resort in Colorado, Giant City Lodge in Illinois, and Pere Marquette Lodge on the

Mississippi. The first lodge they decided to visit was Pere Marquette Lodge near St. Louis on the Mississippi River.

Rose prepared for the trip by gathering information about the lodge and other historic sites around it. She wanted to make the most of their visit and try to make it distracting, so they wouldn't feel sorry for themselves that Aunt Joan was not around any longer. The drive to the lodge would take four hours. They would be able to stop somewhere interesting along the way and still make it to eat Thanksgiving dinner by five o'clock on Thanksgiving Day. After dinner they would drive to a hotel near St Charles, Missouri. Saint Charles is a city in Missouri, the ninth-largest city. It lies to the northwest, and is a suburb of Saint Louis, Missouri on the Missouri River. It was founded about 1769 as Les Petites Cotes, "The Little Hills" in French by Louis Blanchette, a French-Canadian fur trader. The area was nominally ruled by Spain following the Seven Years' War and is the third-oldest city in Missouri. For a time, it played a significant role in the United States' westward expansion as a river port and starting point of the Boone's Lick Road to Boonslick. It was settled primarily by French-speaking colonists from Canada in its early days and was considered the last "civilized" stop by the Lewis and Clark Expedition in 1804, which was exploring the western territory after the United States made the Louisiana Purchase. The city served as the first Missouri capital from 1821 to 1826.

Today St. Charles Historic District and Main Street area is a central gathering place and focal point for the community. The primary features of the historic riverfront area are residences and businesses. Each block features shops, restaurants, and offices frequented by visitors and locals. It is near the Katy Trail walking trail which is 225-miles long, which is enjoyed by bikers and walkers and adapted from a railroad right-of-way.

The Christmas Traditions Festival, one of the nation's largest Christmas festivals, takes place on the streets of St. Charles annually. This was the event that drew Rose to St. Charles. It starts the day after Thanksgiving and continues until the Saturday after Christmas. Over thirty costumed legends of Christmas stroll the streets and interact with guests, while Victorian-era Christmas Carolers fill the air with old-fashioned carols. Every Saturday and Sunday, the Legends of Christmas and the Lewis & Clark Fife and Drum Corps take part in the Santa Parade as it heads up historic South Main Street to the site of the First Missouri State Capitol. A perfect way to spend their Thanksgiving holiday.

They set off on their journey on Thursday morning. Gabriel was moving slowly and not too motivated. Rose hoped he would cheer up once at the lodge. She noticed it was harder for him to get into the car and fasten his seat belt because of his increasing weight. He wanted to bring snacks in the car for the ride, which irritated Rose, since he really needed to back off from extra food. She felt she was a good example of weight control and exercise and didn't understand Gabriel's need to eat 24-7. Was it a genetic problem that stemmed from his birth mother? Was it depression since he didn't understand why he was taken away from his hometown and birth family? Was it because of the absence of a father figure? Maybe it was a mixture of all these circumstances. All she could do was to go on day-to-day. The car was packed, Gabriel was on board, and it was time to take off!

The first few hours of the drive were noneventful. They stopped for lunch and then drove on to the Pere Marquette Park and Lodge. Their destination was named for one of the early explorers on the Mississippi River, Father Pere Jacques Marquette, a Jesuit priest. When they arrived, they drove around the grounds of the state park, taking in the beauty of the park and the Mississippi River. Gabriel had lived on the great Mississippi, so it was a comfort for him to see it again. Rose would have loved to have gotten out of the car and walked the trails, but Gabriel was so slow because of his weight that she thought it best to drive around. Maybe that was her mistake, maybe she should have forced him to walk more, but she didn't want to make this short vacation a burden. She wanted to forget their troubles and enjoy the weekend.

After they parked, they noticed a statue in front of the lodge, which was a carving of an American Indian woman sitting on a turtle and holding other animals titled "Mother Nature." The park was built on a former location of a Native American village. They asked another visitor to take their picture. Gabriel was wearing his camouflage pants and Army jacket, Rose in her jeans and white shirt. They posed on each side of the statue. A picture that earned its place on Rose's buffet for a long time to follow.

Inside they registered for dinner and were told it would be a forty-five-minute wait. During their wait, they walked around the inside of the lodge, admiring the work done long ago by dubious depression workers earning pay to keep their families fed. The main feature of the lodge is an immense stone fireplace reaching fifty feet to the roof and weighing seven hundred tons. They sat and stared at it for a few minutes.

The lodge was also known for the apparitions, which appeared to staff workers. Employees at the Pere Marquette Lodge reported seeing large images crossing through the lobby when no one was there. The housekeepers working in the older part of the lodge have reported observing nightstands shaking violently while everything else in the room remained calm. For some reason, they felt inclined to call this entity George, who was an old man sometimes noticed sitting by the fireplace. It has been told that he disappears when anyone gets too close to him. One of the park rangers is said to have witnessed a man wearing a Civil War uniform in the lobby. Evidently at one point during the Civil War, a small detachment of Federal soldiers camped near the park to protect access to the Mississippi and Illinois Rivers. Sometimes employees felt that someone was brushing by them or that they were being touched by someone who wasn't visible. Usually these feelings would occur in one of the rooms in the old part of the lodge, or in the lobby. One worker had reported seeing the two sets of heavy doors leading outside open and close by themselves.

Gabriel's second love after history, especially Civil War history, was paranormal activities. This made the visit to Pere Marquette Lodge very appealing for him. He always imagined himself living in the past and fitting into a past time more so than the present.

Another room of the lodge was holding a wine tasting. Rose enjoyed one glass of wine while they decided what to do with the rest of their time. They decided on a walk around the outside.

Gabriel brought his camera and took a few pictures of the timber and stone lodge and the great river. They saw wildlife and other visitors enjoying the scenery. They were lucky that the weather was beautiful. It was a balmy seventy degrees, not typical of a Midwest Thanksgiving Day.

Finally, it was their turn for dinner, which was served buffet style in a great dining room hall. They enjoyed turkey, mashed potatoes, and all the trimmings. The end of the meal was dessert, which consisted of pecan or pumpkin pie. The perfect ending to a wonderful day!

The next morning, they woke up early so that they could walk the main street of old St. Charles. It was beautifully decorated with old-fashioned ornaments and garlands on every building. The characters were dressed in the clothing of the period of history they were depicting. There were carolers, gingerbread houses, railroad displays, and of course Santa Claus at the end of the Thanksgiving parade! Strolling the streets were different versions of St. Nicholas from a variety of countries. It was an awesome place to be on this holiday. Rose thought she had hit it out of the park when she organized this weekend. Nothing could have worked out any better.

They walked around enjoying all the shops and displays. There were millions of things they would like to buy, but they were sticking to their budget. Gabriel looked at the shirts in one shop, and Rose was surprised that he was thinking of asking for one. She then noticed his shirt was tight on him. The shirt he wanted to buy was bigger. She gave in to his request and bought him the shirt. Immediately as they walked out of the store, he took his shirt off and put the new shirt on which fit much better. He was now another size larger.

They finished walking through the entire main street and then walked back to the car for the drive home. This was a trip they would remember forever. Their first Thanksgiving without their Aunt Joan.

Chapter 28

The Drive Home

The drive home started with a recap of the weekend. They both agreed that the entire weekend was memorable. The dinner at Pere Marquette Lodge was better than anticipated. Learning about the history of the lodge and the WPA during the Great Depression was a good addition to the weekend too. St. Charles was charming and historic. They could not think of one aspect of this weekend to improve.

After that discussion, Rose turned to the present and the future.

"Gabriel, how is the job going? What do you think of your salary now and in the future?"

"Mom, I don't want to talk about this right now."

"I know it is a hard thing to discuss, but we have to talk about it. You are growing up and need a job that will support you and your family someday."

"I'm fine right now. I have enough money to pay my bills."

"Gabriel, you are a young man now, you have to start thinking about your life and where you want to go and what you want to do. Time goes by, and you need to finish school or get into a trade job or something to become a self-supporting adult." Rose was tired of reminding Gabriel about life and what was expected of him.

"Okay, Mom, I'll give it some thought." Gabriel said with a huffy attitude.

"Think about taking that job with my company. It pays well, and you could get some experience and get into a job that will support you and a family someday, if that is the life you choose."

Gabriel was upset that his mom was bringing up this subject again. He was only twenty-one, he didn't have a family, and didn't need anything else right now. "Can we talk about something different?"

"What do you want to talk about?" Rose also wanted to change the subject and enjoy the ride home instead of fighting.

"I still do not know the country of my ancestors' origin. I want to sign up for ancestry.com to find out more about my roots."

"Did you ask your half brother and sisters yet?" Rose thought asking his birth family was the first place he should start. They may be able to give him names of grandparents and great-grandparents. This would give him an edge when he signed up for ancestry.com.

"Yes, and they did not have any idea who the great-grandparents were or where they originated." Gabriel wanted to find a birth relation who was a good citizen so that he could feel better about himself.

"Well, it's probably a good idea to buy a month of ancestry.com and see what you can find out. Don't buy more than a month's membership on it, though. Sign on and see where it takes you. Maybe you'll find out enough so that you can do more investigating on your own for free."

Chapter 29

The New Job

Rose went back to work after the four-day weekend. It had been nice to get four days off in a row. She had a demanding job as area controller at the manufacturing company. There was usually never time to get off for the entire weekend or any vacation time. The Thanksgiving break was a good time for both Gabriel and Rose.

Her job entailed travel to three plants located about thirty-five miles apart from each other. She was responsible for the financials for all three plants. Month ends were the busiest. It seemed that no sooner did one month end, than it was time to work on the next month end. She was always swamped with work, and with physical inventories on weekends, she worked six days a week. Sometimes month-end work kept her at the plant seven days a week. The money was good, but her job had become her life.

She used the extra money to foot the bill for the military college that Gabriel had first enjoyed. She wished that he had finished school, and her money had been better spent. It all seemed such a waste. Should she have sent Gabriel to trade school or bought him a place to live? She needed to find another way to get Gabriel going on his way to his own life.

The manufacturing manager at one of the plants was hinting for Gabriel to work in his building on the assembly line. He needed a big guy to push the loads of corrugated onto the transfer car and then onto the correct machine line. Rose wanted more than the factory life for Gabriel, but it was a way that he could earn enough money to support himself. About once each week, the plant manager would stop over and remind Rose that he needed Gabriel working for him on the transfer car. She kept telling him that Gabriel was going to finish college and didn't need the job, but the longer the time went on, the harder it was for her to believe that story.

Rose had been an accountant all thirty some years she had worked. She liked the role of an accountant. She didn't like the parts of the job that were more financial analysis. On those days she wanted a different job. Many of her coworkers along the way advised her that her personality was not like an accountant and that she should pursue a different career. Rose only knew accounting and felt that she wouldn't be able to get a job without experience in the new field. She listened to her friends, especially Dennis, who was a financial analyst. He told Rose to become either a trainer or project manager. Rose didn't think of herself as either but decided to give it some thought.

A few weeks later, there was an announcement at work. The mouse was eating the lion. A ten-plant box-manufacturing company was purchasing her one-hundred-plant company! They were told that everything would stay the same, but of course, as time went by some things would eventually change.

Rose decided this might be the perfect time for her to take Dennis's advice. She was going to look for some jobs that were completely different. The next day she started browsing the job-hunting websites for something new.

Within a few days of searching, Rose came across an ad for a software company. The job was a training position teaching the accounting section of the software. It was scary; she didn't like to talk in front of people. Never in her life had she taught a class. It would be an entirely new adventure, and she thought she was due a change.

Rose sent in her résumé and waited for a reply. This was the one and only job she was trying to win. A few days later, the phone rang, and it was the software company expressing their interest in her résumé. They told her they would be sending her a test to take and then afterward they would e-mail her more information.

Rose was elated! A friend of hers worked for a software company, and the long stressful hours like she was experiencing at her present job did not exist. He was always relaxed, and he made good money. Rose decided that she needed more time at home and less stress in her life. If she was offered the job, she would take it. Even if that mean she would earn less money.

The e-mail with the link to the test arrived. She sat down and took the fifteen-minute test and sent it right back.

A few days later Rose received yet another e-mail saying that they wanted her to interview for the position. She could either do a mock training session on Facebook or LinkedIn. Being familiar with LinkedIn, Rose selected it.

The interview day came, and she was a pile of nerves. She drove to the interview, which was about forty-five minutes from her house, but close to her old airline office. The interview was on the seventh floor. The receptionist asked her to wait in the lobby area. After a few minutes she was called into a meeting room. A big screen was in front of her, and two managers from the other side of the world were on the screen. Rose couldn't believe she was going to interview via webcam! She pulled out her note cards and introduced herself. She explained that she was going teach them how to upload a picture into LinkedIn. They understood, and she started. Rose could feel the sweat dripping down her back, and she felt like she was stuttering although she had practiced the speech a hundred times.

Although she was a basket of nerves as she finished, the two managers were smiling and seemed impressed with Rose. She breathed a sigh of relief and answered their questions. There wasn't a chance in the world she would get this job, so she was calm as she spoke. Unlike other interviews, they asked her what salary she required. Rose knew she needed a certain amount to live on but was able to take a drop in salary and still could pay all her bills. She explained her salary requirements as well as vacation and medical-benefit needs. The two managers were satisfied with her answers and decided to end the interview. Rose walked out feeling she did the best she could.

When she returned to her present job the next day, Dennis asked her how the interview had gone. Rose explained the entire day to Dennis, and he assured her she would get the job. She wondered if Dennis wanted her to get the job to keep him more secure in his position. He was a fellow employee in the Finance Department, and if there were fewer employees there was more work, and he would get to stay. Dennis had a new wife and new baby and did not want to leave his present position. He was very good at his financial-analyst position and liked it. It was a perfect fit for him. Even if this was the reason Dennis was so adamant about her leaving, Rose didn't mind. She really believed it was time to leave.

A few days went by, and she received word that she was being offered the position at the salary she needed, but less vacation time than she requested. It wasn't a bad offer, and she was guaranteed a five-day workweek and eight-hour day. She decided to go for it.

Next, it was time to tell Gabriel what it would mean to take this job. She was due a bonus before she would leave her job. She had decided already what she wanted to do with the bonus. Now she had to explain all of this to Gabriel.

It was evening, and Gabriel was home from his job at the armored car company. She asked him to sit down to talk.

"Gabriel, I was offered a new position today with an Australian software company, and I have decided to take the job. I felt that I no longer had a life working the way I did at my present job. You know that I was never home and always working. I was not living a balanced life. I didn't have time to see my friends or go anywhere. The little time I had, I spent with you. I really feel I need a change."

"Okay, Mom, I am happy for you. I know you deserve more time for yourself."

"Gabriel, there is one more thing—money. There won't be as much money after I leave this job and take the new position. We will have to cut back a little, and you may need to work some overtime or reach for a better position. Are there any other positions at your company that you can win?"

"There is some overtime offered in the warehouse, and I can take a few extra runs after work for some extra money too."

"Okay, you may really need to do both. There is one more thing I want to talk to you about. I am due for a big bonus before I leave this job. I want to look for a condo or town house for you that is in foreclosure and therefore a low price. I will put the down payment on the residence and then help you until you can do it all yourself."

"So you want me to move out on my own?"

"Yes, Gabriel, you are a young man and should have your own place."

"Okay, if that is what you want, I will do it." Gabriel thought that he would stay there forever. He took this as a pushout, like from his birth parents. It was happening all over again.

Rose was not trying to be mean. She really thought it was time for Gabriel to learn how to be on his own. She would never abandon him. She would always take care of him. He would understand later.

Gabriel retreated to his room to play video games.

The next day, Rose started looking for condos and town houses for Gabriel. The housing market was in a slump, and the economy was bad. People were losing their homes in foreclosure. She knew she would be able to pick up a bargain. If he rented an apartment, he would be paying double compared to the amount he could pay monthly taking a thirty-year loan on a foreclosure. Also, Rose always wanted to flip a home. She thought it would be a good way to make a little extra money. They could buy a small condo or town house and then fix it up together and sell it for a profit. It would be a win-win situation. Gabriel would have his own place, and they could make some money too!

She contacted a realtor and asked to be shown about five foreclosures. The properties were located within ten miles of their current home. The first one was a second-story condo. The neighborhood was not the best. She didn't feel comfortable with the area. The second was a beautiful duplex. It had a fireplace and a basement. It was definitely the best value for their money. The yard would need upkeep including raking, mowing, and pruning continuously. Rose didn't feel that Gabriel would be up to the challenge. It was a little bit too big of an undertaking. She knew she couldn't buy it even though it was a very nice property. The next two properties fit the situation. They were both in respectable neighborhoods close to Rose. Both properties had associations that took care of all the outside maintenance. One was low priced and located on a second floor. The other was a little higher priced and a ground floor unit that included a patio and garage. It was a no-brainer; the ground floor unit with the garage was the winner!

Rose quickly put a bid on the property and set a closing date. The next step was the mortgage. She hoped that Gabriel could be on the title and the loan. He would gain a good credit rating and, eventually when he made a higher salary, take over the loan. The bank said that Gabriel could not be on the mortgage because he had no credit rating. Even though Rose's credit was outstanding, they would not add him to the mortgage. That was that. Her plan hit a dead end. She would have to take out the mortgage herself or the deal was off. It wasn't exactly the plan she imagined, but it worked out well enough. It would get Gabriel off on his own and start him realizing what real life was all about. The deal was signed, and they had to wait for the closing.

Meanwhile, Rose went to work and gave her two-week notice. She planned to start the new job almost immediately after Gabriel moved into his new place.

A few weeks later, Gabriel and Rose closed on the town house and went there to inspect the unit. Joel, their dear friend, went with them to go through the entire unit. They didn't find anything major that needed repair, only some minor things. There were a few electrical problems. One light on the patio did not work. The kitchen overhead light also had a wiring problem. The doors on the bedroom closet needed to be replaced. They spent the entire day cleaning and fixing things. By the end of the day, it was ready for Gabriel.

Gabriel moved into the town house with an old dining room table from Rose's house and his old bedroom furniture. He bought his own TV and stand. It was enough for a start. He would need some couches and lamps, but it was livable.

The town house association consisted of only twelve units. It was a nice group of people, and the dues were not high. Gabriel did not associate with the neighbors. The older woman who lived next door always greeted him, but that was about it. Gabriel continued to be a bit of a loner. Even when he had lived with Rose, he kept to himself most of the time, either in his room or in the basement family room. He continued to work full-time and made enough money to pay the utilities and grocery bills.

Chapter 30

The Party at Mike's

Sundays came and went by quickly. It was their day to spend together. Sometimes they went to family parties. Rose was really lucky that her mom had her Aunt Joan as a sister. Rose had only one sister, but she had ten cousins all because of Aunt Joan and her ten children. Many of the holidays were spent at either her cousin Mary's house or her cousin Mike's house. This day would be spent at Mike's house.

Mike was the third oldest of Aunt Joan's children. He was approximately the same age as Rose. Theuressa was his wife, who was about ten years younger than him. Mike had built a business and married later in life. He wanted to have children and purposely looked for a woman who did not have children yet but wanted to have a family. Theuressa was perfect. She was pretty and nice, and everyone loved her. She and Mike had four beautiful children, and they were both very generous with their hospitality. Their house was much like the home in the old *My Three Sons* sitcom of the 1960s. Their backyard was large and included a pool, which made it a great place for parties! Prior to buying this home, they lived across the street from his sister, Mary. It was a convenient situation. Their new home was near to Mary too, right down the street.

Mike and Mary were close to each other. They were the two children who were the organizers. They brought everyone together for parties and everything else. When Aunt Joan was alive, it was convenient for her to visit both of her older children at the same time since they lived so close to one another.

Mike was also very protective of his mom. He made sure she had a reliable car to drive and anything else that she might have needed. Years ago, Joan had lived with Mike for a few years. Those were the years before Joan won the job as a full-time nanny for a wonderful couple. While Joan lived at Mike's, Rose would bring her ironing to do. Joan thought ironing was very therapeutic. Bringing the ironing over was a good way to spend time with Joan. Joan had promised her sister long ago that she would watch over the two girls that Dolly had left when she died. Joan always lived up to that promise and watched over Rose and her sister too.

Today's party at Mike's was a summer party to enjoy his back-yard, pool, and friends. Rose told Gabriel that she would pick him up at one o'clock, and they would make the one-hour drive to Mike's house for the party. Prior to arriving at Mike's, Rose intended to stop at the grocery store to pick up some food for the party. She always contributed to the goodies at each party.

As she drove up to Gabriel's town house, she saw him waiting on the corner with a bag in hand. He looked larger. Each time she saw him now that he had moved out, he was appearing to have gained more weight. Rose looked at the landscaping in front of Gabriel's place. She knew that would be next on the list. The landscaping needed a complete overhaul. She saw his car in the driveway and wondered why he had not put it in the garage. Also, why was he wait-ing on the corner instead of inside the house until she arrived? Rose assumed it was because of the uncleanliness of the house. Gabriel didn't want a lecture from Rose, so he chose to stand on the corner versus waiting in his house and inviting Rose inside.

Gabriel lumbered inside Rose's car. Slowly he put on his seat belt and got comfortable. Rose thought that maybe he would lose a few pounds when he moved into his own place since he would have to clean and do dishes himself and wash clothes. It didn't seem to be the case.

"What is in the bag Gabriel?"

"I brought a few snacks and drinks in case I didn't like the food at Mike's house."

"We are stopping at the store for a treat to bring to the party, so you can make sure we bring something you like."

"I didn't know we were doing that. Better to be safe than sorry."

"Okay. How was work this week?"

"It was the same. I've been assigned to the route in nearby Indiana. We are going the same way I drive every day of the week."

"Tell me some stories from this week's pickups."

"One of our stops is Bass Pro Shops just off the expressway. They are supposed to have the money inside the secured bags when our armored truck gets there. We have exactly five minutes to do the pickup and then get on our way to the next stop. They didn't have anything ready for us, and we were going to be late for out next stop, and then we'd need to work faster to make up the time. The manager there told me to go into the safe myself to make things faster. As guards, we are never allowed to go into a safe or cash register to pick up the money. That would be disobeying the rules of our company. We are only allowed to pick up the money once in the secured bags. If we loaded money into the bags, they could accuse us of stealing. I would not disobey orders."

Rose was surprised and proud of Gabriel. "Good for you! Following the rules and being mindful of the consequences is a good thing. I am proud of you."

"Yes, eventually he loaded the bag with the cash himself and made us late, but that is better far better than if I would have disobeyed our orders."

"Wow, you must have learned a great deal at Georgia Military College. It sounds like you are practicing what they taught you at school."

"Yep, and I told our manager about this customer at the end of the day. The manager will talk to him about the rules and why the rules are in place. I shouldn't have to go through that again."

"Good work, Gabriel. Again, I am proud of you. It sounds like this is your kind of thing. I wish they paid more. I think you would do a good job as a manager yourself there. Have you found any other opportunities to grow and get paid more there?"

"No, not really. I know their competitors pay a little more. Maybe I can get a job there?"

"Well, we can try. Life is all about trying. If you don't try you will never know. Wayne Gretzky has a quote, 'You miss 100 percent of the shots you don't take.'"

They rode along and stopped at a grocery store before arriving at Mike's house. Theuressa greeted them with her big "heart to heart" hug. She makes sure each person hugs her with their hearts touching. Rose had to lean to Theuressa's right to have her right side touching Theuressa's right side to get the hearts touching correctly. It was a feel-good gesture.

The usual spread of food covered all the kitchen table and kitchen island. There were salads, desserts, chips, dips, and tons of meat that would be cooked. The grill was heating up, and the guests were outside in the yard. Rose greeted everyone and went out to the yard. Gabriel picked out a chair next to people he knew and sat down.

Everyone there treated Gabriel and Rose with love and respect. There was a comfort level there that was second to none. Rose made a point to go as often as she could to keep the ties strong. Having a very small family made things harder because there was no one to lean on when things got rough. At least with her ten cousins, she and Gabriel always had somewhere to go, people who loved them and people who cared about them.

Each time they came to one of these parties, there was a person or couple from the past that made it much more interesting. People who had hung with the family thirty years ago would appear, and they would talk about old times. Most of the time Gabriel just sat quietly and listened. After about two hours of visiting, Rose would always take off. She never liked sitting around too long. She got antsy. Also, Gabriel liked being by himself. He didn't like it when people looked at him. He felt self-conscious.

The ride home was fun and relaxing. They had some nice stories to talk about. They listened to country songs, sang a little, and danced the cabbage-patch dance. It was always good to spend a day together at the cousin's house.

Chapter 31

The Unpaid Bills

Rose arrived home from work and went to the mailbox to pick up the mail. There was a letter from an attorney. Rose was shocked and horrified. What could she have done wrong? She paid every bill and made sure she did everything right. What had slipped by and gone unnoticed? What could have happened? Was someone suing her for some unknown reason? She tore open the envelope and read it. It was from an attorney who was hired by the town house association for unpaid dues. Gabriel was supposed to be paying the utility bills and association bills. He didn't have anything else to pay except for gas and food. What happened? Rose freaked out. He had not paid the association dues for months. There were in arrears for three months, and now they were adding a five-hundred-dollar fee to the bill for nonpayment. Rose wasn't loaded with money. She paid her bills and saved for retirement. It was hard enough paying for two mortgages and making sure two cars kept running. She didn't need any more bills!

She hopped back in the car and drove over to Gabriel's to show him the letter. She rarely yelled or screamed at Gabriel, but this was one of her pet peeves. Everyone needs to pay their bills. She had made sure to limit the amount of bills that Gabriel needed to pay. She didn't want him to be overwhelmed. She took on more responsibility then needed to keep Gabriel's burden lighter. He had been through enough in his life. He didn't need more stress. Since he wasn't overburdened with bills, this nonpayment of association dues made her furious.

Rose knocked on his door. Gabriel opened the door a few seconds later and was surprised to see Rose. She always called beforehand to give him notice that she was coming. She showed him the letter and asked what happened and why he didn't pay. He said he must have forgotten. Rose yelled and screamed at the top of her lungs, saying she couldn't afford an extra five hundred dollars on top of the association dues. He started to climb the stairs to get away from her. She turned and walked out crying.

When she returned home, she made the phone calls to the attorney and association. She asked why they had not contacted her for the payment. Why hadn't they sent her a statement? She said she would pay in advance, but they said she still needed to pay the five-hundred-dollar fee. Finally, she agreed to pay the fee. This ordeal would set her back a thousand dollars. Another setback that she didn't need.

Maybe Gabriel needed to make more money and take on more responsibility. He loved his job as an armored car driver, but it didn't seem to be paying the bills. He couldn't really have a hobby because he didn't have any extra money each week. Other young men were saving money and buying hobby cars and taking up a sport, but Gabriel didn't do any of those things. Maybe having more money to spend would give him the ability to do something he loved that would keep him busy and away from food?

A few days later, after she cooled down, she decided she would have a talk with Gabriel about taking the union job at her old company. At that job, he would have to work with other men and maybe he would find a friend too. Driving the armored car allowed him access to only one other person each day. There wasn't the chance or opportunity to meet a friend. Her old company was large, and if you did a good job, there were opportunities to climb the corporate ladder. She knew guys there who started out as a laborer and rose to plant manager. Rose had worked there for several years, and they were good to her, except for the long hours. It wouldn't hurt Gabriel to spend some time there either.

The following Sunday she took Gabriel to a gun show at one of the fairgrounds about fifty miles away. He always liked looking at guns and military memorabilia, so they went to quite a few of these shows. Going to the shows on Sundays included walking and learning. Afterward they would stop and have some lunch at a place they had never been to before. A new adventure! Sometimes it was a restaurant that was on the *Diners, Drive-Ins and Dives* show. Other times it was just someplace unique. Rose always loved new places.

When they went to the restaurant afterward, they sat and talked, and there was an opening for Rose to bring up the union job.

"Gabriel how is the job going?"

"It's okay, why?"

"Well, after the fiasco we went through over the nonpayment of the association dues, I have been trying to think about your income and how it could be increased." Rose hated to bring up this job and the problem last week with the money, but it had to be done.

"I tried to get some overtime, but there wasn't any available. What ideas did you have?"

"I know my old company is hiring, and you would make more money there."

"You want me to take that job and quit the armored car company?"

"Gabriel, in all honesty, I wanted you to finish college and be a policeman by now, but that didn't work out. Now, there aren't as many opportunities for you without a college degree."

"I'll go back to school. Maybe I can go to the junior college and finish the two-year degree?"

"You could also call up Georgia Military and see if you can finish that degree over the Internet."

"I will apply at your old company and also call up Georgia Military to see if I can finish it."

"Good, Gabriel. You should be making more money for yourself so that you can afford to buy things you need and want each week. You can apply online for the position, and then they will call you in to take a test. The whole process should take about two weeks. I'll bet you will be making more money in less than a month."

They finished eating their meal, and Rose added a review of the restaurant on her phone app. She liked taking on the role of reviewer and felt she could do a good job because she visited many different restaurants. The bill was paid, and they left. Rose hoped she had gotten through to Gabriel about needing a new job that would give him more money.

Chapter 32

The Friend

It was three o'clock in the afternoon, and Gabriel meandered into the factory and walked to his machine. He passed by many of the other workers, but it wasn't until he arrived at his machine that he received his first greeting.

"Hey, Gabriel, got a minute?"

"Hi, Dan, what's up?

Dan had arrived early and had already looked at the order sheet for their machine.

"Gabriel, we have a long night ahead of us. There are a bunch of orders that need to get out tonight. I'm glad I've got you as an assistant on this machine. Together we can get everything done." Dan gave Gabriel a high five.

Dan understood Gabriel and his weight problem. His father is a large man too. No matter how many diets his father tried, nothing seemed to work. His father was getting older and would need to make a change soon. His knees were getting worse, and he could no longer do the things he had done in the past like climbing ladders and chasing after his grandkids.

There weren't many people like Dan who understood Gabriel's weight problem. Most people looked at a person who was obese and thought that they were lazy people who just sat around and ate all day. Most people stereotyped heavy people. They didn't consider the problems that were going on that caused the overeating, like depression. Since Gabriel had been in several foster homes, bounced around to several schools, and had to move to another city to be adopted, he was depressed. He thought that he was kicked out of many homes because something was wrong with him. He felt like he was unlovable. He knew he wasn't good-looking because of the extra weight. He had low self-esteem too. Gabriel was lucky to have found a friend like Dan.

"What are you up to this weekend, Gabriel? My wife is having some people over, and we would like you to come too. You can meet my family."

"I think I can come. What do you want me to bring?"

"Just bring yourself. No need for anything else. Now, let's get this work done."

Chapter 33

The Party at Dan's

Finding friends was hard for Gabriel and meeting new people even harder. He felt enormous, like a monster. Moving was hard. Walking was hard. Getting in and out of a car was hard. There was nothing easy about being obese. Every look that came his way made him believe that people were judging him. He knew they were thinking that it was easy—just stop eating. It wasn't that easy. There was a hole in his stomach that just never filled up. He tried to concentrate on other things, but there was a cloud in his head. Since he felt so bad inside, the cloud in his brain never allowed him to think normally. The only thing in the world that made him feel a little better was the taste of food, which was the very reason his life was horrible.

He never was promoted on jobs because of his size, so he lived on lower wages. The cost of his food was enormous, and the cost of large clothes was even greater. He never had any extra money for anything. He couldn't even dress to camouflage his weight a little because he couldn't afford many pieces of clothing. He was always hot, so the cost of keeping his house cool was over and above what other people spent. There wasn't a bright spot in the entire picture.

Today, something was going to bring a little bit of happiness into his life. He had received an invitation to a friend's house. He didn't understand why. No one wanted to invite him over. He hadn't gotten an invite for years. It felt good. He had to force himself to move and get over there. The first thing he would do was to drive over by Rose's house and ask her if she could borrow him money for a new shirt. He quickly got dressed and trudged to the car.

It was Saturday, and Rose was home in the backyard tending to her flowers. Her mom had loved gardening, and she remembered some of the flowers her mom had in her childhood backyard. She specifically planted those varieties, and they brought her the most happiness. Her garden was very nice and brought others happiness too. The view was visible to a few houses in the backyard where people had decks and gazebos. These houses overlooked all her flowers and people who visited for parties often called Rose over to compliment how they loved looking at the flowers.

When Rose bought the house, her backyard was a mess. There had been a play set, and the ground under it was bare. There was also a pool. Rose kept the pool for a year or two, and Gabriel had used it a few times. As he increased in size he moved less, and he did not want to expose his body to others, so he did not go in the pool. Rose put an ad on Craigslist and was able to give it to a person who disassembled and removed it. That person had just gone through a divorce and wanted to supply some enjoyment to his children while they were over. Rose felt she had done a good deed.

Rose heard loud music in her driveway, and within a few minutes Gabriel appeared in the backyard. He lumbered over to her and wore a smile.

"Hi, Mom, watcha doing?"

"Hi, Gabriel. I am weeding, trimming, and planting some new flowers. I'm trying to get this whole area where the pool was filled with flowers."

"It looks good. You are doing a nice job."

"What brings you over?"

"I was invited to a friend's house for a party. I was wondering if you can loan me some money so that I can buy a new shirt to wear today."

Rose was surprised that Gabriel had an invite and stopped what she was doing. "Who invited you to a party? What kind of party is it and how far away is the party?

"It's my friend Dan from work. He lives about twenty miles away, and he is having a small party for his kids today."

"That is very nice, Gabriel. Sure, I will give you the money. I want you to look nice. Let me grab my purse in the house."

Rose ran into the house quickly and grabbed her purse and debit card.

"Here, Gabriel, take my debit card and buy yourself a new shirt. Do you need a pair of shoes? I see you are wearing your work boots."

"No, Mom, I like wearing my work boots."

"Well, promise me that you will at least tie them for the party."

"Okay, I will try to tie them."

Tying shoes was easy for most people, but not for Gabriel. It was hard for him to bend over and reach his shoes. He could only reach them if he sat down and bent over. Bending over was tough too. His stomach got in the way. Getting up after bending over was even harder. His shoes were often untied.

"Do you want some company? Do you want me to come to the store with you?"

"Sure, can you go now? I have to get there and still have time to take a shower before the party."

"Yes, I'll change my shoes, and we can go right away."

Rose quickly grabbed her other shoes and made her way to the car. Gabriel climbed into the passenger side. There wasn't any need for conversation about where they would go. There were only a few stores for large people, one of which was near Gabriel's house. That extra-large store was their go-to place to shop for Gabriel. The prices were high, but they did carry some things that were stylish, and they also carried all the accessories for large people, including extra-large shoes and extra-large belts. It was highway robbery that they got away with charging extremely high prices for large clothing. Large people had very few choices, so they paid.

They walked into the store, and it was empty apart from the store clerk. She was a very nice lady who came right over to help. Gabriel didn't like small talk, so he quickly refused the help and started to look around. He found a T-shirt he liked that had graphics on it and looked like something other smaller guys his age would wear. The T-shirt would cost probably twenty dollars at a store with average sizes. Here the same T-shirt cost double that price.

Next, they looked at shoes. The shoes were very basic, and most didn't have ties; they were slip-ons. Rose thought Gabriel would look better in the slip-on black shoes then his work boots. Also, they didn't require tying or bending over. It was too bad that they didn't carry a slip-on athletic shoe because that would make him fit in better.

"Do you want to buy a pair of these shoes to wear today too?"

"Okay, Mom." Gabriel looked at the display until he found his size.

They went to the register and paid for the new items. Rose felt good that Gabriel would be wearing a few new things. She just wished she could help him more. She wanted him to be happy and live a full life. The weight he carried would never allow that to happen.

On the way home, Rose asked him about Dan. Gabriel told her he was a friend at work who he met while working on his machine. He was the assistant operator, and Dan was the operator. Dan wanted to become a supervisor because he had a growing family and needed to earn more money. Dan was always looking for new opportunities at other companies and would move if given the opportunity to become a supervisor. His plan was to gain some experience and then hop to yet another company to go a step further. Dan had told Gabriel that his wife was working as a nurse but quit working when their first child was born. This brought much more stress to Dan's life. He liked the fact that his child was being raised by his wife but didn't like the drop in income.

They arrived back at Rose's house, and Gabriel left with his new shirt and shoes, ready to go to Dan's party. This was a good day because Rose didn't have to worry about Gabriel being alone and lonely.

Gabriel went home and showered and dressed. He looked in the mirror and didn't like what he saw, but he was happy he was wearing a shirt that was cool. He looked around at his home. It was messy: clothes lying all around, cat box overloaded with litter, and dishes piled high in the sink. He just didn't have the energy to clean it. Why bother? Anyway, no one was coming over. He didn't mind the mess for himself. He knew his mom wouldn't come over unless she was invited on a few rare occasions. Rose thought he would only invite her to show how he cleaned the place when he wanted something from her. He fed the cat, Salem, and left for the party.

Dan's house was near work. Gabriel put the address in his GPS and started on his way. He thought of turning around several times, not knowing who would be at the party and what they would think of him and his size. He made himself keep driving. He figured if Dan was there, all would be fine. Dan was always polite and kind to Gabriel. He never made fun of his size. He never minded Gabriel's slow movements because of his size. He accepted Gabriel as he was. There weren't many people like Dan. Gabriel knew he was a rare friend, and he wanted to keep Dan happy, so he kept driving to his house.

He turned into Dan's street and looked for a parking spot. He tried to find a space that was close to his house. There weren't any available, so he picked one a little further away and slowly got out of the car and walked to Dan's house. As he approached, he heard children playing and saw a great deal of activity inside the house. He knocked on the door, and Dan answered quickly with a smile.

"Hi, Gabriel! What's up? Glad you could make it. Come on in!" Dan led Gabriel into the house where quite a few people were sitting, eating, and enjoying the party.

"I want you to meet my dad, Jose. He's heard me talk about you, and he wants to meet you."

Gabriel walked in slowly, embarrassed by his size. He had to meander around people, furniture, and toys on the floor. Getting around in tight quarters was not easy when you are extremely large. The family and friends were kind and moved over politely with a smile for him. He entered the kitchen where they found Dan's dad enjoying his meal.

"Dad, look who came to our party! This is Gabriel from work. You don't have to stand up, I know it's hard on your knees."

Jose stood up and reached out his hand to Gabriel. He was an enormous size, but short in stature. Gabriel was surprised to see what he looked like because Dan was a tall, normal-sized guy. He never would have imagined that his dad was extremely overweight. Gabriel shook his hand with a smile. He understood why Dan treated him just like any other guy. Dan was used to the large size of his father. Gabriel felt comfortable in their home. He relaxed and sat down next to Jose. It was a good feeling. A sigh of relief. There weren't many moments like this where he felt comfortable in the company of others; usually, he'd rather be alone. Today was different. He was a little bit happier.

Jose was a happy guy except for his knee pain. The weight of his body caused his knees to give out before their time. He was unable to walk without pain and unable to run and play with his grandkids. That was the worst part. He yearned to be able to run around with the kids in the yard and play. He also enjoyed hunting, which was another thing he had to give up. In his past he walked the fields and hunted for pheasant and rabbits. He loved a good pheasant or rabbit stew and was proud when he brought home his trophies. He could no longer walk the fields for any amount of time, so his guns and other hunting gear sat alone, unused.

They found they had some things in common. Gabriel liked shooting, and he loved going to the gun range with anyone. He was sad that he didn't have any friends that would go with him. Rose went occasionally, but it wasn't her thing either. She would just go to make Gabriel happy. Gabriel needed some real friends to enjoy his hobbies with him, but at his size, there weren't many people who wanted to be seen with him. At least that was what Gabriel thought. He had low self-esteem after being removed from his birth family. If his family didn't want him, who did?

Jose and Gabriel talked and talked. Soon it was time to leave. The afternoon had gone by fast. Gabriel had a new friend. He looked forward to coming back and hoped that Dan would invite him again. He walked to his car and smiled as he went home. The day had gone much better than he had ever anticipated.

He pulled into his driveway and was met at the door by his cat, Salem. Often, he felt that Salem was the only one who liked him. He would sit in his living room watching TV, with Salem on his lap, purring. It was nice that the cat yearned for his company, but it was no substitute for friends or a girlfriend. Gabriel wanted a girlfriend. When he was in high school, he always had a girlfriend. He was a good-looking guy, a little stocky, but the girls liked him. He had no problem finding a girlfriend; they found him. He enjoyed their company and the attention they gave to him. It had been years now since he had a girlfriend. That was one of the biggest things he missed. He'll try to diet again. Maybe it will work this time.

Chapter 34

The Military Show

Rose called Gabriel to hear about the party. She was excited to hear that Gabriel had a party to go to and hoped that he didn't back out at the last minute. She was ecstatic hearing how Gabriel hit it off with Dan's father. She didn't know yet that Jose was a large man and shared the same problem as Gabriel. She just liked hearing that Jose sat for a long time and talked to Gabriel. He was lacking a male figure in his life and loved to hear that he was getting some attention from a guy.

"Do you want to go to a military show today? There is one right in Joliet at the VFW hall. It starts at ten this morning and ends at four. We could head over there for an hour and then grab a bite to eat. I found a new brewery in a town south of there that is supposed to have some good and unique food as well as a great atmosphere!"

"Okay, Mom, we can go. Give me an hour to take a shower and get ready."

"I'll be there at eleven. See you soon."

Rose hung up the phone and was a little bit happier. It was good that Dan and Jose were friendly with Gabriel. She went out to her yard and did a little yard work while she waited for her son to get ready for the military show. Her plants had come a long way. The yard was starting to look beautiful. She noticed her neighbors were outside. Hopefully, they will shout over the fence to talk to her. She was lonely too. She wished she had a husband. She remembered the days when Bob would be around while she did her planting and trimming outside. He had never liked to do the yard work, but he was there, and it was nice company.

The neighbors also enjoyed being outside. They had a beautiful yard, especially the front yard. Their roses were very appealing. Roses wanted to have roses too, but that would come later. She had to move slowly in her yard, gathering some plants from friends and buying one here or there. Her funds didn't allow her to buy too much all at once. That was another problem about being divorced. Having a double income in one household sure was nice. Together they were able to own a very nice home, go on trips, and buy nice things. Alone, her paycheck only allowed her the basics and helping Gabriel out too, leaving her with even less money. Someday, Gabriel would be better; he would conquer his weight and she would be happy knowing she helped to raise him to become a good person.

After doing some pruning and trimming, she gathered up all her tools and yard bags and put everything back into the garage. She kept her house organized, but the garage was not as nice as she wanted it. When she had more time, she looked forward to cleaning it up, painting the walls and floor, and sprucing it up a bit. Her friend Cindy even put old antique dressers in her garage for cabinets instead of the standard garage shelves and cabinets. It looked awesome, and she wanted to do the same thing in her garage. Time, it would just take time. One step today, another tomorrow. She'd get it all done.

She went inside and washed up a bit and then picked up her purse to go to get Gabriel. The drive to his house was only eight miles and took about ten minutes. He was out there on the corner waiting for her. He was wearing a jacket with his hands in his pocket, his work boots that were untied, and jeans.

Gabriel climbed into the car. He was in his usual somber mood. Rose tried to lighten up the mood.

"Hi, my favorite son!"

"Mom, I am your only son, how can I be your favorite?"

"Even if I had five sons, I know you would be my favorite."

Gabriel smiled a little. Rose was a nice Mom, and he was so thankful that he had been adopted by her. His sister Melissa chose not to be adopted; she chose to go to a foster home. Her life was much different. He heard she was now living in low-cost housing in Michigan. He would like to see her again. He decided he would suggest to his mom that they take a ride there. Rose loved road trips, so he thought it would work.

"I heard from Melissa today."

"That was nice, how is she doing?"

Gabriel paused. "She is living in Michigan. After she turned eighteen, her foster family let her go. She wound up in a shelter and started to work in a grocery store. She met a guy who was deaf, and she started living with him. It seemed he treated her very badly. He hit her and called her bad names, but she stuck with him. He decided that they should move to Michigan for some reason. She really didn't have anyone else, so she moved there with him. After a while, I guess he got tired of her and left. She was there alone living in another shelter."

"That is terrible. What is happening now? Is she still alone?"

"That was a few years ago. She has been in Michigan living in low-cost housing with a black man who is sixty years old. She's had three kids with him already. DCFS is watching her and has placed the kids with their grandmother for now. I'm afraid she'll just get pregnant again and do more stupid things."

"I'm sorry to hear all of this, Gabriel. If you know where she lives or if you can find out, we can take a ride to Michigan and stop to see her. There are lots of fun things to do in Michigan, so we'll make a day out of it.

"Okay, I'll find out where she lives exactly and tell her we will come and visit her."

Gabriel started to text a message to his sister. He was happy that she was talking to him and hoped she would answer back with her address so that they could go and see her.

They drove to the VFW hall and found a good parking spot. The place was busy. It looked like it would be a good show. Gabriel liked looking at the old war guns, ammo, and memorabilia. They paid their five-dollar admission and moved into the hall. There were rows and rows of spaces filled with collectors of all kinds. One vendor specialized in odd ammunition; another had a table full of old patches from uniforms of the past. They stopped at a table with old dog tags. Gabriel looked through them and liked them. He wanted to have one someday. He had always wanted to go into the military, and his dream was still alive. He found a few of them and purchased them for two dollars each. It was his prize of the day. They went down another aisle to look at guns.

The gun booth contained antique guns. There were military guns that were no longer working and just for show, and there were guns that were more expensive because they were operational. Gabriel spent some time looking over them. He also wanted a gun collection someday and a gun cabinet.

After going down each aisle, they called it a day and decided to leave. The next stop was a new brewery. Rose loved stopping at new places and then reviewing them on the restaurant review apps. A few of her friends at work also did the same thing, so after the weekends they would talk about the places they had been and then compare their reviews. It was one of the things that made her workplace a neat place. Everyone got along so well and laughed together. They did a few meetups after work every so many months, and they all became good friends.

The brewery Rose chose was a small one in a strip mall. She didn't expect much when she drove up to it, but they went in to try it out. The place was unique. It was filled with cool things on the walls, and the people were unique too. There were lots of people who decorated their skin with tattoos. They were covered in art! They decided to sit at a high-top table and look at the menu. They each selected a burger, and Rose selected a beer. Rose usually didn't eat burgers but made the occasional exception.

As they were ordering, Gabriel's phone beeped. He looked, and it was a message back from Melissa. She seemed happy to hear that her half brother wanted to meet up with her and gave him the address right away. It was now a plan; they would to go in two weeks to visit Melissa. Meanwhile, Rose would have enough time to make a second selection for a stop while they were on the road trip. She would look to see if there was a restaurant from the TV show *Diners,*

Drive-Ins and Dives. She loved visiting the places she watched on TV. She would also pick out a museum or other touristy attraction to visit. She was looking forward to the trip.

The food arrived, and the burgers looked awesome. Each was piled high with different flavors. Rose had ordered a spicy burger with jalapeños and pepper jack cheese. Gabriel ordered a burger with bacon and cheddar cheese. They both dug into their burgers. They had felt a little out of the norm at this spot, but the food was worth it, and Rose liked being a little adventurous. It was a good find.

The ride home was filled with country music and smiles. Gabriel was happy to be looking forward to the trip to see Melissa, and his stomach was filled with a good burger too. He had his dog tags to hang up on his wall of souvenirs and memorabilia. It was a good weekend. He had met his new friend, Jose, and spent a nice day out with his mom.

Chapter 35

The Trip to See Melissa

It was going to be a long but great day. Rose had found a dune buggy ride on the way to Melissa's place and a *Diners, Drive-Ins and Dives* restaurant not too far from their destination. It was five in the morning, and she was getting showered and ready for the four-hour drive to see Melissa. She texted Gabriel and said she would be picking him up at about six. That would put them at the dune buggy ride at approximately ten o'clock, lunch at noon, and a visit with Melissa at about one. It would be a full day!

Gabriel was ready for her at the time given. He was always on time, never late. It was something that gave him great pride. He didn't like it when others said they would be at a place at one time, and then didn't show up until later, or not at all. That was one of his pet peeves. He made sure he never disappointed anyone by being late.

They spent about two and a half hours in the car and then pulled up at the dune buggy ride. Rose was looking forward to this adventure. She had been on one other dune buggy ride with her Aunt Joan and family. Gabriel had not been there. She wanted to give him this experience that she had enjoyed so much. This wasn't the same ride; the one with Joan had been farther north in Michigan, but she hoped it was just as much fun.

As they waited for their time slot on the dune buggy, they browsed through the store. There were T-shirts, jackets, magnets, and the other normal souvenir items. She liked the coffee mug she saw with Lake Michigan on it but controlled herself and did not buy it. She had bought one while she was with Aunt Joan, and although she loved it, the words were fading on it and it was now just a blue mug. Souvenirs were nice because they brought back the memories, but too many of them were not needed. They just turned into clutter, making her house look overcrowded and messy.

The dune buggy driver came into the store and announced the next trip was about to load and leave. Gabriel and Rose walked out with the rest of the people and started to get into the vehicle. The driver asked Rose and Gabriel to sit up front with him. She thought, why not? So Rose sat next to the driver, and Gabriel sat on the passenger side by the door. They were off. At first, they drove up a road through a forested area. There was a gate that opened as they approached. This land was owned by the tour company. It had been purchased many years ago.

The first story the driver shared was about the ghost town of Singapore, Michigan. It was founded in 1836 by New York land speculator Oshea Wilder who was hoping to build a port town to compete against the big cities of Chicago and Milwaukee. At the height of the town's heyday, it boasted three mills, two hotels, several general stores, and a renowned bank. At that time in history, it had just enough buildings to call it a big town! It was home to Michigan's first schoolhouse. In total, the town consisted of twenty-three buildings and two sawmills.

During 1871, there were four great fires in the Midwest in Chicago, Holland, Peshtigo, and Singapore. The fire in Singapore had destroyed all the tree cover that kept the town safe from the sand and wind of Lake Michigan. Trees couldn't be grown fast enough to keep it safe from the sand. It took four years, but then the sand completely covered the town. Singapore's ruins now sit buried beneath the sand dunes of Lake Michigan shoreline at the mouth of the Kalamazoo River. The town was completely vacated by 1875 except for one man who refused to leave his home. It was told that the sand was so high, the man had to come and go from his house out of the roof. He stayed as long as he could, but eventually the sand completely covered the roof, and he had to leave.

Other stories were not as devastating. He told jokes about leaving mothers-in-law out in the sand, and there were other items set in the sand to tell funny stories about. Most of the ride was a series of staged jokes, but it was fun. After a bit, the driver started to ask trivia questions. Rose was able to answer a few of the questions with the correct answer. Gabriel was a little proud of his mom for having the ability to speak up in front of the crowd and actually get some of the answers right!

The next part was a stop above a high hill with a captivating view of the sand hills and lake. They paused and then suddenly, like a roller-coaster ride, they went down the hill. Most of the twenty people lifted their hands high in the air as they rode down the hill. It was exhilarating.

The ride ended, and everyone cheered. They climbed out of the dune buggy, and most of the riders tipped the driver for giving them a fun adventure.

The next stop was lunch. The restaurant was another hour away. It was a barbecue joint that was getting rave reviews. The place was packed. They had to squish into the middle of the room into a small, two-person table. They ordered their barbecue sandwiches, which came with a choice of sides. Gabriel picked a macaroni and cheese side dish. Rose selected a side of potato salad, which was her favorite. It reminded her of her mom's famous potato salad at the farm parties.

Rose planned on giving this restaurant four stars on her app review. The only disappointment was the crowd. Hopefully, the restaurant would open a second location or expand this one to accommodate all the people that they attracted. It had turned out to be a good spot, and she was glad she made the journey with Gabriel.

Gabriel typed Melissa's address into his GPS on his phone. Next stop, and most important of the day, was seeing his half sister! It had been maybe six or seven years since she had seen her. The last time was when she was just about eighteen years old, and she was about to leave her foster home and go out on her own. There were a few times Gabriel and Rose had tried to convince Melissa to either go to college or into the armed forces. Rose figured that Melissa would be eligible for some assistance for college since she had been in the foster care program. The last suggestion was for Melissa to move in with Gabriel and Rose and find a job nearby and also attend college. Gabriel had sent Melissa a list of nearby stores that Melissa could apply for work. Rose could not afford to bring Melissa to her house and support her. She would accept her, if she wanted to work and improve herself. If Melissa just came to live with them and sat on the couch all day, Rose would have an even harder time trying to motivate Gabriel. Motivating Gabriel was like pulling teeth already, and she could not be burdened with another young adult who needed constant pushing. After thinking about the motivation factor, Rose concluded that the armed forces would be the best place for Melissa. Each time they visited Melissa, they asked about her plans and then suggested she try to get into the armed forces.

Their prodding to get her into the armed forces didn't work. Melissa left her foster home at eighteen and went into a shelter. Foster care had not been the best choice for her. She had made the decision at age eleven or twelve years old. These children who had poor formative years needed support for much longer than a few years to get them going into the right direction. It seemed her foster family did not teach her much about employment or education. Unfortunately, some adults became foster parents for the wrong reason. They took in multiple children and received checks from the state for their clothing, food, and shelter. Then the adults used the money to pay for their own housing and food. The children got the bare minimum of their needs met. They did not gain any self-esteem because they were living in sort of a group home and didn't get much attention. Also, when they went to school, the other children at the school found out that they were living in a foster home. That carried a stigma, and they were teased and bullied. Rose had learned even in her situation that Gabriel's teachers had not believed that Rose was interested in helping her foster child and didn't even call her when they had trouble with Gabriel. It had taken a great deal from Rose to convince the teachers and prove that she was interested in Gabriel's studies. After she met Melissa's foster family years ago, she was convinced they did not make the time or have the motivation to do the same as she did with each one of their foster children.

"Turn left here, then take a right up ahead." Gabriel stared down at his phone, watching as the GPS give the directions.

The neighborhood was run down. It had seen better days. There weren't many stores or places of business. It didn't appear that there were too many places to get a job.

They pulled up to a building that looked like an old motel. It appeared that this structure had been changed over to low-income housing. Imagine a small motel room split in half and now a living room, bedroom, and kitchen. Some of the units had screening over the door to allow air to come into the room. It was a cheap version of a screen door. These places were not nice places to be living.

Rose and Gabriel walked down to the room number given to them by Melissa. She was inside sitting with an old man. She introduced him, and they all sat together in the small room. It was organized but filled with older hand-me-down furniture and accessories. She explained that they had three children who were staying with another family. The Department of Children Services had taken the children and put them in a foster home. Melissa didn't seem that upset about the circumstances. It was a matter of survival. She needed a roof over her head and food to survive. She got these things by living with this old man. The exchange was being intimate with him and producing children that he didn't want, and she couldn't support. It was a terrible situation, but there was nothing that Gabriel or Rose could do. It took a lifetime for Melissa to become who she was, and nothing that they could say was going to change the circumstances. They used the opportunity to visit with Melissa and enjoy the short time with her.

Melissa told them she wanted to get a job and go to school. These were things that Melissa remembered Rose wanted to hear from her days visiting Gabriel and Rose. She was told to get a job and go to school. She knew to repeat these two things to Rose to make her happy. They may never come true, but Rose could hope that since she remembered them, someday they would come true.

After a short visit, they told Melissa they had a long drive home and would need to leave. She walked them to the car, and her boyfriend took a picture of the three of them. This picture would be saved for years and would form a significant memory in Rose's mind. It reminded her that this was not the life that she wanted for Gabriel, and she would do anything to stop this from happening to him.

They got into the car and drove out of Melissa's neighborhood silent.

"Gabriel, can you put on your GPS to get us back to the expressway?"

"Sure, Mom." Gabriel started typing the information into his phone. "Take a right here." Gabriel paused.

Rose turned right and saw the on-ramp for the expressway. She made her way onto the expressway following a few other cars. Once on, she maneuvered her way to the left and started to settle into her path back home. It would be at least four hours until they were back.

After a while, Rose was curious about what Gabriel thought of the whole experience. "Gabriel, what do you think about Melissa's situation?"

"It stinks. She shouldn't be with an old man. She shouldn't have had so many kids with him, and she shouldn't have had her kids taken away from her. It is all wrong."

"Yep, it is. I wish we could do more for her, but it is way beyond what we can do. All we can do now is to listen to her, talk to her when she wants to talk, and maybe give her some advice." Rose was discouraged. She was only one person, and it was hard for her to steer Gabriel in a good direction. Taking on another burden was too much. She admitted it and accepted it.

"I am glad I am not in the same situation." Gabriel sat back and didn't say much more.

The ride was uneventful. They were on the expressway almost the whole way home. It wasn't crowded, and there were no accidents that delayed them. Rose pulled into Gabriel's driveway and stopped. He gathered his things and paused. "Thanks, Mom. I am glad we went to visit Melissa. It's been too long since I saw her. I wish I could do more for her. I'll try to do better so that maybe I can help her or her kids someday."

"Keep thinking positive. Maybe she'll wake up and start to work so she can get out of the circumstance she got herself into. There isn't too much we can do for her right now. Remember, next week we have party at cousin Mike's house to celebrate Aunt Joan's life. I'll give you a call this week to let you know what time we need to get on the road next Sunday."

Gabriel climbed out of the car and walked into his house. Rose waited until he went inside the door. She thought about how people at her job, or her friends, could never imagine a life like Melissa's or the previous life that Gabriel had growing up. They thought all of this just happened to people in Third World countries. They had no idea how bad life could be right here in the United States for people who never had parents to guide them or who cared about their future. It was so sad. She thought of a quote she had read: children don't come with a manual, they come with a mom. That was very true. Every child needs someone in their life to mentor them and keep them on the right track!

Chapter 36

The Party to Celebrate Joan

Rose was worried about Gabriel's mental state. He was depressed. He didn't think anyone liked him because of his size and because of his poor upbringing. He never had any clean clothes when he was little, or shoes that fit. He also didn't take baths on a regular basis, and the kids at school always told him he stunk. The kids at school bullied him, and no one told him he was smart or strong or brave. He didn't have any adults in his life to encourage him when he was young. All these things contributed to his lack of self-esteem. He was so big; it was hard for him to try to do things. Because he didn't try to do things, he never saw for himself that he could accomplish a great deal with effort. Rose tried to help when he lived with her, but nothing seemed to work. After he moved out, he still didn't get it. It seemed she was fighting a losing battle. She knew that people had to hit the bottom in their lives in order to be motivated to improve. Gabriel needed something strong to happen to turn his life around. Something needed to change; otherwise, he would never achieve his wishes of a family and career as a police officer.

Today was Aunt Joan's party to celebrate her life. She had been gone for a year, now and everyone strongly missed her. Rose was picking Gabriel up from his house for the ride out to Indiana for the party. It was the typical party at Cousin Mike's house: an outside barbecue, kids in the pool, and others sitting around talking.

On the drive, Gabriel brought up the idea of sending in his DNA to ancestry.com to find out his ethnic background. Visiting Melissa had not added any information about their bloodline. Melissa did not know anything about her past relatives, their dates of birth, or other surnames. That was a dead end. Rose wanted Gabriel to understand where his roots were from, so she agreed to pay the fee and send in the DNA sample for Gabriel. It usually took around two to three months, but at least this was something they could tackle and finish. He would start the process.

Gabriel was happy to be out of the house with Rose, but going to parties was hard for him. Even though these were his adoptive cousins and they all treated him very well, he still felt a little like an outsider. His size made him feel like everyone was staring at him, and he seldom felt comfortable. He longed to feel normal. He wondered what that would feel like. Conversation was also hard, he wasn't dating, and his job wasn't going anywhere, all because of his weight. He wasn't doing well in school or able to do any projects at home, so there wasn't much to say. This would be just one more awkward occasion, but at least he was out of the house.

They drove up to the usual activities, kids outside playing in the street, noise from the backyard, smoke flying up in the air from the grill, and lots of friendly hellos! They circled around and gave their greetings and made their way to the patio to sit at the table. Rose looked around at the guests and found one from the past. It was Barb, who had been married to Aunt Joan's husband's brother. She looked great! She had to be in her seventies, but she was thin and dressed in a really cute outfit. Rose was pleasantly surprised. She left Gabriel for a bit and walked around to visit. Gabriel stayed at the table and listened to the chatter from the other guests.

Rose found her way to her cousin June and got caught up on the happenings in her life. June was a character. She was very dramatic when she told a story. Listening to her talk always brought a smile to Rose's face. June had been critical of people in the past, but she had gotten divorced a few years ago, and her life got tougher. She realized now that she shouldn't be so critical of other people. Life was not as easy as she had thought. Previously she was harsh to Gabriel, telling him to go on a diet and exercise more. She questioned the things he said and often made him feel bad. Gabriel did not like her at all. Rose was a little more lenient with June. She understood June and gave her some slack. June changed as she grew older and wasn't as bossy or judgmental; perhaps she missed her mom. June was sometimes abrupt with Gabriel, and she said things that were a little harsh. She wasn't as sensitive to other people's problems or needs. Inside she had a good heart, and if you talked to her and explained how her words sometimes hurt people, she understood.

By the time Rose returned to her seat, Gabriel was engaged in a conversation with Barb, the woman that Rose had not seen for years and years. She was curious about the conversation they were having. Gabriel looked engrossed in it. Often Gabriel just sat and listened to the relatives and friends, never joining in, but this time Gabriel seemed very interested. Rose sat down, and Barb told her story in a summarized fashion. Barb had gained a large amount of weight through the years and shed the weight by getting a surgically implanted Lap Band. The Lap Band was an adjustable silicone band placed around the top part of her stomach. It was a laparoscopic surgical procedure and was designed to restrict food intake. Her Lap Band was adjustable, and her doctor could loosen or tighten the band as she needed. The Lap Band surgery has a very low mortality rate of only about .1 percent, which made it attractive.

Barb said she felt wonderful, and she was able to travel and move around much better since the procedure. She recommended it to Gabriel. There couldn't have been a better salesman for the product. Barb was elated. She wanted to spread the joy!

The rest of the party proceeded as normal. They stayed until after the meal was served and then gave everyone hugs and left for their one-hour journey home. In the car, Rose let Gabriel digest the information and events at the party, but she was eager to hear his thoughts about the operation. Gabriel was now about four hundred pounds, and the weight had not hurt his health yet. Any more time, and his knees and back would start to be injured from the large amount of weight they were carrying. Rose hoped they would find an answer to the problem soon.

"So, Gabriel, what did you think of the party?" Rose started the conversation in general to see if Gabriel would bring up Barb and her story by himself.

"It was the same. It was good to see Al. I always like to talk to Al. I remember his father was really nice too. I think Al takes after his father."

Pete, Al's father, had felt compassion for Gabriel. He knew life did not treat him very well, and he was kind to him whenever he had the chance. Pete died a few years earlier, and Gabriel felt the loss even more than Rose knew. Pete was buried close to Joan and close to Al's daughter, Christina, who had died in a car accident around the same time. Al and Mary had gone through some tragedies in the last few years, but they were never bitter and always kind and generous to everyone. They were heroes to all.

"Al is one of a kind, but he was cut from another kind stone. Yes, I remember Al's dad, and he was a very nice man. Too bad he died, but he did live a pretty long life." Rose smiled as she spoke of Pete and Al.

Gabriel smiled too. "It was fun to see the fireworks too. I like the way they remember Joan in a fun way. She would have liked it."

"Yep, Joan loved fun times. She was never one to be down in the dumps about anything. She was kind and accepting of everyone, and I miss her so badly." Rose paused, remembering Joan.

"I am so glad we finally went on that cruise with her. There were ups and downs, but it all worked out in the end. Imagine if we hadn't made the time or spent the money to go with her, we would have regretted it. It was a little sacrifice at the time, but it paid off. We have memories that will last a lifetime. You were able to get to know Aunt Joan in a way that was more than just meeting her at parties."

They drove on for a few moments. "My favorite story of her was when we went to a concert with Mary, Al, and Joan. We were sitting behind Mary and Al. The concert was really bad, but Mary and Al seemed to be enjoying it. They turned around to check on Joan and see how she was doing. Joan told Mary and Al that it was one of the best concerts she had ever been to, and she was so thankful they asked her to go. Then she turned her head to me and said the concert was awful, but she loved going places and being invited, so she would bite her tongue and say she enjoyed it, just so she was kept on the list of invitees. She giggled and smiled and kept it up through the whole event! She was awesome. She never wanted anyone to feel bad about anything."

Rose thought about Joan and remembered how she kept her promise to her sister, Rose's mom, as she was dying. Her mom had asked Joan to watch over her two daughters. Joan had promised that she would. Joan kept that promise until her own dying day. She treated her like she was her own child. Joan had ten children of her own to take care of, and that was a hand full. Joan never complained; in fact, she loved the extra amount of love she had to give out.

When Joan died, and her daughter Karen was cleaning out her apartment, she found loads of pictures and memorabilia from Gabriel and Rose. Karen relayed that information to Rose. Rose loved hearing it and knew that Joan was a minimalist in her older years. If she had kept things to remember her and Gabriel, it meant she loved them very much. She was so grateful that Karen shared that information.

"Aunt Joan loved you so much. She is probably up in heaven telling Grandma all the stories about the adventures she had with me and you. They are probably up there laughing, and maybe they even have God laughing too!"

Rose went on to another subject because she had Gabriel's attention and wanted to know his feeling about Barb and the weight-loss operation.

"Barb was interesting too. Did you know that Jeff at the manu-facturing plant had the same operation?"

"Yes, I knew that! Jeff told me stories about his weight and how he can sort of fool the Lap Band and eat more than he is supposed to at times. He still weighs about 250, but since Jeff is over six foot, he isn't extremely large any longer. He was a lot bigger before the Lap Band surgery."

"Do you remember the time that Jeff and his wife stopped by our town house when it was for sale? It would have been funny if they would have bought it, but luckily for them, they found a house that was a better deal and had more room for their family." Rose thought that it was funny that their paths crossed. She wondered how things always just fell into place if she just gave things some time.

Moving on to get Gabriel to talk about the operation and experience that Barb had gone through, she brought up Barb again. "Barb said she felt wonderful, and it was the best she felt in a long time."

"Do you want to look into that operation? We can make some appointments and find out about it." Rose was happy that Gabriel was thinking about a fix. It was more than he ever said before. Maybe this was just the story he needed to hear. Two people he knew had good experiences with weight-loss surgery.

"Sure." Gabriel wasn't much for words. He sat back and was silent for the rest of the ride.

Rose felt that God was working to help Gabriel and Rose. He placed Barb at the party so that they would find a different way to help Gabriel with his weight problem. Rose would do anything. She just wanted Gabriel to have a happy life.

Chapter 37

The Match Date

Gabriel desperately wanted a girlfriend. He wanted someone to hang with and enjoy life. He was tired of only going places with his mom and maybe a family party at Dan's house. He wanted to go places and do things, but his weight caused him to feel like an outcast and unloved.

He often went to dating sites and would post his old high school picture. The only hits he would receive were from equally large women. He wanted the types of girls that he had dated in high school. They were slim and attractive and fun girls that everyone wanted. At his current weight, none of these girls would look at him. Occasionally a girl would write back to him and use him to get a free dinner. He kept trying. At least Gabriel always had hope. Hope was something that made life worth living. If you didn't have hope, you had nothing.

Today, a girl wrote back to him and wanted to meet him. He was looking forward to some female company, even if it was only a one-time meeting. She said that she would meet him at a restaurant nearby. He got cleaned up, which was very hard for him. His clothes were the same old big tented T-shirts. His jeans were big and unshapely and not very stylish. It was even hard for him to shave. Every movement he made was a struggle. Every time he moved his arms and legs, they were heavy and hurt from the excess weight.

His cat, Salem, looked up at him and watched him as he got ready for his date. He knew it wasn't really a date, but he was excited anyway. It was a chance to get out of the house and sit with someone his own age and talk about things he was interested in, not family things or weight-loss problems. He was tired of the same old things.

The clock on the wall ticked slowly as he waited for the time to leave. He didn't care if he was early, but he also knew he couldn't sit in a restaurant for a long period of time.

Finally, it was time to leave. He was excited. The girl said she was on her way too. He got into his car with a smile on his face, which was very unusual.

She had picked a neighborhood restaurant, nothing fancy, not too special, but nice enough. He would have accepted any place. He just wanted someone to talk to, a girl. He pulled up to the restaurant and walked slowly to the door. There wasn't anyone waiting at the door, so he told the hostess that he needed a table for two. She said she would watch for the girl he was waiting for and show her the way to his table. He sat down and read the menu. The clock ticked by the hour she was supposed to meet him. He texted her but got no response.

He didn't know it, but the girl had watched him enter the restaurant. She recognized his face from his picture, although it was much larger now. She couldn't believe the difference in size. She could not love a person who was that big. She knew she couldn't go through with the date. It was one thing to be a little overweight, but another thing to be obese. She turned her car back on and drove away. A few minutes later she heard a text come through on her phone. Leaving without telling him why was not her thing, but she didn't want to give him any false hope either. She ignored the text and went home.

Meanwhile, Gabriel was starting to realize that this was just another wild-goose chase. The girl saw his enormous size and decided against the date—another lonely meal.

He ordered and then ate his meal in silence. He felt that the others around him were looking at him. As the hostess seated other people near him, she glanced over. Gabriel was embarrassed that he had told her that there would be a girl coming to meet him. He turned his face down to his food. He ate. Food gave him comfort. That was all he had. He was sad, ready to give up. He just wanted what everyone else had and didn't understand why he couldn't have it. Maybe he should try one of those operations. Maybe he would look into it. He knew that Rose would help him. If there was anything in his life that he was sure of, he knew it was Rose helping him. She would do anything for him. At least he had that.

He drove back home and made the long, hard trip up to the top of his stairs to his room. Salem sat waiting for him. She was happy to see her friend. She loved cuddling up to him as he slept.

Gabriel was happy to see his cat. At least it was some sort of companionship. At least there was someone waiting for him to come home each day. Taking care of Salem was a hardship for Gabriel too. It was hard for him to bend down and pick up her bowl to feed her. It was hard to clean out her sandbox. It was hard to carry the big bag of cat food into the house. If he lost weight, things wouldn't be so hard. He would probably be able to get a girlfriend too. Maybe he would start to listen to what Rose always talked about. He knew she only had the best intentions for him. He would give it some thought.

He lumbered through the bedroom and took off his clothes. There were clothes everywhere. His room was a mess. Tomorrow he would straighten things up and wash clothes. Maybe if his home looked nicer, it would make him feel better.

He lay next to Salem and set his alarm before going to sleep. As he lay there, a tear came out of his eye. He was so lonely. He was tired of being fat. Tomorrow was gun class with Rose. Maybe he would meet someone there. He fell asleep with hope.

Chapter 38

The Gun Class

Rose called Gabriel a few minutes before she left the house to make sure he was ready for the gun class. He answered and was getting ready. She knew it was a long ride out to the rural area where the gun class was going to be held that day. They had never been to the place. This was the same company that had run the other classes they attended. Concealed carry was the first one they completed. After that they took a handgun class. This would be the third class they completed. It was going to be a series of lessons, each different. The last phase was shooting moving targets and fast shooting as you walked around barriers and crawled around while concealing your position. The owners were fun guys. They made learning about guns even interesting for Rose. She wasn't really into guns but knew that it was something that Gabriel liked. He classes were not cheap either. Each class was over two hundred dollars, and paying for each was a chore. She would have rather put the money into a new couch or a new pair of jeans or boots, but giving Gabriel some happiness was much more important. Also, as he earned each certificate for each class, his confidence grew. He needed to feel more confident and have more self-esteem. This was important—get him to try harder to get healthy, earn a better job, and take pride in the things he possessed.

Rose pulled up to Gabriel's house, and he was standing on the corner in his typical spot, waiting for her. He had another bag of goodies, probably filled with sugary pops and unhealthy snacks. Rose had always bought him diet pop when he lived with her, but after moving out he went back to drinking regular pop. This bothered her so much. Pop was empty calories. He drank it constantly. If he would just change to water, it would save about one thousand calories a day, plus save him money. He just made so many bad choices each day, and each bad choice led to extra weight and no monetary savings.

Gabriel climbed into her car and, as usual, had a hard time adjusting the seat belt. He tucked his gun into the glove box and settled in for the ride.

"How are your roses doing? Are they growing? Are you taking care of the weeds around them, so they grow?"

"Yep, they are fine. I'll get to the weeding tomorrow. I think I need more flowers in front, and I want to build a bigger patio on the side."

"One thing at a time, Gabriel. You must finish what you started first. The landscaping has been started, and you need to take care of it so that it will grow and fill in the area better."

Gabriel was anxious to change the subject. He knew what he needed to do, but Rose didn't understand how hard it was for him to just bend over. Weeding might be easy for her, but it sure wasn't easy for him. He was glad she didn't want to step inside his house. He hadn't cleaned for a while, and Rose would not be happy. She wanted his floors washed, things put away, and to see progress on the place.

"What time is the class?" Gabriel knew that Rose was usually early for everything. He felt that they would have plenty of time to drive there and wander around before it started.

"We are supposed to be there at 7:00 a.m., but I am not so sure how to get there, so I hope we have time. It's in a field down south, so I am sure the roads will not be well marked. I am a little nervous about the time."

Gabriel knew that Rose was always in control and organized. He was surprised to hear that she was not 100 percent clear on where the class was taking place. He wasn't too worried. He knew she would get them there.

"How are you going to take the class without your own gun?" Gabriel wanted to buy his mom a gun for her birthday or Christmas, but he never quite had the funds to do it.

"I'll rent a gun for the day. They even have ammunition for me to use." Rose never really cared that she didn't have a gun. These classes were all about Gabriel, not Rose. Renting a gun was fine for her.

They drove down the expressway and then got off, following the directions of the gun-class owners. She was familiar with the expressway area, but not once she was far off the expressway. They turned down a farm road and then crossed railroad tracks. Everything seemed to be going well.

Continuing down the same road for a few miles, they looked for the road that was next on the driving directions. There were supposed to find the road about five miles after their last turn, but it wasn't there. Now Rose started to get nervous. She didn't want to miss the beginning of the class, especially since she had to rent the gun and get familiar with it before the class started.

"What do you think, Gabriel? Think we should turn around and go back and find where we messed up?"

"Yes, according to this map we went too far." Gabriel was pretty good at following maps, so Rose trusted his decision.

"I'll call and tell them we will be a few minutes late but are on our way." Rose pulled over and dialed her phone. She waited for an answer and told them they were a little lost and would be a few minutes late.

"He said to watch for a sign for an insurance agency and to turn left there." She pulled out onto the road again and followed the new directions.

"There it is!" Gabriel was happy that they were on the right track now. He got nervous easily and liked to be early too.

Rose took the turn, and then things seemed to fall into place. They saw a bunch of cars parked in a field, and she knew they had found it. Only a few minutes late. Not the end of the world.

They parked and walked over to an area with a few picnic benches. There were about twenty people waiting for the class to start. A few more were still arriving. Rose and Gabriel were not the last ones to get there. She was relieved.

The owners had some ammunition for sale and other gun-related things. They explained that there would be a lunch served that would consist of hamburgers and hot dogs, chips, and pop. The class would last all day long and would be both fun and a learning experience. At the end of the day, would be given their certificates. They also were going to be taking pictures for their website. They signed waivers to relieve the company of liability in case something happened as they took their gun class.

Both Rose and Gabriel did well in the class. They met some nice people and completed all the necessary drills to earn their certificate. Gabriel ran out of ammunition a little early, so he watched Rose as she finished her last rounds of the class.

They walked back to the picnic bench area, returned her rented gun, and waited for their certificates. As they were passed out, the owners congratulated each one of them. It was a proud moment for Gabriel. He had completed a gun class successfully!

"I'm going to hang this certificate on the wall next to all of my others." Gabriel held his certificate proudly. He had many certificates and awards to hang on his walls. The military school had awarded him scholarships, he earned the Silver Presidential Certificate for volunteer hours, and he had other gun-class certificates too. He could fill up an entire wall with these things.

Rose imagined a beautiful wall inside his town house filled with awards and certificates, all arranged skillfully. She could dream and hope. She didn't think it was true. If it had been true, he would have invited her in to see his work. Whenever he did something good, he loved to show it off. She knew he would invite her in if the certificates were displayed. The wall probably didn't exist.

They drove home. Gabriel was feeling better than yesterday. He had earned an award and was now better at shooting his gun. This would help him with his dream of being in the military or becoming a policeman. Things would work out soon. He knew they would.

Chapter 39

The Call from the Hospital

It was a busy day at work for Rose. There was a huge deadline coming up for material that she was responsible to finish. She was having a hard time getting cooperation from some of the managers she worked with to gather information. Rose was able to clear her mind as she drove home. Some would say she had a long commute, but the time in the car helped her wind down and think about all the items on her to-do list. She needed to meet her deadline for work materials. At home, she needed to finish her current redecorating project. She always tried to keep her home decorated in the latest colors and trends to keep the market value as high as it could be. Her house was small, a two-story with three bedrooms and one-and-a-half baths, but with the upgrades—wood floors and finished basement. It stayed at the high end of the market value for the size and neighborhood. Retirement was, hopefully, ten years away, and she needed to increase the amount of money in her 401K funds and pay off her house and Gabriel's house. It would also help if Gabriel could take over the payments on his own place. That would really decrease her burden, but at his weight and mindset, that didn't seem possible. It would take a miracle. She marched on, hoping for good things around the next bend of her life.

Next stop, the gym for her daily workout. If nothing else, she was going to stay trim and fit. She always noticed others around her as they aged, and the older women who were slim and fit did not show their age as much. Being a good weight for your height and body allowed you to dress more attractively and wear the current styles. She vowed she would always stay at the same weight. It was funny, but her mom had told her the weight that she would look the best at, and she followed what her mom had told her. Everyday Rose would hop on the scale and be within a pound or two of one hundred and thirty-five pounds, just as her mom had instructed. Even though her mom had been gone for thirty years, the lessons she taught her carried forward. She hoped that people raising children would understand this point. Things you say and do during those precious years with your parents are embedded solidly in your brain. It is amazing how those things just stay with you your whole life!

Forty-five minutes on the elliptical would do for today. Those minutes were fat burning and kept her metabolism going through the rest of the day. Exercising every day was a good habit. She hoped that Gabriel was watching and learning the good things she did each day. Maybe someday exercise would be a part of his routine.

Pulling into the driveway, she noticed that her neighbor's yard was full of flowers. They did such a nice job keeping their house beautiful! Living next door to a beautiful house increased the value of her home. She only wished that the neighbor on the other side would do the same. All it would take was a little time and effort and the front yard would look clean and neat. Oh well, she would hope for new neighbors on that side for the future.

Rose turned on the TV to get some noise in the house. It felt less lonely with the sounds of laugher of the old sitcoms. She changed out of her gym clothes and into comfortable clothes for her chores. One load of laundry and she'd start back on her refinishing project. She was changing the bathroom from the 1990s style to the new farmhouse style. The dark wood on the cabinet would be changed to a white and beige distressed sort of finish, and the wall hangings would be changed to match. She always felt proud of her accomplishments. On a beer budget, she made things looks really cute. Visitors loved her work, and that made her feel tremendously good!

Over the sound of the TV from the living room, she heard the phone ring. She wasn't expecting any calls, but sometimes Gabriel checked in with her. She knew he was lonely and didn't have many friends, so she always tried to pick up the phone and chat a little, even when she was deeply involved in her projects.

She got up, straightened up, and walked over to the phone. The picture showed Gabriel on one of their trips, half smiling. Clicking on the green icon, she answered the call.

"Hi, Gabriel!" Rose waited for his reply. Usually there wasn't much to talk about; Gabriel just liked to call and talk to someone.

"Mom, I had to come to the hospital. I felt awful." Gabriel was slightly afraid to report another problem to his mom. He didn't want her to worry or go through more stress. A hospital stay could mean more bills and ongoing issues for her to stress over.

"What's wrong?" Rose wasn't surprised to hear that he was in the hospital, but hoped it was an issue that could be solved with Gabriel following some new eating rules and exercise. She hoped a doctor would help her by telling him how dangerous his weight level was, and his future would be bad if he didn't stop the upward climb.

"They ran some tests and found my sugar level was really high. I have type 2 diabetes, and now I must take metformin every day. The doctor told me that metformin is the first medication prescribed for type 2 diabetes, and he wants it to be the last too. This medicine works by improving the sensitivity of your body tissues to insulin so that your body uses insulin more effectively. He also said that the metformin will lower glucose production in my liver. The good thing is, he said that if I follow a diet and lose weight, I could get off this medicine. You know how much I hate medicine!"

Rose wasn't surprised at all. She knew this was caused by his bad habits and low metabolism. She had hoped that it would not come to this point. On the positive side, maybe this is what it would take for Gabriel to understand how important it was to control his weight.

Type 2 diabetes is the most common form of diabetes. Gabriel's younger brother has the other type, which is much more serious. He was lucky not to have his brother's type 1 diabetes.

Type 2 is much more common, and it affects 90 to 95 percent of the thirteen million men with diabetes. People with type 2 diabetes produce insulin, but it is usually not enough, or the body is unable to recognize the insulin and use it properly. When the body doesn't have enough insulin, or the insulin is not used as it should be, sugar can't get into the body's cells to be used for fuel. Then, the sugar builds up in the bloodstream instead of going into the cells. The body's cells are not able to function properly.

"The doctor said that I had symptoms. After he listed the symptoms, I remembered how I suffered from each one of them. I just didn't know what my body was telling me. I guess I felt all of these symptoms slowly and didn't realize it." Gabriel sounded sad but more educated.

"One of the things he said I probably felt was dehydration from going to the bathroom too much. Once he mentioned that, I realized he was right. It seemed when I was at work, I would go more than the other guys at the machines. I was always asking for an extra break." Gabriel paused.

"Other things that I had that were caused by this were increased hunger, even right after I ate. He also asked if I felt tingling in my hands or feet, which is sometimes also associated with this. The doctor also told me this was one of the reasons I was always so tired. I just thought it was the extra weight, but it was my body's reaction to the extra weight, so my organs are suffering too. Not only that, but if I don't control it there are more serious side effects. Over time, high sugar levels in the blood may damage the nerves and small blood vessels of the eyes, kidneys, and heart and maybe in the future I'd get hardening of the arteries and have a heart attack. This is all because of my eating habits and not exercising. Also, if I don't fix this, I could lose my toes, or my legs too!" Gabriel sounded scared.

"Well, it's good you had the sense to go to the hospital. Hopefully, you will learn from this and start doing a better job at taking care of your body. Do you need anything? How long will you be there?"

"I have to stay overnight. Can you bring me a change of clothes and my phone charger?" Gabriel was always apprehensive when he had to confess to his mom.

"You'll need to go into my house. Mom, I haven't had time to clean. It's a mess, but when I get out, I will start cleaning and taking better care of the things you gave me. Maybe when I take this new medicine, I will have more energy and not be as tired." Gabriel listened and prayed that his mom would understand. He hated for his mom to find out just how bad his place was, but he had to send her there.

"The cat has to be fed. I don't want her to starve. She is always there to greet me, and I want to take care of her. If it wasn't for her, I wouldn't send you there, but she deserves to be fed and given water."

"Okay, Gabriel, give me about an hour and I'll be at the hospital with the stuff you need. I will feed Salem and make sure she is okay. Don't worry about your messy house, we can deal with that later. Just take care of yourself and think about what the doctor said."

They hung up the phone, and Rose started running around to get things together. She changed and gathered some things for Gabriel. She grabbed the spare key to his house. She had not gone into his house for months. She wondered how bad the place could be.

Meanwhile, in the hospital, Gabriel looked at his phone. He had sent out messages to several people in his life. He texted his half brothers and sisters. He texted guys he knew at work. He was waiting for them to return the texts. There was nothing there. As always, he was alone.

Rose drove over to Gabriel's house. She knew it would be a mess. The last time she was inside was when the air-conditioning went out and he needed a new system. She had helped clean up the place prior to the service man coming out. She hated to be embarrassed. She felt it was her own fault that his place was unkempt. Rose knew that Gabriel had to take responsibility for his things, but was it her fault for not teaching him correctly? Was it her fault because she didn't force him to keep things clean when he was living with her? Right after she was divorced, Gabriel had a nice room in the town house, and it was always clean. Then he had helped her friend build the basement room, and that was never very messy either. She really didn't remember dreading going into either of his rooms. However, his bedroom in Rose's new house was a disaster, and she never liked looking at it. As he grew older and was in greater charge of his room, it started to go downhill. This was one of the reasons she thought it was important for him to move out. Maybe if he lived in a house that was unkempt, he would start realizing the difference it meant and start cleaning up? She tried everything. She read, and she listened to others with the same problems. So far, she had not found the right formula, but that didn't mean the right formula wasn't in the future. Patience, that was all that was needed. Someday Gabriel would start to value a clean atmosphere.

Arriving at his house, she noticed some papers flying around in his landscaping and the weeds that needed pulling. She didn't have time to do much, but she picked up some of the garbage and pulled some of the taller weeds. There, just a few minutes and it looked much better. Next thing was to walk inside. Was she just delaying walking in the door? She braced herself and turned the key. She couldn't believe what she saw. It was much worse than she ever imagined. It was filthy. There were pizza boxes all over the place. The floors were dirty. Tons of dishes were in the sink. The cat litter box was a nightmare. The toilets looked as if they had never been cleaned. She broke down and started weeping loudly. She knew he had been depressed, but seeing the condition of the house told her it was much worse than she ever imagined. She cried on the floor for a few minutes, thinking she had failed. How sad Gabriel must be to live like this? He had to feel like he didn't deserve to have nice things. She knew that coming home to a clean house each day lifted her spirits and made her feel good. If Gabriel came home to this house, he had to feel even sadder than ever when he walked in each day. She felt so sad for her son and wanted to help him so badly.

Salem appeared. Rose decided she had to do something before getting the things Gabriel needed at the hospital. She quickly wiped her tears and got a plastic garbage bag. She starting to dump all the empty boxes into a bag and then sealed it with a twist tie and got a second bag. Within a few minutes, things were better.

Next, she emptied the litter box and found new litter. She made things better for now. She could deal with more cleaning later. Maybe another talk, or maybe being on the medication, would give him more energy. After cleaning all the leftovers and garbage from around the rooms, it didn't look as bad. She felt that she had buried her head in the sand for a few years by not coming into Gabriel's house and seeing the huge disaster. Then again, there was only so much she could do. She remembered that when she went to the classes before adoption, they told the class that these kids were lacking love. Everyone has a cup that should be full of love, but theirs was empty. The most important part of taking on one of these children was to make sure you filled their cup with love each day. Once they felt loved, they would grow in other ways. She listened to what they had taught her all these years and made that the priority. An unkempt house could be cleaned. A heart without love was much worse and needed much more attention.

Rose said goodbye to Salem the cat and closed the door. She needed to get to the hospital to make sure Gabriel knew it was important for her to see him.

When she arrived, she rode the elevator up to the second floor. He had texted her his room number. One thing she didn't have to worry about was insurance. Gabriel was a good worker. He always went to work and therefore had good insurance coverage. One less thing to worry about. Even if there was a deductible to be covered, it would only be about two thousand dollars. It wouldn't break them financially.

Rose stuck her head into Gabriel's door. He was sitting on the bed in a hospital gown. He looked a little healthier. His skin was a better color.

"Hi, Mom! Thanks for coming," Gabriel smiled.

"I brought your phone charger and stopped at the store for new underwear, a T-shirt, and shorts. Hopefully, they will fit you." Rose dropped the bag and handed Gabriel the phone charger.

"My phone is almost dead. Thanks for bringing me the charger."

Rose smiled and said, "No problem. I would bring you anything you needed. Just let me know."

"I noticed that you are the only one who really cares. You came right away and brought what I needed and fed my cat. I had left messages with the other people who said they were my friends, and no one else came to visit or even said they would be here. Some didn't even respond!" Gabriel looked like he had given this some thought.

"How are you feeling?" Rose was hoping for a good answer.

"I feel better. They haven't given me any food. They said I'll be able to eat before I leave tomorrow. I'll have to start all new eating habits and try to eat the things you have been telling me about for all of these years." Gabriel was serious. This didn't seem to be a snow job. Maybe the doctor got to him.

"The doctor said carbohydrates are the worst and have the largest effect on my blood glucose. I'll have to track how many carbohydrates I eat each day. He also said regular exercise will lower by blood glucose and lower insulin resistance. They gave me an A1C test, and my sugar was at ten. He wants it down to about five, which is healthy. This A1C test measures the average glucose levels in my blood for the past two or three months. I'll have to go to the doctor in a few months and get it done again to see if it goes down. Until it goes down to the level he wants, I'll have to get tested every three months. The better I do, the less I'll have to come back to the doctor, and the less medicine I'll have to take. He also said the hospital has classes and sessions for patients with diabetes."

Rose was impressed. It sounded like Gabriel listened to the doctor, which meant he was concerned about his health and wanted to do something about it.

"Tomorrow they are giving me my own home-testing kit, so I can monitor my blood sugar and learn how to control it. They will show me how to use it. I'll have to test my sugar several times a day. If you still want to help me, I'll go to any of the appointments you have suggested in the past. I just don't want to lose my eyes or legs or anything!" Gabriel looked like he was shaken up by everything the doctor said, which was good. Maybe he hit bottom and will start getting better and take control of his life.

"Gabriel, I'll take you or accompany you to any doctor, psychologist, or weight-loss session there is. I want to support you so that you can get better." Rose was happier.

"Let's get you out of here first. Oh, and don't worry about Salem, she is fed, and the litter box is clean. She will be fine until tomorrow."

The appearance of his place didn't matter right now. They could talk about it later. She just wanted Gabriel to live a better life. "I'll go and let you sleep. Call me in the morning when you get out of here. If you can't drive home, we'll find a way to get your car home. Did you call work?"

"Yeah, Mom, I called my boss. He said to take it easy, and he'd see me on Wednesday. The doctor said I could work and drive as soon as they release me." He was glad that he didn't have to burden his mother with trying to get someone to help her drive his car home. He was also happy that he wouldn't lose much pay. He would only be short one day of pay, and it would not affect his job security. His company used a point system, and his points were in a good state. People were let go when they reached ten points. He had nothing to worry about. He'd be able to bring in a note from the doctor and wouldn't receive a penalty point. He was in the clear.

The next day Rose sent e-mails to a few of her friends to tell them about her son's hospital visit. She received an e-mail back from her old friend Joel. He also worked at the hospital where Gabriel was admitted. He said he would stop by this morning and check on him. He also told her that there was going to be a diabetes event at the hospital the next weekend. It was an event that was near and dear to his heart because he also suffered from diabetes. He was always watching his weight and testing his sugar. He exercised and chose the right food too. Joel said that he would be willing to take Gabriel to the grocery store with him and teach him all about labels.

The friends and family that reached out to her were awesome. Gabriel didn't realize it, but there were many people who were concerned about his welfare. When she heard from Gabriel, she would be sure to tell her about all the pleasant notes she received about his health. One of the most concerned was Al, Rose's cousin Mary's husband. His dad had always loved Gabriel, and now that Pete was gone, Al took over Pete's commitment to Gabriel's welfare. Gabriel admired both Pete and Al, and Rose knew he would be happy to hear about their kind notes and wishes.

As Gabriel left the hospital, he called Rose. "Hi, Mom. The nurse just left. She showed me how to test my blood-sugar level and gave me a list of the foods I can't eat. Can you go to the food store with me to look for the right types of groceries?"

"Sure, Gabriel, I can go with you. Also, Joel knows you were in the hospital and offered to help you learn how to read labels. Remember, he also has diabetes."

This was progress. Gabriel was finally talking about fixing his problem. Prior to this hospital stay, he was in denial. Now, he had accepted that he had a problem and was willing to learn how to deal with it. Rose knew she had to build on his newfound momentum. She would search for ways to keep pushing him along to his new goal.

"Gabriel, I have another idea. I think I could help you stay on a low-sugar diet." Rose waited for Gabriel to react.

"How would you do that?" Gabriel knew he had his mom's support and listened.

"Well, we both get up bright and early each morning. Why don't you stop by for breakfast? I'll cook a low-sugar breakfast and have your lunch ready for you too. That way, you'll only have to worry about cooking a low-sugar dinner for yourself. It will be less work for you, plus I will get to see you each morning!" Rose hoped he would say yes. She would be less worried knowing he was getting two good meals a day that were low sugar.

"That works for me! I'll be there at 4:00 a.m. tomorrow morning before work." Gabriel was happy to have some company in the morning.

"Okay, I'll look into that diabetes festival at the hospital that Joel was telling us about too." Rose was happy things were going in the right direction.

"Bye, Mom." Gabriel hung up the phone.

Chapter 40

The Morning Ritual

Gabriel had been coming to Rose's house for breakfast for a few weeks, and this morning they were headed for the diabetes festival at the hospital. Joel had said that he would be working today, so he would pop up to see them at the fest. He was very proud of the hospital he maintained. His first job with the hospital started at the old facility founded in 1895. The job was tough, and the hospital building was very old and hard to keep running. The heating and air-conditioning systems kept him busy enough; then there was everything else. Most of the staff had been working there for quite some time, and they were stuck in their ways. Joel had a tough time changing them. The workers often resisted his ideas, and they had an attitude since he was new. He ran a tight ship and worked very hard. Although he held two associate degrees, and not a bachelor's, he was very smart and was able to figure things out on his own. Rose admired him greatly. He loved mechanics and probably should have been an engineer. Joel was taught heating and air-conditioning by his father, who ran his own small business. During high school, instead of having fun at football games or dances, he went home to work with his father. The first few years he learned as he worked, but then as he started junior college, he started to teach his father better ways to accomplish the same things. At first he received some resistance from his dad, because his dad felt he should be the one teaching, but there were days when his father gave in to the new ideas and that would make Joel feel good.

A few years later Joel's father died. He kept going to school and soon had a good job in building maintenance. He loved his job but always wanted to maintain a hospital. He took a step down in order to get into building management for health care. After a few years of learning the ropes at a hospital, he ventured out and found a job as a supervisor of maintenance at his current hospital. The years went by, and after a few years of hard work at the old facility, the hospital built a brand-new facility with state-of-the-art equipment. It was his dream come true. Since the hospital gave him a chance, he felt loyalty to the hospital. He knew he would continue working at the hospital until his retirement.

Gabriel drove over to his mom's house. He was smiling and happier these days. He had lost twenty pounds, and his sugar was going down. He hated being on medication and was hopeful he could stop taking the metformin his doctor had prescribed. Also, he was happy for the company in the mornings.

Today would be a good day too. In the past he viewed Joel as a little pushy, but these days he felt that Joel had earned the ability to be a little demanding. He was a self-taught man, learning from experience and from a great deal of reading and watching. Joel suffered from type 2 diabetes too. He had managed his numbers for years now. Since he actually learned the rules about diabetes and then followed those same rules, Gabriel felt he needed to give respect to Joel, and he did.

Rose was home, ready to go. As soon as Gabriel walked into the house, she grabbed her purse and headed out the door, saying her hellos to her son at the very same time.

"How is your oil lately? Have you checked it? Remember, this car eats oil. We are hoping to get a few years out of it, and to do that, you need to keep feeding it oil." Rose unlocked her own car door and backed out of the garage in order to let Gabriel into the passenger door. It was hard for him to squeeze in between the car and the other items in the garage.

"Are you excited about going to this diabetes festival?" Rose hoped he was curious and anxious to get his sugar under control.

"What do you think it will be like? Will there be lots of people there?" Gabriel hated crowds and didn't really like meeting new people either.

"I have no idea if it will be crowded or not. Joel was excited about the event. He said many people at the hospital helped him learn about his diabetes, and it was all through attending things like this." Rose knew Joel took full advantage of anything provided by the hospital. He didn't let moss grow under his feet. If there was a way to feel better or be better, he put his mind to it and got it done.

They drove off the expressway and down to the hospital. The new building was out in a wide-open area. The parking lot was large, and there wasn't a problem finding a space close to the building that housed the festival.

Entering the building, they were ushered into the room where the festivities were taking place. The greeter handed Rose a program of the speakers and times. There was one going on in about twenty minutes, so they had time to walk around the booth area. As they approached the first booth, a friendly nurse greeted them. She asked why they were attending.

"I was in the hospital for high blood sugar about a month ago. I already lost twenty pounds, and my sugar is staying in the normal range." Gabriel was smiling. He loved it when he was able to tell people that he was doing something well.

The nurse was excited. "That is such great news! What is your goal? Are you on a diet? Do you understand the foods that you can and cannot eat? I have some brochures for you." She turned and gathered a large group of pamphlets and brochures and put them in a canvas bag for Gabriel.

"I think I understand what I can eat and what I cannot eat. Bread was the big thing that I must limit. I love pizza and sandwiches. All the things that are filled with bread." Just as Gabriel was ending his sentence, Joel approached.

"Hi, Linda. These are my friends. I told them we have a good program and to come and take advantage of it. I also heard Gabriel say that he loves bread. That is my weakness too. I love the smell of fresh baked bread when I take it out of my oven. I had many recipes that I used to enjoy making for myself. But now I only make bread if company is coming over, and if there is any left I give it away." Joel was smiling. He enjoyed all these people who worked with him at his hospital.

"The main event is about to start. You two better go in and get some seats before they are all taken." Linda urged Gabriel and Rose to move into the main theater.

Linda was right; most of the seats were filled. There had to be about one hundred people seated and waiting for the doctors to speak. They found two seats over to the left of the room in the back. One of the nurses in the room came over and handed them some flyers about diabetes. Just as they were getting comfortable, a doctor approached the podium and introduced himself.

"Hi, I'm Doctor Dey, and I am a specialist in the care of patients with type 2 diabetes. Today, I'll help you understand what type 2 diabetes is and how you can manage it. I have a few other doctors here with me who will guide you through the offerings at Silver Cross Hospital." The doctor went on for about five more minutes and then introduced another of his colleagues. Rose and Gabriel listened to all the doctors talk and filled out cards to hand in to the nurse for additional information and invitations to other similar events. As they walked out of the room, Joel was there waiting for them.

"Well, what did you think? Did you learn anything? Were the speeches helpful?" Joel was smiling ear to ear.

Gabriel smiled. He knew that when it came to learning, Joel was always excited.

"The speeches were helpful. This is a great facility. You should be proud that you work for such a great place!" Rose liked to see Joel excited about anything.

"Gabriel, anytime you want to go food shopping, I will take you and show you all of the fascinating labels and products I have found with little or no sugar in them. I can go to the grocery store and stay for hours looking and reading the various labels." Joel smiled.

Gabriel smiled too. "Okay, Joel, I'll let you know."

Rose was happy that Joel wanted to help Gabriel. There was a time when he wasn't too excited about helping him out. Things have changed. It was a big improvement. Rose was happy to see the change.

"Gabriel, do you need to walk around some more, or do you think we are done?" Rose was just about ready to get out of there. She liked to see new things and learn about new things, but she had a time range, and this was getting to the end of her range. She was getting antsy.

"I'm good. We can leave." Gabriel inherited Rose's need to move out of a place after about two hours.

"Okay, let's get out of here. Joel, it was good to see you. Thank you so much for telling us about this great event, and thank you for caring so much." Rose smiled. She really enjoyed Joel's company. She hated to leave. She loved it when he was happy too.

They drove away and were heading back to Rose's house. Gabriel looked through the items that they had gathered at the diabetes festival. There was a health bar that was in the bag of stuff, which was more interesting to Gabriel than anything else. It didn't seem that he was reading anything that they picked up. Rose thought she'd see a total turnaround, but it didn't seem to be happening. Even with everything that Joel and the nurse had said, he was still not gobbling up the information. If this health problem was happening to Rose, she would be reading everything she could get her hands. Not only that, she would be exercising and eating better too. She didn't understand why Gabriel didn't try to help himself. Maybe it was depression? Maybe he didn't think anyone loved him, so he didn't think he was lovable? Maybe because of that he didn't think he was worthy of any love, even the love of his own self. He had such a terrible childhood; it would make sense that he felt like it was his fault. He saw other kids with families and homes, but he hadn't had a family and home. He probably felt that if his birth mom and dad had a better child, maybe they would have been a better family. She tried many times to take him to a psychologist. If he didn't agree to go, taking him would be useless. He would have just sat there, not saying anything. The doctor wouldn't be able to analyze a person who didn't

185

speak. There were copayments too, so it would be a huge burden financially. She probably should have forced him to go. She heard too that if a person isn't open to help from a counselor, they wouldn't get anything out of it. Gabriel had to want it.

Chapter 41

The Talk with Jose

Gabriel returned to work with a little bit of optimism. Dan was surprised to see him smiling while working on his machine.

"Got a minute, Gabriel?" Dan wanted to find out what happened to make his friend smile.

"Yeah, Dan, what's up?" Gabriel walked over to Dan since they were in between runs of boxes at the manufacturing plant.

"You've got a smile on your face. What brought that on?" Dan slapped Gabriel on the back.

"I've lost twenty pounds already, and with the homemade lunches my sugar numbers have gone down too. I am hoping that I can get off this medicine and that I'll keep losing weight." Gabriel smiled.

"My dad was asking about you. He wants you to come over. He has been going to the doctor and having tests done. He needs both knees replaced, and he'll need to do something about his weight before they perform the operation. Why don't you come over this weekend?"

"Sounds good, I'd like to see your dad." Gabriel smiled. He liked to get invitations and didn't get many. This week was pretty good.

The week went by quickly. The plant was busy with orders. They'd have to work Saturday to get the box orders done on time.

Gabriel didn't like working on Saturdays, but it did fill his time and left less time to feel lonely at home.

"We'll see you at around two in the afternoon. Don't bring anything, we'll have food. See you tomorrow!" Dan walked out of the plant and to his car in the lot.

Gabriel watched and wished he had a family to go home to, just like Dan's. He hoped that someday he would find a girl to call his own. At least he had something to look forward to tomorrow. He walked slowly to his car and drove home.

The morning came quickly. He did a load of laundry and tested his sugar. It was still on target. He would try not to eat too much at Dan's house. He wanted to give Dan's dad, Jose, a good report. He didn't have much energy to clean the house, but he fed Salem and tried to clean his sandbox a little. He didn't ever want to leave his house in the same condition that Rose had found it when he was in the hospital. It caused him pain to bend over to pick things up off the floor, but he was forcing himself to struggle through the motions. He had to drop some of this weight in order to make his place look better. He didn't have the stamina to clean for more than about ten minutes at a time. Sleeping was difficult too because of his enormous weight. He wasn't comfortable on his back, and no matter which way he moved, his back was sore when he got up in the morning. The sore back didn't help at work or when he tried to clean the house or pull weeds in the front yard. He climbed the stairs and pulled his clothes out of the dryer. He didn't have much of a wardrobe. Big sizes were very expensive and not very fashionable. He tried, the best he could, to hide his weight by wearing dark colors. It was very hard to bend over, so his shoes were rarely tied. It was time to leave. He walked out the door and went to his car.

Gabriel was greeted by Dan's wife. She gave him a hug and escorted him to a seat next to Jose. Jose reached out and shook Gabriel's hand. Dan walked over quickly and did the same.

"How are you doing, Gabriel? It's great to see you again." Jose was in good spirits. His weight hadn't changed much, but he didn't seem sad about it.

"Great to see you too. Dan said that you had some news for me." Gabriel wanted Jose to get new knees so that he could have his wish to run and play with the grandkids.

"The doctor said they can replace my knees, and they will work as good as new, but first I'll have to lose this extra weight. They are going to give me gastric bypass surgery. I should lose the weight quickly and then be able to get the operation for the new knees. I wanted to tell you about it because I was thinking that surgery may be an option for you too." Jose knew how Gabriel felt with his extra weight. He also knew that he would eventually destroy his knees too if he didn't do something soon.

"Hey, I'm glad they are going to do something for you. I know you want your new knees. That will be good. I have a feeling that this operation will be good for you. I'll think about what you said and maybe investigate it. Do you know anything else about it?" Gabriel didn't know anything about the process of having surgery. He didn't like going to the doctor either because they always gave him a lecture about his weight. He had lost twenty pounds, but that wasn't even a dent in the total weight he needed to lose. Two hundred pounds would be closer to the amount he needed to shed.

"So after listening to the doctor about one hundred times, I finally understand what it is. Gastric bypass surgery refers to a surgery where my stomach is divided into a small upper pouch and a much larger lower pouch, which is the old stomach. Then what they do is rearrange the small intestine to connect to both. The doc said there are several different ways they can reconnect the intestine, but I didn't need to know all that stuff. The changes they make causes a reduction in the size of my stomach and a difference in the way I respond to the food I eat. The reason I can have this type of surgery is because of the extreme amount of weight I am carrying along with all the medical problems I have because of the extra weight. There are other surgeries, but I needed this extreme surgery. Doc said I'd live longer after the surgery. He also said only about 15 percent of patients experience complications. So I am not too worried."

Gabriel thought for a minute. "I never heard much about this surgery. A little while ago I met a family member at a party who had

Lap Band surgery. That one seemed very simple, but you needed to go back for adjustments. I didn't think it sounded right for me. This one seems very invasive. I wonder if there are any other kinds of surgery? Since I know a few people now that are going through this process, I may look into it more."

"Going through the surgery will be scary, but life like this isn't good, and the doctors said that my heart is working really hard with all of this extra weight. I don't want to die before my time. I must go through with this surgery even though it is drastic. They have done this to many people, so they know what they are doing." Jose hoped that Gabriel would understand all these things applied to him too.

"I don't know if Dan told you, but I had a serious problem and ended up in the hospital a few weeks ago. My sugar skyrocketed, and I felt awful. After that I have been on a diet and going to some health fairs to learn more." Gabriel felt good talking about everything he went through with a friend who had similar problems.

"Sometimes it takes something really big to push you into doing something to help yourself. I think it was good that you went to the hospital to check up on your health when you were feeling bad. That was a good thing." Jose was happy that his friend was getting to a point where he might get some help.

They sat and didn't speak for a few minutes, then Jose spoke up. "Just because we have problems with eating, doesn't mean we have to starve ourselves today. We've made a whole bunch of food. Let's enjoy some of it while we can, but at the same time we should control ourselves too!"

Gabriel nodded. They both stood up and wandered over to the buffet table. The food was always good at Dan's. They both enjoyed a reasonable plate. This was one of the better days in a long while.

The following day Rose picked up Gabriel to go to a diabetes seminar at the local grocery store. Anything and everything that could teach them both something about diabetes, they took advantage of and went.

When they got to the grocery store, they were escorted to the second floor. Rose had been in this store a million times and didn't know there was a second floor. The upstairs contained a meeting room with about twelve chairs and a few tables. The tables were filled with gifts for the participants. There were snacks that were low in sugar and other treats. They were also given a bag filled with handouts.

They sat down, and attendance was called. Next, they were given cards to fill out with their name and address. There was also an area for the reason you were attending this talk. Gabriel was never much for words, so he put down to learn about diabetes. Other cards were filled with paragraphs telling their story about how they got there. Rose entered her information, and she said she was here to support her son.

The lecturer came in and collected all the cards. She glanced over them quickly and asked everyone to go around the room and introduce themselves. Gabriel was shy and didn't like to speak up, but after he heard some of the others talk, he felt more comfortable. There were all shapes and sizes of people, some big, some small. He started to think that he wasn't the only misfit. He felt a little better about himself.

After the talk was over, they wandered through the store picking up products that they had learned about during the talk.

"Let's buy some of these products for you. I can use some to make your breakfast and lunch."

"Okay. Dan brings things to share with me. Can you make a little extra so that I can share some of my lunch with him?" Gabriel wanted to make sure he was nice to Dan to keep the friendship.

"Sounds like a good idea. Also, next time he has a party I'll make something healthy that you can share with Jose." Rose knew that Jose was an important person in his life.

"Yep, he needs help with his diet too." Gabriel smiled.

They finished shopping and got into the car and smiled and did a little bit of the cabbage-patch dance to celebrate.

"Did I tell you that Jose likes to hunt and has given me a few things that he had from his past hunting days when he was healthy?"

"Yes, I think you mentioned it before." Rose smiled. "I hope he gets his operation and gets to do the things he used to enjoy!"

They pulled up to Gabriel's, and he waved goodbye to his mom. "Bye, Mom, I'll see you at 4:00 a.m. for breakfast!"

Rose loved seeing the smile on Gabriel's face. She watched him go into his house and then pulled away. It was already late, and she had lots to do to get his breakfast and lunch ready for the morning. She wanted to do one more thing: call Joel and give him the progress report. He would be so happy to hear that everything was going so well. She dialed the phone and waited for him to answer.

"Hello?" said Joel in his usual happy voice. He always liked to get phone calls.

"Hi, Joel! How are you? Guess where Mike and I went to tonight?" Rose waited for the reply. She knew he would come back with a smart aleck remark.

"I don't know, maybe the zoo to see the llamas?" Joel tried to stay as serious as he could while he answered with his silly answer.

"No, not the zoo. We went to Jewel to listen to their seminar on diabetes." Rose was used to Joel's kidding around with her.

"Oh wow. I didn't know. How was it? Did they give you and Mike some good information?" Joel just liked having the news about Mike and Rose; any news was good news. "Did you learn anything? Find any new food products? Remember, anytime Mike wants to come to the store with me, I would be happy to take him."

"I know and I'm hoping he will take the offer. I'll keep pushing. I'll let you know if we can meet you at Caputo's this coming weekend. You said that was one of your favorite stores to browse through." Rose liked meeting Joel at various places; she enjoyed his friendship. He was a very smart guy and was very organized. Trouble was, he had been hurt when going through his divorce, and he really didn't get over it. It was hard to break through the wall he put up.

"Okay, Rose, I'm glad Mike is open to going to all of these places that can help him. Keep giving me the updates. You're doing a good job." Joel was very glad that Rose called.

"Thanks, Joel, I'll keep you informed. Maybe I'll talk to you before the weekend. Have a good night!" Rose hung up the phone and smiled. It was so good to give people good news for a change. Things were so sad for such a long time. Hopefully, this was the start of an upward swing!

Chapter 42

The Neighbors

It was a summer weekend, and that meant yard work for Rose. Working in her yard was both relaxing and fun at the same time. She loved planting new flowers and watching them grow. Sometimes it was a surprise when new growth appeared, and she had to try to remember which plant it was.

Over the past eight years that she lived in the house, she transformed the yard. When she first moved in, it was pretty bare. There was a pool, a patio, and grass—that was all. After about two years, she put an ad in the paper for the pool, and she got a call from a man who would dismantle the pool and take it away. What was left was a large hole in her yard. Rather than spending a large sum of money filling the hole with dirt, she decided to put in a lower patio and start filling the area with plants. Looking at the area now, you would never know there was a pool. The neighbors enjoyed looking at the yard, and they also enjoyed watching Rose work. They often said she was the hardest-working girl in the neighborhood. The other women joked that she was making them look bad, so she should slow down. Rose didn't think it was work; she enjoyed every moment of carrying dirt, raking, planting, laying stones, and dead-heading flowers.

"Hey, girlie, how are you? What are you up to?" It was Devi next door. She was the greatest neighbor in the world. Even though Rose wasn't married and often wished for a man in her life, Devi made sure she wasn't lonely. Devi and her husband, Al, invited her over for meals almost every single Sunday. They were always asking if she needed help and always knew Rose would decline.

"I'm good, Devi. How are you? What are you up to?" Rose was grateful for the pause in her work.

"Hey, when you are done, grab a beer and come over to our deck. It's time we caught up." Devi always loved company. She invited all the neighbors over, not just Rose. They were always cooking, always sprucing up their yard. Their house was the nicest in the neighborhood. Their lawn was almost perfect, except for the leaves that often blew over from Rose's tree.

Rose finished her task and grabbed a beer from her fridge. She purposely walked across their beautiful lawn while Devi's brother Bill watched. She knew it bothered Bill that Rose stepped on the lawn, so just to tease him she walked across the lawn and landscaping and giggled. Bill looked up and shook his head.

"Sorry, Bill, I just did that to annoy you." Rose smiled.

"It's not you that annoys me, it's the water-meter reader and the guy from the electric company. They are the ones that don't know how to step in places where there are no flowers." Bill shook his head while he complained. "Devi's on the deck in back waiting for you. You can go through the house if you want."

Talk about wonderful people. Everyone in Devi's house treats Rose like a queen. She never had it so good. Rose pulled open the front door and walked through the living room and kitchen to the sliding patio door.

"Hi, Devi. Thanks for inviting me over. I needed a break." Rose walked over to the couch on the deck and took a seat. She was happy to see that Charlotte is over too. "I've got a story."

"Wait, wait, we have a story to tell you first!" Charlotte said with a big smile on her face.

"What! I can't wait to hear. What happened?" Rose sat back and was ready to listen to the story.

"Notice anything at all that is different?" Devi asked Rose.

Rose looked around. Devi was always decorating and putting new things out on the deck. She didn't recognize anything new. "No, sorry, I don't notice anything new."

"No smokes on the table! No ashtrays! We both quit smoking. Charlotte has quit after forty years of smoking, and I have been smoking for thirty years. We both went cold turkey for two weeks now. Haven't touched a cigarette. It feels great!" Devi had a huge smile on her face. "You know I was supposed to quit when Al had those heart problems. He quit and I kept smoking, which isn't good for him. Secondhand smoke is harmful too."

"How did you do it? What made you quit? How did you finally make it work?" Rose was stunned. She loved her neighbors and knew that cigarette smoking was bad for Al and Devi. She always hoped they would both quit. Devi's brother Bill smokes too, and he is a type 2 diabetic. He shouldn't be smoking either.

"Two weeks ago, we went to a hypnotist. This guy travels around the country and gives one-day seminars. The seminars are for smoking and weight loss too. It cost us seventy-five dollars for the seminar. He hypnotized all the people in the room at the same time. It was amazing." Devi was so excited about the process.

Rose's wheels started to turn. She thought of Gabriel and how this could be a kick-start to his much-needed weight loss.

"Is he still in town? Can I go and take Gabriel for weight loss? It sounds like it has worked wonders for you two." Rose was just as happy as her two friends. This might be the solution for all of them.

"Hmmmm. I am not sure he is still in town, but he will be back. Let me run in the house and get you his card. You can call and find out if he will be back in the neighborhood." Devi opened the patio door and watched so Layla, her boxer, didn't run out. She sneaked in to find the business card for the hypnotist.

Rose waited for Devi to come back out of the house with the card. "Thanks, you are a lifesaver! I'm going to talk to Gabriel about this and find out when this hypnotist is coming back to town. This is awesome!"

Charlotte sipped her beer and then asked Rose for the other news. Rose told her neighbors about Mike's hospital stay a few months ago and the seminars they had been attending. She was happy to tell them that Gabriel had lost a little weight and that he was at least open to learning about how to diet and help himself. It was much better than it was. Gabriel was so depressed before and had no desire to diet or exercise.

Devi told Rose that she had noticed Gabriel coming over every morning. She was curious why he stopped by each day. Rose told both of them about the healthy breakfast she was making every day and the lunches she was packing for him. Not only was Gabriel eating better, but it also gave them a chance to catch up each morning. They had gotten closer since this all happened. It was good for both of them. Having Gabriel in her life gave her life meaning. She was grateful for him. Rose felt that her life was so much more important because Gabriel was in it. Even though things didn't work out like a dream, she wouldn't have gone back to change anything about her life.

Rose continued to tell Devi and Charlotte about the drop in sugar level Gabriel has had in the past few months. They could tell that Rose was happy; they knew their friend suffered knowing her son was so depressed. Rose wanted Gabriel to have friends and a good job, and neither were possible because of the way he felt about his body. There were obese people who were able to have friends and family, but Gabriel lacked self-esteem and didn't believe anyone would be interested in him at his present size.

Devi told Rose to keep them updated about Gabriel's progress and to come and tell them if they make it to the hypnotist. Then Devi started to inform Rose of the other activity in the neighborhood. There were new neighbors moving in and old neighbors moving out. Even Charlotte and her husband were planning on moving out of their house soon. They were ready for retirement and thinking of moving to Montana. Just as they were winding up their conversation, they heard loud music coming from the driveway in front. It sounded like Gabriel was here. His music was always so loud that he never snuck into the area.

Gabriel pulled up out front and saw the back gate open. He wandered through the yard and noticed Rose on the deck at the neighbor's house. He knew this was the second place to look if Rose wasn't in the house or yard, and she was home. He headed over to Devi's deck and greeted everyone with a smile. He felt comfortable there. They were always so nice to him. He picked a seat and sat down.

"Can I get you a drink or anything?" Devi was quick to make people anything they wanted.

"No, I don't need anything, but thanks." Gabriel got comfortable in his chair. No matter where he sat, the chairs were not big enough for him, and he was not comfortable. It was the same in school. He hated taking classes because he feared he wouldn't fit in the seat, and it was bad enough that the other students stared at his enormous size when he walked into the room.

"Mom, I got the ancestry.com DNA test in the mail today." Gabriel smiled. This was something he had been waiting to receive for a few weeks. "I wanted to complete the steps and get it in the mail today. The quicker we mail it, the sooner I will know about my ancestry. I want to know whether I am German or English.

"Okay, Gabriel. Sounds like we need to go in the house and have you spit in a cup. Let's go! See you guys later." Rose waved goodbye to her friends and followed Gabriel back inside her house.

They read the directions to the test, and Gabriel spits in the cup and sealed it shut. He put the label on the cup and placed it into the small box that is already addressed to ancestry.com.

"It won't be long now. I should get some information about my background. It's driving me crazy that no one in my family knows anything about our heritage. It's frustrating." Gabriel got a little upset. He had wanted to know about his heritage for years. It's now possible through these DNA tests. Years ago, nothing liked this existed. He was happy about the progress in science to make this possible.

"I'm leaving. I want to go and drop it in the mailbox at the post office. It takes about six weeks as it is. If I drop it by the post office instead of in a mailbox, I'll eliminate one day of waiting." Gabriel shut the door and was on his way.

Rose was happy that he was moving quickly. There wasn't much that excited him these days. Maybe finding his heritage would close one of the open doors and make him feel more complete. She guessed that if she didn't know her own background, she might feel a bit empty too.

Chapter 43

The Hunt for the Surgery

The ride from work seemed a bit long today. Rose was excited about the seminar with the hypnotist this evening. If the hypnotist eliminated Devi's desire to smoke, just think what he could do with Gabriel's food cravings. She hoped this would work. They had heard a few stories about weight-loss surgeries, but she hated to think that he would have to go through such drastic measures to lose weight. She found out that the surgeries were not as uncommon as she believed. Not only did they run into a relative; a fellow employee, Jeff, where Gabriel now worked; and Jose; but she just heard that a girl at her own office was getting the operation. She would get to see the whole progression right in front of her eyes by watching Suzie go through the operation and weight loss afterward. The type of operation that Suzie was having was different than the other operations. This was called a sleeve operation where they cut the stomach down to the shape of a sleeve. It was reduced to 15 percent of the original size. The procedure was irreversible. The sleeve operation started as the initial phase of the gastric bypass surgery for extremely obese people. It had such success, and surgeons started performing it as a stand-alone procedure. Today, sleeve gastrectomy is the fastest-growing weight-loss option in North America and Asia. The only real complication is the sleeve leaking, which happens in only one in two hundred patents. One of the restrictions was cost. Not all insurance plans cover the procedure. Because of this, many people went to

Mexico to get the surgery where it was done for about four thousand dollars. Going to Mexico was a bit scary to Rose. It would be scary enough for Gabriel to get this surgery; she didn't want to even think of him having to have the surgery in a foreign country.

Rose had done some research about the amount of weight lost with these operations. They don't make you skinny; there is a calculation where they can predict the weight loss number, almost exactly. This must mean that these operations have been done on millions of people, if they had it down to a calculation. It was beginning to make her feel a bit more comfortable, but not totally sold. Maybe the hypnosis would be the thing that works.

The seminar was in a town about twenty miles from her house. That was the closest location that this hypnotist was appearing. He wouldn't be around for a long time, so they were going a little distance to grab the opportunity. Gabriel was open to the idea, but not sold. He was willing to go with Rose. He trusted Rose's opinion and her ideas.

She was going straight to pick up Gabriel. They could grab a small meal beforehand. The seminar was inside a hotel, but Rose was not familiar with the hotel and wasn't sure there was a restaurant there.

As she pulled up to Gabriel's town house, she saw him in the same spot as usual, waiting for her. He was definitely a person of habit. She stopped the car, and he climbed into the passenger seat.

"Hi, Gabriel. Are you excited about this thing tonight?" Rose hoped that he believed in it. She heard that you need to believe in hypnosis for it to work.

"I'll give it a try. Not so sure it will work, but who knows." Gabriel didn't really seem too excited about this chance. She wasn't sure whether that meant he was giving up hope, or if he was getting interested in the operation options.

"Don't hold back your enthusiasm!" Rose teased to get Gabriel to smile.

Well, at least he agreed to give it a try. In the past he would have said no. It would have been like pulling teeth for him to give it a try. This was a whole new Gabriel since his time in the hospital. That doctor must have really laid it into him and scared him to death. Something had to have opened his eyes and made him listen.

"Let's stop for a quick bite to eat on the way to the seminar. I'll get a small salad. I don't know how long this thing will be, and I don't want to starve while waiting. My stomach will start to growl, and everyone will be looking at me." Rose smiled. She was trying to lighten their spirits.

After eating they found the hotel and started to look for the conference room. The signs led them upstairs where there was a check-in table. Rose paid the fee for both of them. She would not be able to sit inside the seminar unless she was a paying customer.

They found a seat and tried to get comfortable. There were all types of people attending. She guessed that the attendees, who were an average weight, were trying to quit smoking. The others who were overweight were most likely coming for weight loss. It was interesting that everyone was in the same room. She thought that they may split up the groups into two.

The clock ticked, and finally it was time for the speaker to introduce himself. He talked for about twenty minutes. Much of the talk was about the vitamins and natural products to lose weight, sleep better, and stop smoking. These products were not cheap. Gabriel did have some interest in the sleep product. It contained the same thing in turkey, tryptophan. Since Gabriel had felt sleepy after devouring a turkey dinner at Thanksgiving, he seemed to believe in the power of tryptophan. Rose thought it might be worth buying it for him.

Finally, it was time to be hypnotized. Everyone would stay in their own chair and be hypnotized all at the same time. The presenter said to picture a blackboard with the item that you want to give up written on it. Rose didn't need to lose weight, so she thought about something that she would want to give up to test the hypnosis. She didn't ask Gabriel what he was going to picture on the chalkboard. She assumed he would imagine food written on the chalkboard. Slowly during the hypnosis process, you would see the writing being erased on the board, which would be equal to your desire being erased for that item. The hypnosis created a hyperattentive and hyperresponsive mental state, in which the subject's subconscious mind is highly open to suggestion.

The room got quiet. Everyone was ready. The hypnotist started to talk. It seemed to Rose that the suggestions were given for about fifteen minutes. When the hypnotist asked them to open their eyes, he went around the room to find out how long individuals felt they were under. There were various amounts of time. Gabriel thought he was out for about forty-five minutes. The hypnotist explained that the longer you thought you were under, the better the hypnosis worked. Rose was happy to hear that since Gabriel thought he was under longer than her.

After the hypnosis section of the talk was over, he explained how long the suggestion would work. He said it depended on several factors, including the willingness of the subject and the skill of the hypnotherapist. Generally, you could say that the changes last exactly as long as they last and not one second longer. The more thorough the preparation phase, the faster, deeper, and longer lasting the change.

Rose had imagined Crystal Light being erased from the board. She had eliminated soda from her diet in the past and was only drinking coffee, water, and Crystal Light. She knew that Crystal Light contained aspartame, an artificial flavoring that could be harmful to your health. This sweetener was marketed as safe and was approved way back in 1976. It got its low-calorie name because it was two hundred times sweeter than sugar. Since it was so sweet, less aspartame needed to be added to foods, therefore it reduced the total number of calories you put in the food. There were several studies on both sides of the aspartame sides, ranging from harmless to scary. The US Food and Drug Administration still stands behind it, as well as other organizations too. On the other hand, other studies show that it causes cancer in the liver and lungs in mice and increases leukemia and non-Hodgkin's lymphoma too. It may also increase dementia, stroke, the risk of obesity, and the risk of depression. There were enough evils about it to cause Rose to believe she should quit drinking it.

The seminar was over, and as they moved out the door, they had the opportunity to buy the products that were discussed during the meeting. Rose stopped and purchased the sleep aid for Gabriel.

It was over, now the wait to see if hypnosis would work. She asked Gabriel what he thought of the process, and she received the usual amount of feedback, which was not much. She still prayed that this was the answer.

Weeks went by, and she had no desire to drink Crystal Light. She went to the fridge to pour it once, but then set it down and didn't want to drink it. The hypnosis seemed to be working. That was enough for her to seek out another hypnotist for Gabriel. She found a counselor who used hypnosis in his therapy. He was also in the Navy, and Gabriel always looked up to military people. She hoped that this would be another way to get Gabriel to be a believer. Next, she needed to sell the idea to him, which was never easy. She needed to make a great pitch. This would never have worked years ago, but now he was a bit more open to new ideas, so she would give it a go. "Give it a go" was a phrase she learned from her Australian employer. They had different ways of expressing things, and this was one phrase she enjoyed and found herself using.

"Hi, Gabriel, I have some news for you. I found a hypnotist nearby, and you can start going for hypnosis sessions to lower your desire for food. What do you think?" Rose stopped and listened for an answer.

"Whatever you think. I'll go if you want me to." Gabriel wasn't into it at all. This was the usual answer she received. It was obvious that he didn't believe in the process, but since the hypnotist was a counselor in addition to the hypnosis, maybe it would help in some way.

"The appointment is for Wednesday night. Do you have school or anything going on that day?" Rose waited and hoped he would say he would go to the counselor.

"I can go. Are you driving?" He didn't want to go alone. If he had to go alone, he would have to explain why he was there and the whole situation of his life.

"Yep, I'll pick you up. Maybe afterward we can stop for dinner, my treat." Maybe that wasn't the best type of reward for going to a counselor for weight loss, but she knew that it would be an incentive to go. She was willing to do anything to get him help.

This didn't seem like the real answer for this problem, but the way Rose dealt with problems was to try new ideas until there was an idea that worked.

Rose picked up Gabriel, and as normal, he was out waiting. He slowly entered the car and settled in, pulling the seat belt in and out until it fit around his large body. As usual, he was disgusted with the process. She hoped that as he went through this process, he would gain some enthusiasm for the counselor. She wasn't good at express-ing her feelings because she didn't want Gabriel to be mad at her for saying that she was worried about his weight. Embarrassment was another one of her feelings, which she knew was wrong. Aunt Joan accepted people for who they were, but Rose wasn't as open. She wanted her son to look good. It was important for him to be presentable. When she introduced Gabriel to people, she felt that they were judging her. She felt that everyone thought she overfed him. That she gave him too many treats. That she wanted him to be fat so no one else would love him, and he'd have to stay with her. That was the total opposite of how she felt. She wanted Gabriel to be attractive, to have many friends, to go out into the world, and to live his dreams and be who he wanted to be. She knew Gabriel loved the armed forces and wanted to be a husband and father. His weight was not helping with any of these desires.

The counselor's office was thirty minutes from his house. As they drove, they talked about their days. Rose gave Gabriel the scoop on her responsibilities at work. She was changing from accounting to customs duties. Rose had worked in the accounting area for her whole life, but there was a need for someone to train and create US Customs material for the customers of her software company. Rose thought she would give it a try. She loved new challenges.

Gabriel listened but didn't contribute much to the conversa-tion. When Rose asked him how his job was going, he said it was the same as always. They arrived at the address and parked. The parking lot was practically empty. They walked into the building and took the elevator to the second floor. They were told by the doctor to just sit in the waiting-room area. When he was done with his last session, he would come out and get them.

Rose noticed a home-decorating magazine on the table and starting to browse through it while waiting. Gabriel looked through apps on this phone. Soon the counselor walked down the hallway. His previous patient left, and then the counselor introduced himself. They both followed him to his office. Inside was a lounge chair, incense, and soft music. He asked a few questions about why they were there, and then Rose left the office. She decided to walk around the building outside to get some of her daily exercise. She worked out every day by either going to the gym and riding the elliptical or walking or biking outside. Tonight, she wouldn't be able to go to the gym because she went directly to pick up Gabriel after work, and they wouldn't get home until nearly nine o'clock. She normally got up at four in the morning to start preparing breakfast and lunch for Gabriel. It was a long day.

After thirty minutes, she went back to the waiting room. She paged through a magazine, and soon Gabriel was on his way out of the office with the counselor walking behind him. He was smiling and yawning as he walked. Maybe this was good. Maybe the hypnosis suggestions would stick with him. Maybe he would like coming here, and things would get better.

The cost was not covered by medical insurance. Rose was paying for it herself. She felt the investment would be well worth it, if it would help move Gabriel in the right direction. The counselor said it would be best to come every week, but Rose saw with the hypnosis she had that the suggestion worked for about six weeks. Also, she remembered her neighbor was able to quit smoking for quite a few weeks. For these reasons, Rose thought an appointment once a month may be enough. Once a month would have to do, because she really couldn't afford much more.

They left the office and started to drive home. Gabriel wanted to stop for a beef sandwich. Rose had promised to stop with him if he didn't overeat. He bought a six-inch beef sandwich and a diet pop. That wasn't overeating at all. Plus, he wasn't in a hurry to eat it, which was a very good sign.

She dropped him off and went straight home to bed. The morning would come early.

Rose heard loud music in the driveway and knew it was Gabriel. She had the breakfast done and was packing his lunch.

"Hi, Mom." Gabriel sounded happy as he shouted out the morning greeting.

"What's up? Did you sleep well?" Rose was elated that something was making her son smile.

"I got the DNA results back today. There was an e-mail from ancestry.com, and it listed the countries where my ancestors lived. I am both English and German. Look, there is a long list of my cousins. Many are fourth cousins, but there are a few third cousins. My ancestors also came to America very early." Gabriel was smiling all through the discussion.

"Let me see the list of your cousins. Can you write to them?" Rose started reading the list of relatives.

"Yes, I can write to them through ancestry." Gabriel watched as Rose went through the list.

"Gabriel, here is one cousin that has a family tree with thousands of names on it. She must know more than the average user. Maybe you should write to her and tell her your situation. Maybe she can help you find some other relatives that are closer to you?" Rose was excited that Gabriel was interested in ancestry and history. This was something he could take on as a hobby.

"Okay, I'll write to her tonight. I'll tell her a little about my background and see if she knows my grandfather or grandmother. I gotta get going to work now." Gabriel smiled as he grabbed his lunch off the counter.

Rose walked out the door and watched him go to his car. She waved her hand goodbye like Granny on *The Beverly Hillbillies* and shouted, "Y'all come back now y'here!" Rose laughed and loved to goof around to make Gabriel smile.

Gabriel shook his head like he was embarrassed but smiled anyway.

Chapter 44

The Seminar

After everything that happened over the past several months, Gabriel knew it was time to start looking to the future. He parked his car and headed into the hospital. This was the same hospital that he ended up at when his sugar went up and the same one where he attended the diabetes seminar. This time he was there was there for another reason, a weight-loss seminar involving surgery. He had heard stories from three friends about their surgeries. Two people he knew had Lap Band surgery, and Jose was waiting to receive gastric bypass surgery. Gabriel didn't think either of those were the right surgeries for him, but he thought maybe there was another solution that was better for him.

He walked in and was given a packet of information. There were about thirty people attending the seminar. Most of them were large people. They were of all ages. The clock ticked slowly, but the seminar finally started. It was led by the two surgeons who had performed about five thousand weight loss surgeries. They explained the new surgery that they were performing on most individuals. It was called the sleeve surgery. Sleeve gastrectomy or vertical-sleeve gastrectomy is another bariatric surgical option. This operation removes approximately 75 percent of the stomach and leaves a smaller stomach portion, shaped like a banana. This surgery was performed under general anesthesia and laparoscopically. Usually a one- to two-night stay in the hospital was necessary. The sleeve surgery restricts your food intake. This means that the same process for food stays in place in your body. It goes through all your organs just like before the surgery. On the other hand, the gastric bypass type changes how the food travels in your body. They are similar, though, because the same vitamins are necessary after a sleeve as with a gastric bypass. After the surgery, Gabriel will have to follow up with the bariatric team for the rest of his life. That was a big responsibility! This was a change of life and not an easy decision.

Next, the surgeons went over the benefits of the sleeve surgery. The Lap Band uses a foreign object placed in your body to control the amount of food that flows into your stomach. The sleeve surgery gives you better weight loss. Also, there is a lower risk of an ulcer than the gastric bypass option.

They also said there were a few disadvantages, which included that it is nonreversible since the stomach is actually cut out and cannot be replaced. This was scary to Gabriel. Weight loss with the gastric bypass would be greater, but there really wasn't enough long-term data yet with the sleeve operation. There is also a slight risk of a leak following the sleeve surgery. All in all, the surgeons said there really wasn't much negative about the sleeve surgery.

Gabriel determined he really wasn't scared about the risks. He kept observing the people in the room. He saw an older man who came in with a walker. The man spoke and said that he was told to have weight-loss surgery years ago, but never went through with it. Now his knees were shot, and he must get the surgery. It was life or death now. He was just like Jose; unless he received weight-loss surgery, his doctor would not replace his knees.

The meeting ended, and Gabriel left with lots of information and hope that maybe this would be a solution for him. The very next thing he did was call Rose.

"Hi, Mom!" Gabriel was calling with a hint of hope in his voice.

"Hi, Gabriel, what do you need?" Rose caught herself asking this same question whenever Gabriel called her.

"Nothing, I just got out of the meeting at the hospital for weight-loss surgery." Gabriel waited for his mom's reaction.

"Wow, Gabriel! That is great! What did you learn?" Rose was excited that Gabriel took the initiative to go to this meeting on his own. This meant that he was truly interested and ready to make a change.

"It sounds like the sleeve operation might be a good choice for me. I spoke to the doctor, and he said because I was young it would be good for me to get this done now before my knees gave out and high sugar hurt my internal organs." Gabriel was excited and full of hope!

"I am glad you are excited about this option. Do you know how much time you need off work? What is the process? How much does it cost? Does insurance cover it?" Rose was always full of questions. She wanted to make sure Gabriel thought about all these questions before he got too excited. Unfortunately, she was very responsible, and the money and time off work questions always came out of her mouth first. She wanted him to be happy and hoped that he didn't think she only worried about the cost.

"I am not sure about everything. Can you come with me to the next meeting? The meetings take place every Wednesday night." Gabriel knew Rose would go with him.

"Sure, I'll go. Just let me know the time, and we'll go next Wednesday." Rose was elated that Gabriel wanted to pursue this option.

"Okay. Thanks, Mom." Gabriel was feeling a little bit better about his future.

The following Wednesday's meeting was a mirror of the previous week. The same two surgeons presented the three types of weight-loss surgeries, the problems, and the good points. After the presentation there was a question-and-answer session. Many of the attendees had various health problems and asked how their health would be after the surgery. The surgeons had statistics showing how many ailments were eliminated after the surgery. This was really good news. Some of the problems that Gabriel had may dissolve, which included the type 2 diabetes. This would save his organs from further damage caused by the high sugar in his body.

Rose and Gabriel reviewed the paperwork that was handed out and looked at papers that were supplied offering loans for the surgery. Of course, the best way to go about paying for the surgery would be insurance coverage. Lots of research and phone calls would be needed to find out how this all could come together. Gabriel set up the first appointment to determine if he would be a good candidate. If he was deemed to be a good candidate, there would be a succession of several visits with specialists.

Unfortunately, Gabriel's employer's health insurance would not cover the operation. There were a few options. The operation was available in Mexico, and there were several companies offering a package that included a hospital stay and transportation to and from the United States. That option seemed a little risky. What would happen if there were complications? The operation was low cost, but if there were other complications and it wasn't covered by insurance, it could be a financial nightmare.

The second option would be to find other insurance, but that would mean Gabriel would have to move to a different employer and find one that covered the operation. At his present weight, it was hard to find a job, and Gabriel never felt comfortable with new people. He dreaded meeting new people and trying to fit into a new place.

The surgeon would not send him to any of the specialists until he found a way to pay for the surgery. They were at a standstill. Something needed to happen. As Rose's mom used to say, "Something will come up." She remembered and always had a positive attitude. It would happen. They just needed to be patient.

Gabriel continued his normal routine. He sent in his résumé to many jobs asking about the insurance coverage before he went any further with the interviews. At his current job, he inquired about the different options for health insurance that would be available at year end, but none would cover the operation. It was pretty depressing. There was a solution to his weight problem, but he just couldn't get all of the pieces to fit in order to obtain the solution.

At work, Gabriel continued to work alongside Dan. His friend was trying to get a job as a supervisor. He wanted to become a supervisor for their present employer, but that would take time. He had a growing family because his wife just announced that she was pregnant with their second child. A supervisor position at another company would probably come up faster, and he was willing to move. Gabriel wasn't too thrilled about Dan moving to a different company. He felt comfortable with Dan, and he wanted him to stay. Gabriel knew it was only a matter of time and Dan would leave. Another sad thought.

"Hey, Dan! How was your weekend?" Gabriel enjoyed listening to Dan talk about his life with his wife and baby. That was the type of life that Gabriel wanted. He just listened, trying to think how it would be to have his own family someday.

"Good news, Gabriel, my father had the gastric bypass operation a few weeks ago, and he is doing great. We are going to have a party on Saturday, and he wants to you come and see his progress. He is already able to walk much better and is having a great time with his grandchildren. After he loses more and gets down to a normal weight, they will operate on his knees. His spirits are up, and he can see the light at the end of the rainbow. He wants the same bright future for you. Come over so he can tell you himself." Dan was really happy that his father was losing weight. It meant that he would live longer and be able to see his grandchildren grow up.

"Okay. Okay. You don't need to tell me anymore. Of course I will be there on Saturday! I am really happy to hear about your dad. He is a good man and deserves a better life. He is lucky that his insurance covered his operation. I am not having the same kind of luck." Gabriel had mixed feelings now. He was happy that Jose was able to get the operation completed and was doing well, but it brought up his own dilemma about not being able to get his weight-loss operation because his employer didn't cover the insurance.

"It's at two o'clock Saturday afternoon. No need to bring anything. My dad will be really happy to talk to you. Let's get to work and get these orders run. Saturday will be here before we know it." Dan turned to the machine and started the next order.

Rose had the same situation where she worked. A fellow employee had a weight problem, and their employer covered the operation. She had the surgery a month ago, and Rose was watching the weight fall off her. She was happy that someone she knew was going through the process, and she could watch her progress. Each day she came to work and watched how her friend ate post-surgery and how it was changing her life. She looked happier and didn't complain about any complications. It seemed that the operation worked for her. This was another indication that she needed to try to find a solution to pay for the surgery for her son.

Saturday finally came, and Gabriel was curious about Jose. He wondered if Jose would look the same at a lower weight. What would happen to all the skin? How was he reacting to food after the operation? How much weight would he lose? Would all his health problems disappear? Could this be what would happen to him in the near future?

He got out of his car and approached the house. The main door was open, and he could see into the house. The party was lively, and there was Jose on his feet walking to the door to greet Gabriel. He couldn't believe the change in Jose. He was smiling and moving much quicker than he ever saw before.

"Hi, my friend! Come on in. Join the party!" Jose extended his arm for a handshake and pulled in Gabriel for a big hug.

A huge smile ran across Gabriel's face as he felt the happiness in his friend. He knew he had to do the same. He wanted to get the operation.

The day went on, and Jose explained the entire process of the gastric bypass surgery, which was much more extensive than the sleeve surgery that Gabriel was hoping to receive. The post-op recovery wasn't too bad. First, he had to use an incentive spirometry bottle, which encourages patients to take long, deep breaths. The device provided patients with visual or other positive feedback when they inhaled. There was a predetermined flow rate or volume, and the patient was told to keep the inflation for a minimum of three seconds. The objective of this process was to increase the transpulmonary pressure and inspiratory volumes. It was technical, but in other words, it brought you back to normal. When the procedure was repeated regularly, it helped rule out any problems you may have with your lungs.

Another step included exercise. Jose needed to walk, go upstairs, and do a little more each day. The object was to get moving and eventually make exercise a part of his life forever.

Jose could no longer take anti-inflammatory pain medications like ibuprofen. He could only take Tylenol products. This was a little scary because headaches, backaches, and any slight pain was always relieved in the past by taking medication. Now, it was important to try to work through the pain without taking pain relievers.

His lifting was limited to twenty-five pounds, but that was temporary. Eventually he would be able to lift anything he could naturally handle. Exercise could include weights.

One of the bad reactions immediately following surgery was gas pain. He was able to take over-the-counter gas-reducing drugs for relief. Soon that subsided too.

Vitamins would be part of his daily routine for the rest of his life. He needed to take vitamins to ensure his body was getting all the nutrients he needed. Calcium supplements were also part of the vitamin routine.

There was one negative—after the operation he would never be able to donate blood for the rest of his life.

Jose needed to follow a special diet after the surgery, and it was very similar to the diet Gabriel would need to follow too. The diet was divided into three stages to allow for gradual adjustment. The first stage was a liquid diet for two weeks. One of the products he drank was a protein drink. These have just become popular and were liquid packaged in a small paper container that was coated to preserve the protein drink. It was like drinking a milkshake and came in a variety of flavors. They weren't as bad as they sounded!

The second stage was a soft diet for four weeks. Soft foods included bananas, melons, and strawberries. Cooked vegetables could be eaten except for corn. Rice and soft bread were also banned from this section of the diet. A huge part of this section of the diet was learning how to chew very well to ease the food into the stomach.

Lastly, the final stage was a regular diet. He was supposed to eat only at set mealtimes and a set snack time. He needed to change his eating patterns. This was important to maintain a healthy lifestyle. Liquids were prohibited for thirty minutes after each meal or snack. Only solid food, which filled the stomach pouch and emptied very slowly, would relieve his hunger.

None of this sounded too complicated to Gabriel. He would be so happy losing his excess weight that a few weeks of changed eating would be a welcome addition to his life. If Jose could do it, he knew he could too. The results were amazing. Jose had lost forty pounds in the first month after surgery, and he was down sixty pounds now after two months. The weight was melting off him. He looked better, and his outlook on life was amazing now.

Gabriel left the party even more determined to find a way to get the surgery.

The next week at work Rose went on one of her daily health walks with her two friends Shannon and Christen. She explained the whole dilemma to her friends. They both knew how passionate Rose was about this surgery because at one point during the walk Rose broke down and cried. She didn't think it was fair that Gabriel was stopped from the surgery because of the limits of his health insurance. She reminded them about their own health insurance, which enabled their fellow employee to have this same operation. They knew that Rose would find a way to go forward. She was tenacious and didn't stop until the work was done. They believed in their friend. It was good to see their support.

Back at her desk she received an e-mail from her good friend Joel who offered to pay for the surgery. She was shocked and a happy tear came to her eye. He was always so frugal and didn't give loans to anyone. He had broken his rule and was offering her a gift. She thought it over and declined. Maybe after exploring all other options she would give it another thought, but she didn't think so. She always depended on herself. She could do it. She knew something would happen.

She called the surgeon's office and explained the situation to their assistant. They were experts at this problem and knew the exact insurance companies and plans that they needed to look for when Gabriel was exploring job offers. At least she was becoming more knowledgeable, and knowledge was power.

Chapter 45

The Insurance

The summer turned to fall, and Gabriel continued to go to work at the same company. He kept inquiring about potential changes in their insurance policy. More calls from potential new employers came in, and he questioned their health-insurance coverage. He was honest with them and told them he was trying to improve his life and needed special insurance coverage.

After the morning meeting, he and Dan walked to their machine. Dan told Gabriel about his weekend, and when they got to the machine and they were alone, he hesitated.

"Gabriel, I have some really good news. I got that call from the manufacturing plant that I was waiting for, and they offered me a supervisor job. We negotiated back and forth on a few things that I wanted, but eventually they gave in to my list of needs and offered me the position. I start in two weeks." Dan watched for his friend's reaction before he went on to tell him the rest. Gabriel was filled with mixed feelings. This meant that he would no longer have his good friend with him each day. He would miss the stories of his family and might even lose touch with Jose. He was sad for himself, but happy for Dan. Dan's wife was at home with two children now, and they needed extra money. He had to take the new job. There was no question about it. He knew this was a step to the future management position that Dan dreamed about. Also, the new company would pay for him to attend college. This had been one of the things that Dan had on his list of needs. Gabriel knew that Dan was impressed that his friend continued to go to class to finish his degree even though it was hard to be surrounded by new people in the classes.

"That is great, Dan." Gabriel extended his hand to shake his friend's hand.

Dan saw the look in Gabriel's eyes, the sadness of losing his friend in his daily work routine. He couldn't hold off any longer. He had to tell Gabriel the best part of the offer.

"Their call was amazing. I got everything I wanted. I couldn't believe they made me such a great offer. The news is good for you too." Dan waited again to see his friend's expression.

"Why is it good for me? You are getting more money, a better position, money for college, and will have a shorter commute to work. I will still be here, and I'll have to retrain someone on this machine." Gabriel tried not to let Dan see his sadness.

"Friend, the deal included the ability to hire someone to work under me. No questions asked. Of course, it is you who I intend to bring over with me, that is if you want to move to the new company." Dan was pleased he could make this offer to his friend. He was excited that he could also improve Gabriel's life.

Gabriel's expression changed and a smile appeared on his face. "Wow, I would love to leave this place and come with you. I can't believe you thought of me. I know how important it is that you make a great impression at the new company. I hope I can live up to your expectations."

"Don't worry. You are a hard worker and smart. You exceed my expectations on this machine every day. You have nothing to worry about." Dan stopped again. There was even better good news.

"Well, tell me more about it. What does the company make? What will I be doing? Do I have to fill out an application? Do they have good benefits?" Gabriel's mind was filled with questions, but the one about benefits topped the list.

"That is the best part. I was saving the best for last. Believe it or not, their health insurance will cover your operation. You will just need to wait three months after your first day of employment, and you will have the insurance you need." Dan had a tremendous smile on his face.

Gabriel was shocked. He didn't know what to say. His dreams were becoming reality. His friend had gone out of his way to make his surgery possible. His friend changed his life. He couldn't wait to call his mom and tell her everything. She would be so happy.

"Let's get back to work. Later you can give the company a call and set up an appointment. Don't worry, you are in. This is just a formality." Dan started the setup on their machine. It would be a great day.

Lunchtime came, and Gabriel called Rose. She wasn't used to getting a call from her son during his lunchtime, so she was a bit worried as she picked up the phone.

"Hi, Gabriel, what's up? Rose waited for his reply, worried that there might be some sort of problem. She knew that if there was a small problem, he got very nervous right away instead of staying calm and thinking of a good solution.

"I got a new job!" He was excited about the news that Dan gave him.

"What? How? At work? Did they move you to a different machine?" She asked a few questions to try to understand what he was saying.

"Dan is taking me with him to his new job. He needs an assistant. He is going to be a supervisor now."

"Oh wow, are you sure this is good for your résumé? It's not good to jump jobs. What about the insurance coverage? Did you ask the HR person at the new job already?" Rose didn't want him to keep moving around, and if this new job didn't have the right coverage either, he would end up moving again.

"Dan already looked into it before he told me about it. That is why this is so cool. Dan wanted me to come with him. He asked all the right questions and asked if he could hire his own person to work under him. They agreed to everything he wanted."

"This is incredible news. He must really value your friendship, Gabriel. He is a such good person. You are so lucky!" Rose was truly amazed at the entire story. She didn't know much about Dan's family since her son didn't say much. All she knew was Dan understood the problems that went along with obesity since his dad suffered from it too. It was so fortunate that Gabriel had met Dan at work. It is funny how things just end up working out. If it wasn't for Dan, Gabriel might not be able to have the surgery.

"I know, Mom. I can't believe it myself." It would take him a little while for this to all sink in; so much was changing suddenly.

"Okay, I'll let you get back to work. Tell me more later when you get home." Rose hung up with a smile on her face. This was like a mini miracle. She wanted to tell everyone how things were looking up!

The next day, Gabriel called the new employer and set up an appointment. Then he called the surgeon, and said it would be just three months, and he could start going through the process for the surgery. They had said the appointments would take time to get with the specialists, so they agreed to give him the list of doctors to call to set up the appointments in advance. It was only a matter of time now. Gabriel was very healthy apart from the high sugar and obesity. The other doctors shouldn't find any reason for him not to have the surgery.

Rose went to work and told everyone at work about the good news. She couldn't wait for her daily health walk with Shannon and Christen to explain the whole situation. What a difference a day made!

She also called her cousins and sent a text message to Al, who was always especially concerned for Gabriel's well-being. Everyone who received the news was excited that things were finally turning around for Rose and Gabriel.

Another consideration was the hypnotist counselor that they had been seeing for the last year. Gabriel had never had the type of therapy recommended by family services after his adoption. Rose thought the counselor may be helping him a little, and she didn't really want to stop the sessions. After all, they were only going about once a month, so it wasn't too much time taken out of their daily schedule. She knew Gabriel didn't want to go, so it would take some finagling to get him to continue the sessions until the surgery.

She approached him about the subject, and he wasn't too enthusiastic about it at all. This was going to take some doing. On the flip side, if he wasn't into it, the hypnosis or therapy may not be as beneficial. She decided to take him to at least one more session before the surgery. Part of his process was to visit a psychiatrist to determine if he was mentally ready, so Rose thought that if the psychiatrist thought he was mentally healthy, she would be okay with it too.

Another weekend came, and they did their normal Sunday outing. The countdown to the surgery was continuing, so they would visit a few of the places they liked before he was on the liquid diet. Today they would go to a few antique stores and a brewery that had great burgers. This wasn't necessarily an unhealthy meal as long as it was a moderate portion without appetizers.

"Hey, Gabriel, how was your workweek?" Rose picked him up outside of his house in the usual spot. Maybe she should demand to go in occasionally. One thing at a time. *Let's worry about the weight before starting on improving his other skills.* Was this the right approach, or should she have always tried to improve everything at once? Nagging wasn't the way to go. Everyone hated to be nagged at all the time. She thought that all his bad habits were attributed to his early years of life, or maybe he just lacked motivation. She always went back to the thinking that if his weight were lower, his energy level would go up, and he would be doing more each and every day.

"Work was good. I am training with Dan. Soon I'll be able to work on a machine on my own. The machines there are small. I'll be running the machine and maintaining the machine. If it breaks down, I'll be responsible for letting management know, so they can call someone in to fix it. I'm pretty much on my own, which I like. I also like being on straight days. It is better for going to school, and it is better for all of my doctor appointments."

"Good, I'm glad it's working out. Have you set up all of the doctor appointments yet?"

"I have four doctors that I have to see to get the go-ahead for the surgery. There is a psychiatrist, heart doctor, lung doctor, and a sleep study. I have most done, but I am having a hard time with the sleep study. They want me to have my insurance card before I make the appointment."

"Well, if you can get the rest of the appointments made and leave that one for the end, you are doing pretty good." Rose was smiling because it appeared that Gabriel was really enthusiastic about the surgery. He had to be. He was making all the appointments without any prompting from anyone!

They rode on and stopped at a few antique shops in nearby towns. There was nothing new that day, just a repeat of places they had gone to before. The last stop was a brewery with great burgers. "I'm not going to be able to eat like this anymore after the surgery. I'll miss going to all of the new restaurants." There were good things and bad things about getting the surgery. They had been going on weekend outings for about five years. It was a ritual.

"I'll miss it too, Gabriel. By the way, there is someone I want you to meet next weekend. How about a movie? I'll make plans for us to meet with my friend, Robo, to watch the movie. You'll like him." Rose knew that Robo was a guy who didn't judge anyone. He wouldn't even notice her son's weight; he would talk to him exactly the same way he spoke to everyone. She thought it was someone who would make him feel comfortable. It had been a long search for a guy like this, but finally she found him.

They finished their meal, and as they were eating, Rose took pictures of the plates of food. She posted them on the Yelp website and wrote her review. She posted so many reviews that she was a Yelp Elite reviewer. The nomination for this position came from the girl at work who had the weight-loss surgery a year and a half ago. She was still doing well, and her weight had dropped about one hundred pounds. It was a perfect example of success through weight-loss surgery, and watching her progress gave Rose incentive and motivation that was needed to support her son.

"Everything takes such a long time. I wish I could have the surgery today. I am so tired of waiting for everything to happen." Gabriel was ready to get this over. He was tired of his life, which consisted of carrying around a large amount of weight. He was tired of the pain that came with each and every step he took. He was tired of not being able to bend down and tie his shoes. He was tired of not having friends, not going places, and not having any plans. He wanted a girlfriend. He wanted a family. He wanted a better life.

"It will be here before you know it. Just take one step at a time. Only two more months before you can start the doctor visits. Hopefully, the sleep test can be done right after you get the insurance card and book the appointment. If you have any problems, remember to call the surgeon's office. The administrative assistant said she will help in any way. They want you to get the operation because it is another success story for their record." Rose was happy to have another person on her side helping her son. The surgeon would help things along because the operation created income for them, and they want people to go through the process and have the surgery.

The next weekend came quickly. Rose and Gabriel met Robo at the movies. He wore his typical golf attire, which Gabriel felt was odd. He had never known an avid golfer before. Robo did not judge Gabriel at all. Rose had been right about that. He shook Gabriel's hand and smiled and made Gabriel smile. He was a good man. Aunt Joan would have liked him too. Too bad she didn't live long enough to meet him. Rose knew she was looking down from heaven, smiling, knowing Rose finally found a good man to keep her company.

After telling them that it took twenty-two minutes for him to drive from his house to the movie, Robo turned his attention to Gabriel.

"Hey, Gabriel, I heard you just started a new job. How is it going?" Robo was a talker, but he stopped talking about golf long enough to ask Gabriel a question about himself. He was an avid golfer and curler. It was good for him socially and physically, since it kept him moving. He had retired early at fifty. He was lucky. He was able to spend much of his lifetime doing things he enjoyed. His life wasn't all luck, though; he spent many hours, days, and weeks taking care of family members who needed his care. He got through it all with a smile. Many people admired his good spirit.

"The job is pretty good. I get to work with my good friend, Dan, all day and that makes it enjoyable. Someday I'd like to become a cop, though. I am going to school for criminal justice." That was the most Rose ever heard Gabriel say about himself to anyone. It showed that he also felt comfortable with Robo.

"Good, keep at it, you'll do well." Robo went back to talking about his last golf game.

They ate lunch together and then split up to drive home. It was a good meeting. Hopefully, Robo would remain in their lives.

The weeks flew by for Rose, and soon Gabriel was able to start all the specialist appointments, so he could get the go-ahead for the surgery. The heart doctor was the first one to approve him. Gabriel had a strong heart and never had a problem with any heart condition. He learned that the heart doctor had the same surgery himself. He said that Gabriel would have so much energy after the surgery that he would be amazed. This was yet another positive review of the sleeve surgery.

The second doctor was the psychiatrist. At this appointment, Gabriel had to take some written tests to determine if he was of sound mind. He had suffered from some depression, but it was because of his quality of life and nothing else. He had never tried to commit suicide or was hospitalized for any type of mental condition. There was no history of any medications for mental health either. Gabriel got the go-ahead from the second doctor too. Things were moving ahead.

Gabriel spent a day at Dan's house again. He was very curious about how Jose was doing after the surgery. It had been months ago already, and Jose was still losing weight. He told Gabriel that his whole life was changing because of the surgery. He was able to sit in any chair now. He was no longer concerned about going to public places or other people's houses, not knowing if there would be a place he could sit down that would fit around his large body. He was also wearing clothes that were stylish. Jose said that he was so tired of wearing T-shirts that were as big as tents. He was also tired of paying high prices for extra-large clothing. Now he could go into regular stores and buy clothing. He liked buying something that was stylish. It made him feel good about himself. Jose also told him that he was happy that his family wasn't embarrassed to be with him any longer. They had never said that, but he felt it. He had been so big that people stared. It was an awkward feeling. Gabriel knew how he felt. He had all the same feelings. He hated people always looking at him for his size and making judgements. He also didn't like wearing the huge tent-sized clothing. He was tired of all of it.

"How is the search for your father going? Have you heard anything from your cousin who is helping you with the DNA results?" Jose wanted all the best for his friend.

"Yes, she has contacted me via e-mail. It only took her a few weeks, and she traced back my DNA to my real birth father." Gabriel was happy to announce the news to Jose.

"Were you able to confirm this is the right guy? Do you know who this guy is?" Jose was surprised to hear this information came so quickly. He had no knowledge of DNA at all. He didn't realize so much information could be found so quickly just by looking at the DNA results.

"I told my half sister Melissa, and she confronted my birth mother, who confirmed the information was correct." Gabriel never spoke to his birth mother. He felt she had let him down long ago and didn't want to have anything to do with her.

"What is the next step? Do you get to meet him?" Jose thought meeting his father would bring closure to Gabriel.

"No, he died three years ago. I found out he was an okay guy, though. He had two other sons and was married for a long time to their mother. He always worked. I'm okay not meeting him. I am just very happy that the scumbag I was told was my father wasn't my father after all."

Gabriel was always ashamed that his birth father was such a horrible man. He was an alcoholic and abuser. He hardly worked either, and was on the run from the police for the abuse he did to his children. He crossed into the next state to run away from the law and took his children with him. Gabriel was very glad he had gotten away from him. He did reunite with the half siblings, after they turned eighteen and left their father. Those children weren't really half siblings, but Gabriel decided not to tell them. There would really be no reason seeing that his actual birth father was already dead. He had a relationship with these half siblings, so he left it just as it was. Gabriel was very kind and always thinking of others' feelings.

"Good, I'm glad you got the answers you were wanting. I was also impressed when you told me you aren't going to let your half siblings know that they are not really related to you. You are a very mature man." Jose was proud of his young friend. He thought Gabriel made some very good decisions. He was a good young man.

"What good would it do to tell them? I have thought them to be my half brothers and sisters for twenty years. I am going to continue to be the same person I have been." Gabriel had put some long hours of thought into this decision.

"It sounds like you have everything all figured out. I am proud of you." Jose really meant it. He was very proud to know Gabriel and wanted everything to work out for him.

"I have some cool stories about my grandfather to tell you too. He was one of the original horsekeepers for the Budweiser Clydesdales." Gabriel was smiling to know something pretty cool about one of his ancestors. He loved looking into history and wanted to go further on his search of his ancestors.

"I'm looking forward to hearing more as you dig up more knowledge about your grandfather and other relatives. Good for you!" Jose sat and listened to more of what Gabriel had to say about the DNA findings. He had become very fond of him and knew the hardship of the enormous weight he carried. People often judge when they see a large person, but it is a sickness that is not that easy to overcome. He knew that Gabriel had two sisters who lived apart from him, yet they put on weight in the same way that their brother did. There was something in their bodies that caused the massive weight gain. It was not all controllable. He also knew that when your mind was always thinking about curing the insatiable hunger, you could not concentrate on anything else. Your work suffers, as well as your ability to socialize, to meet goals, to concentrate on education, or even cleanliness. Everything is tied together. When you had all this extra weight, each step, each movement was extremely difficult. Compared to a man of average weight, a heavy man needed to work ten times harder to get out of bed, get into a shower, and drive to work each day. He knew that if any thin person could walk one mile in his shoes, they would begin to have empathy for his plight.

Gabriel left his friend with added incentive to get all the testing done. It was the extra push he needed. The calls, the waiting, and the added stress of the doctors' bills were all deterrents, but he strived on to accomplish his goal. His goal was to obtain a normal life, have friends his age, fall in love, and have a family. In addition, he wanted a career and excel at his daily work. Most of all, he just wanted to be a normal guy.

The test results were all normal. Normal meant that yes, he was depressed, but only because of the weight and the sickness that came with it. His heart was good; his lungs were good. He had some sleep apnea, but the problem would subside with the loss of fat around his neck area. There were so many problems in his life that would be solved with the bariatric surgery. The next step was waiting. The surgery was scheduled for July 17.

Gabriel decided that he wanted to wait and stop appearing at parties until he had the surgery. He wanted everyone to see him after the weight loss. He was so excited that the end now had a date. He was a little happier. He knew he would become the person he wanted to be. No longer would he have to go to the extra-large clothing store or look for the largest seat in a restaurant or struggle with the seat belt when he got into a car. The car, that was another thing that made him feel bad. Because of his current employment situation and being stuck in low-paying jobs, he drove an economy car, which was small. He always felt like a large clown getting out of the small economy car. Every time he approached the car, he felt bad and thought that people were looking at him funny. He just wanted it all to end.

He called upon his faith again to ask God to help him through the surgery. Rose and Gabriel planned a journey to the Passions of Christ, which was an exhibit of life-sized stations of the cross, depicting Christ's journey to his crucifixion. Since it was near to her dear friend, Cindy's house, she let Cindy know of their plans.

This time Gabriel drove to Rose's house and arrived early for the excursion. He was excited. The time for the surgery was drawing near. He had lived in this body for too long now, and nothing could stop him from getting this operation, yet he wanted to have everyone on his side, including Jesus, who he asked for help so many years ago when he was with his birth family.

They drove to the exhibit in near silence. They both knew there was no going back. The operation was not reversible. It was all or nothing. They both needed faith that everything would go well.

The last time Rose had been to the Shrine of Christ was with her mother fifty years ago. Her mom always visited holy places when she was feeling doubt. One of her favorite places of worship was the National Shrine of Saint Jude in Chicago, which was founded in 1929 by the Claretian Missionaries. Hundreds and thousands of devotees went there to pray. This was because St. Jude was the patron saint of hope and impossible causes and one of Jesus's original twelve Apostles. Sometimes people referred to him as the saint of hopeless cases. He was known for preaching the Gospel with great passion, and often in the most difficult circumstances. Through the power of the Holy Spirit, he had made profound differences in people's lives as he offered them the Word of God.

The Gospel tells us that St. Jude was a brother of St. James the Less, also one of the Apostles. They are described St. Jude in the Gospel of Matthew as the "brethren" of Jesus, which most likely meant they were cousins.

St. Jude was traditionally shown carrying the image of Jesus in his hand. This is because of one of his miracles during his work spreading the Word of God. It was told that King Abagar of Edessa asked Jesus to cure him of leprosy and sent an artist to bring him a drawing of Jesus. Impressed with Abagar's great faith, Jesus pressed his face on a cloth, leaving the image of his face on it. He gave the cloth to St. Jude, who took the image to Abagar and cured him.

When Rose was a young child, she didn't really understand her mom's devotion to St. Jude. As she grew older, she understood more. Now on her way with her son on his journey through surgery, her faith grew stronger, and she believed their prayer this day would be heard. Her son suffered too long. He was good and kind, and he was helping himself as best he could. This was his time.

Her Aunt Joan had a different opinion of St. Jude, who was the patron saint of hopeless cases. Joan told Rose that problems were not hopeless, that every problem could be solved. What a very positive way to look at it! Another reason Rose loved her Aunt Joan so much.

They parked in the lot and walked into the gift shop. They bought their tickets, to contribute to the maintenance of the shrine, and walked out to the garden and the start of the exhibit. It was a beautiful day, and the walk around the garden was enjoyable.

The grounds were not empty but far from crowded. They walked to each station of the cross and listened to the story. The stations of the cross refer to a series of images or displays depicting Jesus Christ on the day of his crucifixion and including accompanying prayers. The stations grew out of imitations of Via Dolorosa in Jerusalem, which are believed to be the actual path Jesus walked to Mount Calvary. The object of the stations is to help the faithful Christians make a spiritual pilgrimage through contemplation of the Passion of Christ. Through the ages, it has become one of the most popular devotions, and the stations can be found in many Western Christian churches.

It is a series of fourteen images or, in this case, life-sized statues arranged in numbered order along a path. The visitors walk from display to display, in order, stopping at each station to say the selected prayers and reflect. Many people come to walk through the stations individually or in a procession during Lent, especially on Good Friday, in a spirit of making amends for the sufferings and insults that Jesus endured during his passion. Rose remembered doing this during her years in Catholic grade school.

Afterward, they went back inside the gift shop. Gabriel bought a pendant of St. Michael to help him through the surgery and recovery. They went to the cashier and paid for the purchase. On the way out, they ran into Cindy, who came to meet them and give Gabriel her best wishes for a safe surgery and recovery. She told him that she always admired him.

"Gabriel, you will do fine. You always pull through. Things will work out perfectly. You have always had a good head on your shoulders and act very mature. I am sure you will listen to everything the doctors say and have a quick recovery." Cindy gave him a hug.

"Thanks." Gabriel was brief as always with his reply.

"Thanks for coming out to see us. I know you live pretty far and won't be at the hospital. I'll keep you updated during the operation." Rose hugged her friend too. Cindy was always good to Gabriel. She was one of the people who never judged him. Rose knew she was sincere in her good wishes.

"After this, we are stopping at the butcher down the street to pick up some tomahawk rib eyes for Robo's birthday party."

"Oh, I have been at that butcher. They have some good meat. I'm sure they will have exactly what you want! Why are you getting him steaks for his birthday gift?" Cindy was a little surprised at the choice. She knew Rose liked Robo and thought she would select something more personal.

"He is the man who has everything. I cannot think of anything that I could buy him that would make an impression besides these steaks. He loves a good steak, and he is always barbecuing and smoking meats. It's one of his hobbies. Believe me, he will love it." Rose smiled.

"Okay, you know him best!" Cindy laughed.

They hugged again, and all got into their cars and drove away. Gabriel was very happy that Cindy had come to see him. He never believed people cared as much as they did. Cindy knew him for years. Of course she cared and would wish him well.

Their next stop was the butcher and then onto Robo's birthday bash. It was a backyard party, so very casual. The butcher shop was a big place with lots of prepared food and cuts of all types of meats. Their shelves were full of different sauces and rubs. After walking around the store, Rose found the tomahawk rib eyes. They were perfect! She picked out two and had them wrapped. Gabriel selected a few of the hot sauces, and she added them to the order. The store also sold ice. She had anticipated buying the steaks and brought a cooler, which was in the car. They finished their purchase and carried everything to the car.

They put the steaks inside the cooler and got situated for the hour drive to the party. The timing was working out well. The traffic was light for a Saturday, and they should be there in plenty of time for the start of the party. The gang that would be there included friends and relatives, all of whom were very nice to both Rose and her son. That was one of the best parts about Robo. His kids were really wonderful. She had never met anyone who had children that were accepting of her. The blending of a family was usually tough to create. There were differences in lifestyles, religion, politics, education, and everything that you lived through in the past fifty or so years.

The party was lively. Robo loved competition. He had a net set up for badminton, and games were already started. There were a few other lawn games too. Some of the relatives and friends were not athletic and sat and talked around the patio. Gus, a former restaurant owner and master chef, was grilling the food. Robo really knew how to make people feel comfortable!

After an hour or so, Rose's girlfriend, Janice, who now lived up near Robo, stopped by with her boyfriend. They were welcomed with open arms, and Robo made them feel like they had been part of the group for years and years.

Everyone hugged Rose and Gabriel. Rose had never been a hugger, but Robo was changing that part of her personality. The hugs were welcome, and Gabriel probably needed thousands of hugs to make up for his early years of life.

Some of the people at the party knew Gabriel was having the operation tomorrow, and others did not. The wonderful thing was, no one treated him like he was different or overweight. They treated him just like everyone else. The group reminded Rose of her dear Aunt Joan who accepted everyone no matter what shape, form, job, or religion they had now or in the past. It was a rare quality, and this whole group had it.

The party ended after about six hours. Everyone was overstuffed, except for Gabriel who was fasting, preparing for the surgery.

The yard game also tired everyone out. It was time to go home and get ready for the next day. Robo promised to show up at the hospital to wait during the operation for support. She was happy to have had the offer. It would be stressful. This operation could be awesome for Gabriel, but it was also an operation that could not be reversed. Once it was done, it was done. There was a chance too that once inside, the surgeon could find a reason why they might not be able to finish the surgery. Rose hoped and prayed that did not happen to her son.

Chapter 46

The Operation

They arrived at the hospital at seven in the morning. The hospital surgery area was quiet; not many people were there. Almost immediately, they took Gabriel out to prep him for the surgery. They told Rose that she could come in after he was ready in order to wait with him to be wheeled to surgery.

Rose was ushered into the surgical waiting room and saw Gabriel with a tube in his arm for the anesthesia. They sat there quietly. Rose asked him if he was nervous. He said he was just anxious for it to be over and for his new life to begin.

Soon the surgeon appeared to go over the surgery again. He said it would take about two hours. Gabriel had few questions and told the doctor he was ready.

It was time for Rose to leave. She gave Gabriel a hug and walked to the waiting area. A few minutes later, Robo showed up. This was not his first time in a surgical waiting room. He suggested they take a walk to get a nice cup of coffee. The sitting and watching the board for the surgery to begin and end would be stressful, so it was a good time to leave now before it started.

The coffee shop was on the first floor and offered many different flavors just like the premium coffee chains. She ordered her absolute favorite flavor. This was a treat for her; she didn't normally get herself anything fancy. Robo was a prince. He treated her well and was happy to buy her a special treat.

They walked back to the surgical waiting area and took a seat for the long, anguishing wait. The board changed to say Gabriel's surgery was starting. Now the clocked ticked slower, and a minute seemed like an hour. Rose paced back and forth to read the board. As they waited, they watched some surgeons come out to confer with the patients' families. After listening to the doctor, the families smiled and hugged. Other surgeons gathered the families into a small conference room attached to the waiting room. That was when they received less-than-happy news. The faces of the family leaving that room wore concerned looks. The news they received was not as positive. Rose now knew after watching that she wanted the surgeon to give her the update about Gabriel right out in the open room. If he ushered them to the conference room, the news wouldn't be what she wanted.

Robo sat next to Rose and said not to worry. Worrying wouldn't help. This wasn't his first rodeo. "Try to stay calm and keep your mind off of it." How was that possible? These one or two hours could change the course of Gabriel's entire life.

She wandered over to the board once again. It had changed. Gabriel was out of surgery. It was too soon. The operation should have lasted longer. She was stunned and nervous. If the operation couldn't be done, she knew they would stop right away, and she would get the news that something was not right. This would not be the solution. That would be the worst news of all. Gabriel had waited so long for this surgery. He wanted it so badly. She couldn't go through this. This couldn't be the news she would get. Tears rolled down her face. Robo said, "Don't think of the worst. Maybe it was just so easy, and everything went perfectly, which made it quick."

They both waited. Finally, the surgeon appeared, and he looked around the room. His face was stern, but that didn't mean anything because his personality was serious. No matter if the news was good or bad, his face would not have had a smile on it.

He looked over their heads, and then Rose called over to get his attention.

"Oh there you are." The surgeon walked over to their chairs. Rose and Robo stood.

"What happened? How did the surgery go?" Rose couldn't wait for the answer. She half expected to be led to the room, but the surgeon just stood there.

"The surgery was perfect. The best procedure yet. He is in recovery. You'll be able to see him soon."

Rose was elated. The news couldn't have been better. Gabriel's surgery was a success, and he would start to lose weight. Rose smiled, and another tear rolled down her face.

"The best news is that I still have time to get in a round of golf." Robo chuckled.

Rose gave him a punch in the arm and laughed. "Go on, I'm fine here by myself."

"Are you sure? I was just kidding!" Robo smiled.

"I am good. The worst is over. I'll just wait here until he wakes up." Rose gave him a hug.

"Thanks for being here." Rose waved as he walked out the door.

The surgeon walked away. Rose sat back down and waited until Gabriel was out of recovery and in his room.

A few hours later, Gabriel opened his eyes and saw his mom sitting in the room with him.

"Glad to see you are waking up." Rose smiled.

"I'm okay." Gabriel added groggily.

"I brought your bag of stuff and plugged in your phone. I'll leave you to get some sleep, and I'll come back to visit you tomorrow. Have a good night." Rose walked out of the room feeling blessed that the surgery had gone well.

Two days later, Rose picked him up from the hospital. He was moving slowly but doing fine. She took him back to her house for a while and went to work the following day. By the time she arrived home, Gabriel asked to be taken back to his own place to check on his cat, Salem. Rose agreed to drive him back under strict orders that he call her if he needed help.

Gabriel's employer was very nice and gave him two weeks off to recover from surgery and then agreed to allow him to come back to work and do only light duty. He couldn't pick up more than twenty pounds for the next few weeks.

For two weeks, Gabriel had to follow a liquid diet. He drank protein shakes and started to take the new vitamins that he would need for the rest of his life. Gradually he added solid foods to his diet, but it would take a full year to be able to eat certain foods.

The change was miraculous. In the first month he lost forty pounds, and after three months he was down about ninety pounds. The weight loss started to slow, but he continued to lose. The only downfall was the excess skin. He was thirty years old, and his skin was still young enough to bounce back, but it was a very slow process. He retained some excess skin around the middle section of his stomach. It may take years for that skin to fit to his new body. Some patients of bariatric surgery have skin surgery to remove the excess skin. This was something he would need to think about after his weight loss leveled out, and he kept the weight off for a significant period of time.

Gabriel found that he was able to bend down and tie his shoes. Daily household chores didn't take his breath away. His sugar was now normal. His back was in less pain. His feet felt better. The acid reflux he had always experienced after eating disappeared.

Chapter 47

The Outcome

Months went by, and Gabriel lost nearly two hundred pounds. He began doing things he never was able to do, which included simple tasks such as picking up things in his front yard that didn't belong there. He straightened out his house and decluttered it. He cleaned his garage, and he went back to website dating. The most significant thing was his head. The cloud was released. He was able to think clearly. He explained that before the weight loss he couldn't remember anything. It was either he was so involved in the constant thoughts of fitting in or being overweight or not having a girlfriend, or maybe it was a medical reason related to the weight. Either way, the cloud was gone. His thoughts were clearer. He remembered the things he was supposed to do each day. He passed his classes in school without too much effort. Everything was different and better.

Since everything was a little clearer, he gained a little confidence. He had enough confidence to reply to some of the online-dating responses he received. The girls spoke back to him. They didn't run and hide. He was a little happier because most messages he sent received a response. He wasn't sure how to respond. He didn't know what to say. This was because of the long, ten-year gap between dates. The best thing, though, was that now he had someone to message back and forth. He looked like everyone else answering texts on his phone!

A few months went by, and finally a really nice girl kept replying, and they went on a date and afterward she kept texting. It was such a significant surprise and change in Gabriel's life. They went on another date, and she asked when she would see him again. It was working! He had a real girlfriend. After all of the lonely years, after all of the dates where he was stood up, he found someone who wanted more of him.

The best part was, she was a wonderful girl! She loved to do things. She loved to go places. She lived on a budget, used coupons and Groupons. Her job was challenging. She wanted a family. There wasn't a thing that Gabriel didn't like about her. She even liked decorating and trying to make his place look nicer. This was something he always wanted to do. Life was good!

The weekend events with Mom became almost nonexistent. Rose didn't mind, she was ecstatic. This was what she always wanted. She wanted Gabriel to have a good life, to have fun, to be happy. Finally, her dream and her mom's dream was coming true.

He also continued his studies and worked his way to his criminal-justice degree. There was a downside. He had to retake a few classes because of the poor grades he received when he was at his heavier weight. It wasn't all that hard. The classes and studying came easier. He was able to concentrate. The walk to each class wasn't bad at all. His knees didn't cry out with pain.

His friendship with Dan and his father Jose grew. Jose and Gabriel now talked about their successes with weight loss. Not only that, but now they talked about going hunting. Hunting was something that Jose loved, but had to give up years ago because of his weight. Gabriel always wanted to hunt, but by the time he got into it, he was too big to do it. The hunting would lead to more exercise and more weight loss. It was a win-win situation. Everything kept getting better and better!

Rose finally felt that it was okay to do her own things on the weekends. She left the house and went on adventures with her friends, and her relationship with Robo progressed. She felt a warmth inside that was like nothing she ever felt. The adventure that started out because of her mom turned into a nineteen-year journey that made her life worth living. It gave her a purpose. It made her feel that she was important and completed something worth doing. She never ever thought during the adoption process that anything would give her as much pride and joy as this journey she lived with Gabriel.

Now, Rose and Gabriel each had their own lives, plus a life with each other. The things they had gone through together gave them a history together, a mutual bond, as tight as if Rose had given birth to Gabriel. There are people who say that the birth mother's love for her children is like nothing else. Well, those people did not go through the journey that Rose and Gabriel lived through. Only they would know the bond they felt. She felt that her love for Gabriel was just as strong as a birth mom's love for her child.

Life was not over, and they would go on together and separately. However, each knew they now had a permanent mom and a permanent son. It wasn't just a piece of paper that bonded them together; it was the mission they undertook together that got them to this good place in their life.

Finally, the time would come when Gabriel and Kelly, his girlfriend, would get married and have a child. Rose knew it would happen. When the baby is born, Rose would have a speech prepared for that child. She would tell the baby to make sure to let Rose know if there were any problems with Gabriel and Kelly. Rose would stand by that baby and go head to head with both parents and make sure they knew that their baby would never ever suffer the way Gabriel did in foster care. They would never fight or break up, at least not if Rose had any say in it. That baby was due a lifelong commitment from both of his or her parents to stay together and create a good family life together. Rose would stand over them and keep watch. That was her oath, and she would live by it forever.

The End

About the Author

Betsy Naglich has spent her life pursuing her dreams—from company controller to airline employee, from writing scripts to designing e-learning lessons. Each career choice has been one more step up the staircase on this incredible journey called life. Her journey has led her to hike the Appalachian Trail, go white water rafting, and explore the world. She often volunteers to help others and loves road trips and gardening. These continue to be mainstays in her life, but her greatest accomplishment was adopting and raising her son, teaching him to understand that life is a journey to be enjoyed. Her debut novel, *The Length of Our Staircase*, tells the story of a woman who, by taking it one step at a time, helps her child make his dreams and her own come true.

CPSIA information can be obtained
at www.ICGtesting.com
Printed in the USA
BVHW071205170521
607542BV00003B/292